I0628729

50-Out:
Calling the Regretful

Book One:
50-Out

Christian V. Reinhardt
02/17/2021

Published by: Artisan Publishing Guild, LLC
APGuild@outlook.com

50-Out: Calling the Regretful
Book One: 50-Out

By Christian V. Reinhardt

Copyright 2021 by Artisan Publishing Guild, LLC
ISBN: **9781942935216**

Author's note:

Hello and welcome to a whole new world. Today, you'll get to meet a new band of miscreants. All seven of this team are people that you may know in the real world... well, except for Ananias Dare, being the richest man in North America. All seven are men you may strive to be... well, except for Mason Patrick, he's a cat burglar.

Ok, I completely blew that, how about this... All seven members of this team have regrets, as do most people, but as it turns out, they share one in common, and all seven have an opportunity to remove that regret from their lives. As you journey into their story, remember that every world has politics, understand theirs are not ours.

Take time to lose yourself in the exploits of this odd group of men, find yourself in them, find your friends in them, find fun and laughter in their attempt to save the world through corporate team-building exercises, because as Ananias says, "If we can't laugh, why bother?"

A Tiny little thing, both the editor and a couple pre-readers of this book have said, some of the training chapters, are interesting but... Well perhaps Leif says it best, "Just sayin'... ZZZZ." Trying to zhuzh them up took away from the team building that it was meant to show.

Love and Strength,

C.V. Reinhardt

Introduction

Too many men reach an age when they realize they should have served their country, putting their lives on the line for every person in their homeland. In generations previous, serving one's country was not voluntary—each male was required to do it for a set period, which was achieved through a process called conscription, or the draft as it is more commonly known. The driving body behind the draft was the Selective Service System (SSS), their role was to identify young men and place them within the armed forces.

While the United States remained a country, the draft came and went. The first version of conscription was removed from the lives of all men in 1918. However, in 1926, a new revamped version reared its head, based upon the new needs within the military. In 1940, it morphed once again, into the Selective Training and Service Act (STAT). Later that same year, STAT was put to work, becoming the first peacetime draft, remaining in place through 1969, when the pressures from the Vietnam Conflict forced another change.

During this time, some felt compelled to enlist, while others used family ties to earn deferments to follow or pursue college degrees they may not have otherwise pursued. Receiving a deferred or exempt status became a positive social consequence, being presented as a method of staunching the loss of the country's "best and brightest" who had historically died in war at a young age.

History moved forward, and in 1973, the US government terminated the draft in favor of an all-volunteer armed forces. With the removal of the draft, the men and, later, the women who served in the armed forces were cut dramatically. As fewer men and women served, fewer also saw the gifts America offered and the truth of what America meant to the world.

In 2022, with the United States' divisiveness on its way to a second civil war, the Parting Pact was put in place, and the world recognized three independent sovereign countries. The southern states became American Springs Politica (ASP), their capital was in Dallas, Texas. The Northwest became the New World Order (NWO), their capital was in San Francisco, California. Leaving the Northeast to become New Roanoke, their capital remained Washington, DC.

The Parting Pact also established the North American Land and Air Military, to be run by the elected officials from each state in the new countries, enter the Congress of Governors, or COG. The NALAM took over the entire state of Missouri and Arch Master Base was formed. Additionally, three Naval Master Bases were built, one in each new country. In 2030, conscription was imposed once again. As with feudal systems throughout the ages, a set number of healthy people of a specific age group from each region must serve in the military for a set number of months.

As for the residency of the people in these areas, small cities were allowed to establish themselves as remote provinces of one of the three nations by vote. During the initial parting, however, these provinces were to be turned over to the region within a 20-year time period, allowing those in the area time to sell and relocate. The 40-year window quickly moved to 20, and then 10 years when the obvious issue of dual citizenship became too overbearing for the countries.

In 2035, when the NWO had reached a point of bankruptcy and disillusionment, they negotiated with New Roanoke, and they merged. Today, the world is waiting… as two-thirds of the United States have reformed, could a reclamation of the world power be in the cards?

Chapter 1
Silence of the Exposed

The table took up more than three-quarters of the room. If one hadn't understood it was actually crafted within the confines of the 50x50 single-doored enclosure, they would marvel in disbelief at its magnificence. The chairman of this think tank known as the Camelot, while being an Arthurian scholar, was also one of the showiest assholes in the capital city of New Roanoke, Croatoah.

Due to the room's architecture, each of the 30 people sitting in their equally spaced seats at the enormous round table could hear even their furthest contemporary. The meeting had gone like all those from the past 25 years, where members of the Camelot were treated to the latest record-breaking quarter results. Smiles filled the room as the ebony-skinned CFO closed her notebook and retook her seat.

"Thank you, Ms. Lane. Fantastic summary as usual." The man who had commissioned the table stood, drawing surprised gasps from those in attendance. He took center stage, or perhaps claiming the head of the table for the first time since the formation of the Camelot. "My friends, today will be my last meeting…"

"Mr. Dare?" several voices said, in sequence with others saying, "Ananias?"

"Please." Not raising his voice, he patted the air, calmly waiting. His hair, which was too long for any trillionaire, was primarily white, except for a single three-inch swath that was as black as when he was a teenager. The black hair was pulled into a braid that fell across his left eye, drawn in three places with iron rings, each with a precious stone — one blood-red garnet, one white diamond, and a deep blue sapphire. Tucking the braid behind his ear, he began to lose his composure, "Friends, this is not up for debate. As is laid out in our bi-laws, I will leave it to the remaining Camelot to determine the best path to replace me."

"Why, Ananias?" Ms. Lane's voice was as unemotional as it was moments earlier when she read the results of their financial foray.

"It's just time, my darling. That is all." He allowed his sympathy for her remaining here with these jackals to show in his eyes for just a moment.

"And your shares?" a small Indian woman sitting directly across from him asked.

"Saanvi, I again return to our bi-laws, section 4.2i.c Member Shares, and I quote, when any member leaves, their shares will go solely to whomever their chosen successor is, so too shall mine. When I leave, I relinquish all, including this beautiful table. Although, should you ever choose not to use it, I would like first right of refusal as I had it commissioned out of my personal bank account."

"Of course, Ananias, that will be entered into the minutes, alongside your request to leave," the ruggedly handsome man to the left of Saanvi replied. "Secretary Marshals, please initiate the dissociation protocols. Mr. Dare, please securely place your hands on your voting discs." Ananias complied.

When he had placed his hands upon the two discs inset into the tabletop at his location, Marshals stood. "You, Ananias Dare, have requested to be removed from the Camelot. Do you understand that you will have no memory of this body, nor what this body does?"

"I do."

"Do you, Ananias Dare, understand that you will have no memory of the members of this body, nor will any of the members have memories of you?"

"I do."

"Do you, Ananias Dare, understand that you are relinquishing all shares in the Camelot?"

"I do."

"Do you, Ananias Dare, understand that you will, after the quarter that was reported upon today, never receive payments from the Camelot or the remaining and future members herein?" the secretary continued.

"I do." Ananias closed his eyes, preparing for what he had seen several dozen times over the 25 years that he, as the founding member of the Camelot, sat in.

"Is there a specific medical facility you wish to be delivered to?" Ms. Lane asked.

Opening his eyes, he said, "St. Elmo's, I've written a note... I know it's a bit far." He touched his jacket pocket and smiled at her.

"It will be done, sir. And, sir, good luck in whatever you plan on doing." Saanvi smiled at the man she had argued with routinely over the past years. A man who she would have gladly seen walk out of this building in shame more times than she could recall, but today, she understood everything they had accomplished in this grand experiment would never have come to be without this man. She stood, bowing deeply in his direction. The gesture traveled like a wave around the glorious table. As it skipped over him, he placed his hands back on the voting discs. The show of respect returned to Marshals, who also placed his hands on the pads.

The braid fell from behind Ananias' ear a second before he crumpled to the floor. The effects of the dissociation caused his body to convulse uncontrollably, and his eyes rolled back in his head.

"Security?" Marshals lifted the phone, calling for help while everyone else watched the poor man, who had fallen victim to some kind of seizure, twitching on the floor. "We're going to need the med staff to move this man from the penthouse conference room to the lobby, and then call an ambulance."

"Of course, sir." The phone connection ended.

A short time later, the emergency responders were led into the lobby where a man lay on the floor in a suit worth 10,000 standard gold. "My name is Captain Green. What happened here?" the woman to the rear of the gurney asked.

"This man came in and said he needed help. Apparently, someone had been following him. He paced around for a while before he went into some form of seizure," the short man behind the desk said. "It looks like his name is Brioni."

"Most likely that's the suit he's wearing," she replied.

"I managed to stabilize him while attempting to make certain he didn't swallow his tongue," another man, who had been unseen until that moment, said. "As it turned out, things went differently, he tried to bite off my fingers."

"Are those bites ok?" she indicated the injury to his left hand.

"I poured a bit of everything we had in the pantry on it, including bleach. If you have better, have at it." He smiled.

"I'll look after we see to this man."

"Vitals are steady, eyes fully reactive. Should we use smelling salts?" the younger of the two emergency responders asked.

"Take a look at all his fingers and toes, check for any peculiarities."

"Yes, ma'am," he replied, then began taking off the fallen man's shoes. "Damn."

"Even rich people can have stinky feet, Bret" the commanding officer laughed.

"Actually, that's not it at all, these shoes are amazing." He held one out to her.

"What is it with you and feet or shoes?" The bald woman inspecting the downed man's fingers laughed.

"Telly, we all have our things, you of all people should know that." He winked at her.

"Smartass. Captain, there's nothing odd on his fingers but he appears to have raised marks on both palms."

"I'm sorry?" She strode over and took a knee, examining the palm on her side of the body. Finding there were indeed uniquely raised areas, interestingly, they appeared to be on top of several identical older scars. "Let me see that one," setting the hand down gently and taking the other when Telly presented it.

After relinquishing the extremity to her boss, she nervously ran her palms over her bald pate. "What is it?"

"Did you notice there are older marks as well?" she asked, turning the palm up to allow both of her charges to see. "Sir, can I see the video recording of what occurred here?" she turned to the security guards.

"Ma'am?" the man to the side stopped wrapping his hand.

"I'm wondering if he possibly got shocked or burned by something in here." The captain began walking in an expanding circle around the area, trying to locate the odd square symbol with what looked like five vertical lines forming a staircase up and down or… "Wait, maybe a pyramid with an odd eye?" Her statement came off like a question, no one was meant to answer.

"The old symbols, yes, that's what I see. But this newer one is simpler, two interlocked Js with a crescent moon, perhaps," Bret commented.

"About the recording the Captain requested to see?" Telly inquired.

"There has been servicing of the system for the last seven days. We should be back online next Tuesday." The short man behind the desk came back into the game.

"Ma'am, I found a letter in his pocket,"

"Excellent what does it say?"

Unfolding the thick bonded paper, Telly read:

'To whom it may concern:

My name is Ananias Dare. Fate must have taken an odd turn for you to be reading this letter. If you make certain I am taken to St. Elmo's Hospital on the outer ring, you will, of course, be greatly rewarded for your simple act of kindness.

In advanced appreciation,

Ananias Dare'

"Well, I'd hate to let down the richest man in North America. Let's get him to the hospital. At this point, I'm just wasting my time. I can't find a darn thing that matches these marks." The captain walked back to the body, securing him to the gurney, and as abruptly as they entered, they exited, wheeling him out to their ambulance.

"You forgot to look at that guy's fingers," Telly remembered.

"He'll live, we've got shit to do!" the captain replied excitedly.

Chapter 2
The Influence of the Majority

JaLen sat at another bar, filling another night with stupid trivia and drinks, which didn't even help to distract him from the same time every year since his brother failed to keep his promise to return from his third tour in Afghanistan. His wasn't the only promise that was broken; the President of the United States had promised to remove all the troops from that 18-year-long war zone. But when he tried, the Washington complex stopped him, so he caved and his brother and many others died.

"Another?" the attractive 40-something waitress asked, placing a hand on his shoulder.

"You got it." She handed him the check, walking away.

"Ok, no number works too." He removed his wallet, pulling out his favorite plastic, showing the helmet of his home town team from the defunct football league. Opening the docket, he found the missing number along with his bar tab. Grinning and glancing at the number, he read the little note, 'I get off at 10 pm. Suzie', he removed the number, tucking it in his wallet. Like a skilled professional, he slid the credit card in the top of the vinyl folder.

"I'll be back in a moment," she said as she scooped it up. "Would you like coffee while you wait?" she gave him an innocent wink.

"That would be great, Suzie," he said with a smile in his voice. He looked down at his watch while passively glancing up at the shapely rear-end heading to the waitress stand. He stood and walked in the opposite direction to the restroom, next to the entrance. The man next to the hostess stand took an involuntary step back as he closed the distance. Trying not to roll his eyes, JaLen pulled his mask over his chin and shouldered into the bathroom, appreciating the density of the door. After finishing up, he took the few steps to the sink and, stooping, he washed his hands while looking in the mirror, checking his teeth.

"They didn't take into account someone of your size when they put this bathroom together, eh?" an old man laughed as he walked into a stall, closing the door.

"You can say that again," JaLen chuckled, wiping his hand on a paper towel before rubbing another towel across his shaven head. Tossing the papers in the trash as the old man released in the stall, JaLen found himself rushing from the bathroom. A memory came unbidden to his mind, the odd day he decided to shave off his cornrows that had adorned his head from early in his high school years. Shaking off the memory of the braids falling to the floor, reminding him he was no longer a child.

He sat at the bar, finding his coffee along with the vinyl folder. He removed his credit card and returned it to its home before signing the receipt and adding 20% to the tab.

"Nice tip, but I already propositioned you." She looped her arm, intertwining it with his. "Justine, punch me out." Reaching over, she slid the nasty vinyl folder under the bar.

"See you tomorrow, girl," the bartender

waved.

"Do you always take charge as such?" JaLen looked down at the short red-head.

"You won't be complaining later, trust me." Her small hand smacked his ass as they walked from the tavern.

"If you say so. Not to be cliché, but your place or mine?" He shook his head at his stupid comment.

"Hmm, I'd say mine but I don't think I'd be able to sneak you past my spouse." She cocked her head, looking to see if he had any reaction to this declaration.

"It's like that, eh?" His eyebrow rose. "Am I some kinda revenge?"

"Something like that." Suzi attempted to look strong, but it came off quite sheepish.

"Don't get me wrong, I'm ok with playing my role in this, but what if you fall truly, madly, deeply in love with me tonight?"

"That, handsome man, would be my cross to bear."

"So then, to my hotel?" JaLen held out an elbow to escort her to his car.

"My car?"

"You can bring it if you'd like, but if you are going for the big revenge, leave it here for him to find when he comes looking."

"Perhaps you've been here a time or two?" she asked as he closed the door, leaving her in the front seat of his car as he walked around.

"I was once the fool on the other side." The rental car was a mid-size POS. "Now I travel and try to stay away from my hometown." He drove to the hotel three blocks away.

"That was close, why didn't you walk?"

"What and miss out on the chance to get a DUI and lose my job? Fuck that." When the laughter stopped, he turned to her with a serious expression, "Suzi, just because your spouse decided to be a fool, doesn't mean you have to do it. We can go back and forget about this, go for a walk and chat. Or go for a drive."

"You really did go through this, didn't you?"

"I did," he continued driving. "And to be honest, I was drunk and didn't even know what happened. My wife planned her revenge and executed the plan. But as the saying goes... 'No battle plan survives first contact.' She tried to back out and got raped for my mistake."

"Wait... you didn't rape her."

"I guess I see that differently. Don't you understand that men are all assholes? To most of us, an offer is as good as a buy."

"Sorry? Never mind, it doesn't matter. So, in other words, I luckily chose a non-asshole?"

"No, I'm an asshole too, just the right kind of asshole for you right now." He pulled into the driveway to the tavern. "Where is your car?"

"That pickup, right there." Her pointing hand was shaking.

"Relax, no need to shake." He stepped from the car, walking around and letting her back out.

"I'm confused. Are you rejecting me?"

"No, not even a bit, your aura gave you away, you wanted this right up until you didn't." JaLen held a hand to help her out of the car. "Go back to your husband, scream and yell, tell him how wrong he was. Make him know that you are better than whatever chippy he hooked up with."

"Two things in that, first, my chippy hooked up with a man."

"I did not see that one coming." The laugh that came unbidden echoed in the parking lot.

"Which part didn't you see coming?"

Ignoring her question, he presented his own, "Have you ever been with a man?"

"No, never wanted to before yesterday. Been a tomboy since I could walk. Went to an all-girls school and got married right out of college."

"Good for you. Now, go fight for that again." He closed the car door and leaned against it.

"So, you didn't fight for your relationship?"

"I fight for it every day in trying to seek redemption."

"Redemption?"

"For my part in her death. The rape also became a homicide."

"What makes you think she was going to find…" Suzi started.

"She left me a note, which I still carry. Want to

see?"

"No, I think I know what she probably wrote... I thank you for being the right kind of asshole." She scampered over to her truck, starting to drive away. Stopping beside him, she rolled down the passenger window, "What did you mean by my aura?"

"Look it up." JaLen laughed and walked back into the tavern. Four hours later, he returned to his hotel room, unfolding an aged piece of paper, "I'm sorry, Victoria-Lynn." He touched the old paper to his heart, weeping as he sat on the bed and kicked off his work boots. "I sure hope Suzi made it home before her wife read that note." Walking into the bathroom, he folded the paper and returned it to his wallet. Stripping, he stepped into an ice-cold shower. "Fuck, I can feel my blood stalling." Drying off, he went to bed.

Yellow, black, green. Yellow, black, green. The silent room flashed through a series of colored messages from the forgotten television.

"What the..." JaLen rolled over in bed. Yellow, black, green. He patted the bed looking for the remote control. Yellow, black, green. "It fell on the floor..." mumbling to the empty room, he tried to ignore it as he threw his face back into the pillow. Yellow, black, green. Yellow, black, green. "Fine, fine." He rolled over, pushing back against the headboard and started to read the flashing screen.

'Ever feel bad for electing to not serve your country?' The text was written in black, on a yellow screen. The room went dark, 'Wish you could undo that decision?' Red letters asked on the black screen. 'Reach out and ask us how: iamthetraveler@outlook.com'. The green screen with white lettering. Yellow, black, green. Yellow, black, green.

"What?" He watched the words flash by again. Turning on the bedside light, he wrote the email address on a pad of paper, found the remote which had fallen on the floor, and shut off the TV. "I gotta remember to shut you off before I crash."

His head fell into his pillow and his mind tried to understand what that message actually meant. Elsewhere in the country, hundreds of other minds raced down the same track after being awoken by the yellow, black, and green screens.

Chapter 3
When Shit Breaks

Today marked his 100th straight night driving in circles around the city, rescuing the fools who pushed their luck one too many times. Thinking that not all events he interjected himself into involved people driving their cars that one time too many. One of the aforementioned rescues was playing out in front of him currently — a girl standing next to her broken car on the side of the highway was being ushered into a car right in front of him. As his grandmother used to say, 'If you smell the turkey burning, don't just sit on your ass basking in stupidity. Do something about it!' She wasn't exactly the bard, but the point stayed with him, and at that moment, following the burning turkey seemed like the right thing to do. After a few miles, the Rolls-Royce Cullinan pulled off the highway, the tow truck continued trailing at what he thought was a close enough distance. He radioed a friend at the State Police department.

"Collins," the familiar voice popped into life over the music in his earpiece.

"Terry, it's Leif."

"Hey, Chief, everything ok?" the police sergeant asked.

"Well, can you get me some info on a car?"

"Plate?"

"ABGX22," Leif read off as the car turned to the right.

"It's a rental car. We don't have…"

"I think the driver just abducted a girl."

"Fuck! Ok, I've activated the tracking on the car. That is the first Rolls-Royce I've ever seen as a rental, and of course, you're in a shitty part of town too... great," Sgt. Collins laughed.

The car turned right again.

"Anything? He may have seen me."

"Leif, I have him, you don't have to..." he started.

"What do you want?" A 30-something man stood in the middle of the road, waving a gun around like a fool while yelling like an idiot.

"Is that him I hear?" Collins asked.

"Yup. Name?" Leif pulled up behind the car, he angled the truck such that the lights showed the pleading girl's face. "She definitely isn't choosing to be in that car, that's for certain."

"Deter, his name is Deter Von Schlept..."

"Deter, I'm just making certain the young lady in your car is ok." Opening the door to the wrecker, he stepped out, speaking through the open window of his truck. "Miss, please step out of the car."

"Who in the fuck do you think you are? How do you know my name?" The clipped speech identified the man's homeland.

"I know more than that, Deter Von Schlept... you're a German businessman here on a work Visa," Leif replied calmly.

"Go fuck yourself, she's not going anywhere with an overaged moron driving an even older tow truck." The flailing gun stilled and aimed at the windshield. Bang! Bang! Bang! As if the gun was aimed at her, the girl started bucking against the car door. "Now, get out of here before you get yourself hurt."

"Let me guess, child safety locks engaged? So that door won't open from the inside. You freak." Bang! This time, the bullet hit the door right in front of him. "Miss, calm down." Bang! Bang! Two more in the door.

"I'm giving you to the count of three, and if you don't get in your tow truck," he gave a condescending laugh, "I'll blow your head off."

"Hmm. Do you see that dot on your chest? Go ahead and look…" he paused, giving him a moment to see exactly what he meant. "That is the site of my trucker's special. It happens to be loaded with buckshot, so even if I didn't have the laser site, I would most likely clip you with a couple of pellets." Deter was reasonably quick. Bang! The impact on the door was center mass. Click, click! "I guess that would be all your bullets."

"Fuck you!" the man threw his gun to the ground and put his hands up.

"Move to the side, and if you even think about reaching a hand out to her, I will shoot you." The green dot lowered to the man's crotch. "Miss, what's your name?"

"Tina." The answer came quickly. Good, she was responsive.

"Excellent, Tina, I need you to slide over—"

"No! He said he'd hurt me!" she cut him off.

"Move to the front of the car, you sick fucker. Give her room!" This time, the laser was trained on Deter's forehead.

"Fine! Fine!" He started to shuffle slowly until the sound of sirens in the distance gave him pause.

"Miss, now!" he ordered, the authority in his voice shook her from her fear-induced paralysis.

"Shit, shit, shit." She scampered out of the car, falling to her knees. Her movement never slowed, her hands and feet pushed her forward, crossing the broken concrete through all matter of detritus. When she was outside of the pervert's reach, she slowed just long enough to get back to her feet.

"Get in, get in." Leif pulled her forward, she slid into the bench behind the driver's seat.

"Are those cops coming here?"

"Yes, Tina, they are." He released the breath he hadn't realized he was holding.

"What the hell is wrong with me?" She let the tears start to fall, her body reacted by curling into the fetal position amongst the glass strewn over the back seat of the wrecker.

"Don't even think about making a run for it, Deter. I'm not opposed to shooting you in the back. Oh ya, you can trust that." His Wisconsin slipped in. "Yes?"

"Listen, I have $10,000 on me right now. You let me leave and you can have it."

"I want you to hear me, my name is Sedulous HouLeiff, which means 'the never-ending pursuit'.

Does that sound like the name of a man who would accept a payoff?"

"Is that really your name?" Tina asked, looking up from the bench.

"Yes. I know, kinda strange but it's mine." The police car turned the corner.

"Leif," the voice of his friend in his earpiece startled him.

"Shit, Collins."

"Sorry, I didn't want to pester you in the middle of what was going on. You'll need to turn your gun over to the policeman."

"I will, of course, turn my weapon over as soon as they take this jackass into custody. Have you been recording this the entire time?"

"Yes."

"Hmm, well, the shoot you in the back thing," the lights from the police cars strobed off the walls, outlining the area. Leif knelt on the ground with his hands behind his head.

"Just kneel down and turn it over asap, they are engaging now," Collins advised.

"I'm kneeling already, and my hands are behind my head. Oh, and my weapon is on the ground three feet in front of me." He sat patiently waiting.

"Mr. Von Schlept," the voice from the loudspeaker under the police car's hood boomed. "Put your hands on your head and step sideways such that your body is in full view. Slowly." The passenger side door in the squad car opened, and the sound of a shotgun racking a shell into the chamber echoed into the night.

The man complied, beginning a series of accusations against Leif, "He tried to kill me. He and his girlfriend tried to rob me. He shot at me first…"

"Kneel down and clasp your fingers behind your head," the speaker crackled.

"I will, I will, you understand I'm the victim here," the German man shouted.

The policeman ran forward from the passenger side of the car, shotgun trained on Deter Von Schlept. "Clear." The officer began the process of cuffing the man.

"Clear? What do you mean by that? He has my gun, I am the victim!"

"Shut up!" Leif could not take it any longer.

"Leif, not another word," Sgt. Collins ordered over the earpiece.

"Mr. FouLeiff, I will be walking toward you. Stay where you are, in the position you are in." The driver stopped using the PA system. The crunching of gravel walked up behind him. "Where are the weapons?"

"He threw his gun at the grill of my truck after he ran out of bullets."

"And yours?"

"My weapon is directly in front of me," he indicated under the open door with his chin.

"This," the cop grabbed the device off the ground, holding it up. "It's a laser pointer?"

"It is."

"You stood down a man who was shooting at you with a laser pointer?"

"He had more than a laser pointer!" Deter said incredulously. "You fucking—"

"Enough!" Leif cut him off, he knew the man was simply pissed that the story he was making up about him and Tina just died on the vine. "Officer, there's a gun in my locked glove box, inside a safe. The safe has a counter of how long since it was last opened on the front."

"I'll need to see it."

"The key for the glove box is on my key chain, in the ignition."

"And the combination?" the policeman asked.

"Thumbprints, both thumbs." Leif smiled.

"Ok, then." He reached through the open door, taking the keys and walking to the passenger side. Opening the oversized glove box, he removed the safe. The timer on the front read 12 hrs 42 min 32 sec when the officer took a picture with his cell phone. "Would you like me to take a picture with your phone?"

"Yes, that would be good of you."

"I'll need you to operate it, so I can see that it isn't a dummy timer." The officer handed Leif's phone back. "And I'll record it so lawyers can't fuck with you."

"Not a problem, sir. And thank you, sir." Leif placed his thumbs on the readers, the safe clicked and the timer zeroed out.

"I've never seen one like that," he said after stopping the video recording.

"I invented it, brings in a few bucks a month. Can I head out, sir?"

"Collins knows how to reach you, right?"

"Of course. Sir, the girl?" Leif chinned his head toward the back seat.

"I'm not getting out. You can you drive me home?" Tina squealed.

"Of course, I go cha'," he looked at the cop, "Follow me, please," Leif mouthed.

"You got it," he winked.

Chapter 4
Hand in the Cookie Jar

The moonlight seemed inordinately bright tonight, maybe the dilation of his eyes during his optometrist visit, even though they had said the requirement to wear sunglasses would fade within a few hours. Shaking off the stupid concern, he stepped out to his 1960 Fairlady. Popping the trunk, he removed his computer, throwing it over his shoulder. Quietly closing his trunk, knowing a thump may bring his neighbor running out, asking for his help. It wasn't that he didn't like helping people, and it wasn't like spending time with an amazing-looking woman wasn't... well, amazing, but it simply wasn't the time for such activities, he needed to get his mining rigs tuned up. He had just gotten the parts he needed to tweak that little extra processing time without generating so much heat that the local DEA kicked in his door for the third time. 'Whoops,' he thought, turning back to the car and opening the driver's door to grab the bag on the seat. With a smile, he closed the door, 'bam'.

"Blaire?"

"Shit," he mumbled, looking at his reflection in the window of the classic automobile. "Tall, flabby, and stupid!" His positive affirmation finished and he smiled, "At least you don't have a comb-over." Winking at his reflection, he started walking.

"Blaire, is that you?" the call came through the second-story window. He knew he couldn't ignore her, so he waved. "Good, it is you. Do you have a couple of minutes?"

"No more than a couple, I'm actually working late." He walked toward his neighbor's side of the duplex.

"It shouldn't take you long, I froze my computer and I really don't..." blah, blah, blah, he stopped listening as he shuffled his feet to the door. "Just come in, it's open."

Walking in, he padded up to the desk in the corner of the front room, being a mirror image of his flat. "Janey, your computer is off," he yelled toward the steps he walked past when he entered.

"Not that one, my laptop is up here. It's docked or I would bring it down. I'm gonna jump in the shower, can you come up and see if you can unlock it? Password is, all caps, D34THD34L3R. One word."

"Deathdealer? Ok, we'll go with that." He proceeded up the stairs slowly until he heard the door close, at which time he started taking them two at a time. Thinking through a simple troubleshooting routine, "Docking station doesn't seem to have power," he reported to no one in particular. Taking the cord in hand, he followed it to the power supply finding no light. "Hmm?" From there, he tracked it to a surge suppressor. "Tripped." He smiled and pushed the reset button, instantly, inside the desk drawer, the sound of an offset clothes washer on spin cycle reverberated. Opening the drawer, he found an interestingly-shaped massage unit grinding away against a change jar.

"Any luck?" Janey asked through the

bathroom door.

"Yeah, looks like you just overwhelmed your surge suppressor. Be careful of how much you plug into those things." He unplugged the massage unit, wondering why it was J-shaped. He closed the drawer and headed downstairs to his apartment.

"Wait, Blaire, I wanted to…" the voice faded as he closed the front door.

"That was all your fault." He glared at the bag in his left hand. "God help me, gummies really are gonna get me into some serious shit one day." Removing the bag of sour bears, he tore the bottom corner of the bag, allowing some of the lemon sugar gathered there to burn his lips. The warning tones in his house let him know the monthly allotment he had set or his power consumption had elapsed. "Fuck. I just don't get it, I didn't even have the new units online." He walked over to his thermostat, seeing a setting that he knew he hadn't programmed in, "64 degrees? Who the? Why the?" Reaching under the unit, he flipped the automatic/remote/manual switch to manual.

"This is a warning, do not disable remote mode," the voice that filled the room came not only from the temperature control unit, but his lamps, and somewhere in the kitchen area.

"What? Who the…" he started.

"The legal owner of this tenancy has set the yearly control variable," the female voice was obviously an AI simulation.

"She doesn't pay the damn bill. When she

does, I'll leave it in remote."

"You will not be able to alter the previously established criteria," the robotic voice reported.

"Is that a challenge, Red Queen?"

"I am not certain to whom you are addressing your question, Master Blaire."

"Ok, well let's speak again tomorrow. I have some things to do." Walking to his desk, he removed several tools from a small bag. Starting back to the thermostat, he took a simple item from the satchel before dropping it on the floor and starting to swagger his way to the main breaker panel, opening it.

"Master Blaire, there are several regulations pertaining to a renter operating the main breaker panel in an apartment…" the voice dropped as he threw the switch.

"Fuck yourself, you peeping Tom." Placing the elastic band of his flashlight around his head, he switched it on and walked over to the temperamental piece of electronics. "Let's see what we have here." The cover fell away, and a small cable dropped from the concealed area. "Interesting."

"Blaire! Did you shut off the power?" Janey yelled from outside.

"Since when does my power affect her flat?" he asked the silent room. "Fuck it." He grabbed his tablet from the bag and plugged in the loose cable. After a series of buttons, the interface between the two pieces of electronic came to life.

The words that flashed across the screen of his

tablet were a green font. 'I want you to be certain you understand that by interfacing with this unit, you're directly violating the local ordinances as well as federal mandates on manufacturing.' Those words were replaced with an amber font. 'Blaire, you need to choose your next actions carefully. Take a moment to think this through. Perhaps partake in one of those gummy candies you love so much.'

"Hmm, still watching, eh? Next time you ask someone to look in the mirror, perhaps you should be certain they don't have a pocket full of stones." He slid his hand over the screen quickly to the left, then just as quickly to the right, words started to appear. Blaire made a circular motion around the screen as the four fingers on his right made what, to an observer, would appear to be random tapping. A few moments later, the circular event of words stopped.

'Mr. Rivers, I must say I am most impressed. But how can a one-handed soldier expect to defeat a deva like Marici?' In a flash, the pattern worked itself off the screen. 'What a shame, next time, come prepared.' A picture of a topless woman with six arms, each with a bladed weapon in them, popped onto the tablet's display. The arms came together, the blades ending up so close, sliding a hair between any two of them would be impossible. Outside, the sound of a police car took the place of the night's music braying of insects and reptiles.

"Inside the house, please do not make this a larger issue than it already is," the friendly voice of the local sheriff announced over the PA in his squad car.

"Sheriff Ernst?"

"Yes, Blaire, your attempt to alter a predetermined configuration of the apartment controls, established by your landlord…"

"Are you joking me? You've got to be joking, this is the stupidest thing I've ever heard of!"

"Well," the Sheriff replied, "there is that mattress tag law."

"Ok, but I didn't remove the tag on my mattress."

"Perhaps not, if you had, I wouldn't care, that's a federal problem. The falsification of rental property energy management is a locality issue, and we have clear guidelines."

"How in the heck did you even know what I was doing?" Blaire smiled, tapping each corner of his tablet three times before moving to the next.

When Blaire touched the final corner, the six-armed avatar sheathed all six swords, then bowed to him and said, "Well played." Before winking out and being replaced by the words, 'Factory Reset In Process', in small white letters flashed on the tablet's screen. He grabbed the thermostat's cover, stood, and unplugged the cable from his tablet, rolling it back into the cover, returning it as he found it.

"Son, it doesn't matter how I found out. I do know and that's all that matters. We're heading in, unless you—"

"I'm coming out," he cut across the sheriff by kicking the door open. "You never even asked me to come out, you know." His arms were raised over his head as he stood on the stoop.

"Put your arms down, you putz." Sheriff Ernst tossed the microphone onto his seat.

"Would it be an issue if I locked my door?" Blaire waited.

"Please do, I don't want to be blamed for causing a theft. Now, lock it up and get in the backseat."

"Can't I just drive myself? You don't want to drive me back, and you know there are no cabs that come out here. Please, I'm not going to do anything stupid like try to flee."

"I tell you what, I drive your car and you drive mine." Ernst smiled, looking at the Fairlady.

"Sheriff!" Janey's unique voice yelled from her open door. "He cannot drive your squad car."

"For god's sake, woman, I was kidding," he yelled over his shoulder.

"I'll pull over at the end of the street, you can give the Lady a romp," Blaire winked.

"I'll allow you to drive yourself. Good night, ma'am." He waved to Janey. Before walking to his car Sheriff Ernst whispered, "See you up the street."

Chapter 5
A Wrinkle in the Tapestry

The green glow in the night vision monocle allowed Mason to see the doorway as if in a strange stratosphere of smoldering embers. Placing his small fiber-optic camera into the keyhole, he examined the tumbler set for a moment. Pulling the camera to get his picks, a reflection ever so briefly captured his interest.

"Mason," a small whispering voice prompted.

"Don't, Cary. I would have thought you would've learned not to pester me by now," he shot back. Twisting the camera this way and that, it became clear there were actually three fiber-optic readers inside this lock. "We need to go." He stood, pulling his kit back together.

"That isn't going to happen," the cocking of a pistol filled the hallway. "Mason, we signed up to complete this mission."

"This isn't a mission, Cary, this is a job. A job that I'm telling you we need to walk away from, we don't have much time, they know we…"

"You couldn't have tripped anything, you didn't even touch the tumblers. I watched each move you made. Now, get back to it."

"Or what? You gonna shoot me?" he mocked, continuing to put his tools away.

"He may not, well, you may not believe he will, but you feelin' that I will, yes?" a shiny barrel aimed over Cary's shoulder.

"Ryan, what are you doing?" Feeling the gun entering his space, the fucktard swatted away the gun. Blam! The accidental discharge of the SW 40 took his middle and index fingers, covering Mason's monocle with blood. "Fucking asshole!" Cary fell to the floor in a ball.

"I guess, we are done here." Mason removed the night vision from his head, aggressively wiping the back of his hand across his eyes.

"What would possibly lead you to that conclusion?"

"He's really hurt, you may not see it, but I need to get him to—"

'Blam.' The second shot, not so accidental, ended the crying. "I guess we have all the time in the world now." Ryan waited.

"You really are fucked up."

"Indubitably. Now, get your shit together, we have a certain painting to find as it needs to be leaving here with us."

"I tried telling Cary this lock is not a—"

"I don't care what you tried telling him, get to it, or I will shoot you and then that lock."

"Shooting it won't really do a damn thing. I don't even know if I can get through this door at all." Mason held his hands, laden with his craftsmen's tools.

"Then what is your plan? I think I've shown you, we aren't leaving here without—" Ryan started. Crack! In mid-sentence, Mason spun, kicking the wall directly behind the hinges. "You fucking moron, I told you, Dutch said no damage."

"We needed an alternative entrance." He kicked out several more times, making a hole large enough for him to enter the study beyond. "What makes your boss think the painting is in this room?"

"He saw it in a video-conference, the man who owns this building was stupid enough to take a call in his exchequer. Technically, many other pieces of art were on display that are worth much more than this one. But Dutch was born in Nuenen and he feels this piece must be in his collection."

"Ok, well, I'm in. Do you want to stay out there? Or are you making a larger hole for yourself?"

"What difference does it make?" Ryan poked his head through the hole, following the movement of the smaller man in the dark, the best he could.

"You said I'm going to be picking a safe. To do that, I'll need silence. I'd rather you made your way in before I wasted my time. Some of these units are set to mass fail if you attempt to crack it too many times. And seeing how the door had a self-destruct on it, I wouldn't put it past this man."

"Self-destruct?"

"Yes, that is why I didn't try to pick it."

"Jesus fuck." Ryan moved away from the doorknob. "Ck, I'm staying out here, get this done. I hate the smell of blood and shit."

"Maybe you shouldn't have killed Cary then. Never mind, I'm glad you did, he would have done something stupid anyway. We all probably would've died." Mason wiped the night vision unit, hoping to get as much detritus off it as possible. Seeing a room at least 12 feet tall, decorated in all manner of wonder—sculptures, frescos, sepia prints of inventions from the dark ages, cases with jeweled necklaces, and an actual crown. Beneath the crown, an eight-foot-tall tapestry hung on a rod with a golden finial on one end, while the other side, still golden, had an additional cantilevered support. "Gotcha." He pulled the tapestry, exposing more than a mere safe. The vault door most likely covered a strongroom.

"Fuck!" he knelt down, looking at the maker's mark. "Double fuck." This isn't even a vault he had ever heard of, "I fucking hate rich people." Standing again, he removed the fiber-optic camera that had saved his hand earlier and began running it along the seam between the door and the frame.

"Cops. I hear sirens," Ryan said from the darkness beyond the tapestry.

"Deal with them, I have work to do." Hoping the ape would work himself into a stat on some web page titled 'Suicide by Cop'. Smiling, Mason slowly passed the wheel. Seeing no reflection at all, he continued his camera slowly to the floor, finding another self-destruct finger two inches from the bottom. "Almost fucked up, ol' boy. Good, you stayed the course, Gramps is smiling upon us tonight." Running his finger along the cable, he examined the small trip switch. Another fiber-optic? Taking two types of tools and a roll of tape from his pack, he reviewed the finger on the vault door for another moment, and his plan was made. Taping his camera light source to the receiver side of the trip switch.

After that was secured, he removed the emitter from the door. Adding it to the taped receiver, he slowly withdrew his camera, just as the first gunshots went off somewhere in the building.

"You getting close? I got two, but I can see lights heading this way," Ryan's voice sounded a million miles away as Mason finished securing the trip switch with more pieces of tape to the wall beside the vault door.

"Ok, Mr. Rich Guy." He returned the small camera to the wheel, "Did you really just…" he pulled the handle, and the door swung freely open. "Lazy, lazy." Gramps had always told him that people get stupid cocky, especially if locking a personal vault with a knee-buster, and self-destruct mechanism on an outer door. Inside the strongroom, the smell of ozone air, as well as a temperature-controlled 67 degrees with an obvious low dew point management system rattled in the overhead. "A possible exit point?" Mason pondered as he snapped his small oxygen tank over his nose. "I fucking hate ozone machines." The painting, Vincent van Gogh's 'Congregation Leaving the Reformed Church in Nuenen, was there, on the farthest wall. '. "Ugliest painting I ever stole." He shook his head, looking one last time for tripwires, finding none. He removed the frame from the wall, the attachment of the picture was done by a professional, but four cuts later from his CobraTec autoblade, and the canvas fell loose, rolling into a cylinder. To the left of the painting, a brown leather scabbard for carrying art lay on the shelf. Taking an extra moment, Mason found this was where the owner had chosen to put another tripwire.

Following it back, he found it would force what looked like an air piston to draw the door closed. "I like this guy, he's a tricky bastard." Taking the few steps to the entrance, he laid his pack in the path to hopefully stop the door from closing. "Fuck it," he set the painting in the opening as well. "If you break my shit, I break your painting." Once again, he extended the blade of his knife and cut the airline to the piston.

"Come on!" Ryan yelled, closer now.

"Got it." The tripwire cut as his blade retracted. Mason grabbed the art carrier, taking it to the awaiting painting. Stepping from the vault, he slid the art into the tube and slung it over his shoulder and fastened his tool pack around his waist.

"Here." A waving arm in the darkness held something, a box.

"What the fuck is that?"

"Payment," Ryan replied. "My boss is trading for that. Put it on his desk. Oh, don't take anything else... seriously, nothing."

"Seriously? So, I should put back the Shroud of Turin and the Hope Diamond?"

"What?"

"Joking." He tossed the box on top of the desk beside stacks of cash. "Get out of my way, this place is fucking with my mind." Mason kicked a leg through the opening just as another series of gunshots started in the hallway.

"Argh!" Ryan's falling body forced Mason's leg back through the opening as he absorbed the six gunshots.

"This isn't even possible!" he muttered and ran back to the vault, ignoring the sound of shooting still going on. He used his gymnastic ability acquired when his father tried to reduce the effects of his childhood asthma through training. His legs and hands in concert ran up the inside of the vault wall until his face was inches from the rattling HVAC unit. "Come on, Gramps, an idea, any idea." His foot pushed over a box containing an old samurai sword. "Thanks, gramps." The blade worked its way through the grating and the metal roof like butter. Two prying attempts caused the bolts to loosen, and he forced himself into the service area. He kept the sword in case he needed another fulcrum.

"If there's anyone in there, we've gotten your two partners. Give up, we don't want to have to kill you too," the voice finished its coaxing just as the door tripwire blew whoever was over there in half.

Dumbass, why did you think there was a hole in the wall? Mason thought as he worked his way up. Finding the ever-present cliché fan running and blocking his pathway. Dispatching the conduit leading into the motor junction box Gramps referred to as a pecker-head, with another flick of the sword. Stopping the free-spinning fan blade with the sheathe allowed him to climb to the roof. When his feet were out, he dropped the borrowed property down into the darkness. "That may have been a mistake." Bending, he secured the vent cover before starting across the roof, trying to stay out of any light that would provide feedback to his night vision unit, hoping that would also mean the police wouldn't be able to see him either. At the edge of the building, he had to remove the eyepiece and hope for the best as there were no more shadows. There were two possibilities — straight below him was a pond with a fountain in the middle, the other, at the corner a drain spout ran down the frame.

In the courtyard, he could hear the radios of the squad cars squawking. "No replies? No answers to dispatch." Further up the road, more sirens were signaling their path. Most concerning, there were two helicopters inbound. "Ok, Grampa Patrick, show me the way home." As he said this, a large bird landed in the pond, showing the water was no more than a few inches deep. "Drain spout it is."

Chapter 6

Only You Can Prevent... You Know the Rest

The radio crackled. "Base one to any in the range of this transmission. Base one in need of immediate help." The night fell back to silence and an oil lamp that was a mere spark a moment earlier grew bright. "Base one to all those in range to pick up this transmission.. Dammit, Robert, I know you can hear me." The voice was that of a scared woman, and from the sound of it, she had a two-pack-a-day habit that rolled back several decades.

"Go ahead, Base one," the baritone voice replied.

"Robert?" the scarred vocal cords raised their pitch.

"I said go ahead, Base one." Aggravated, he tossed a handful of kindling from inside his tent onto the dead fire pit.

"Yes, yes, of course..." chastised, the voice continued, "Base one reporting three lost children on the mountain. Repeat, three children lost somewhere on the mountain."

"Delta go to three channels up, from my call-sign and count the same. Copy?" Robert asked, lighting a twig on the oil lamp, throwing it into the kindling.

"Copy," the voice replied, and the night grew deadly still. "Delta to 50-Out, do you copy?" the voice came across channel 53, 53 seconds later.

"50-Out, here. Report out on the children."

"Two of them are brother and sister — David, 12, and Cate, 16. And a family friend, Jasmine, also 16. They were camping with Alfred and Ellaine Best, the siblings' parents."

"Best? As in Best Real Estate?" Robert asked.

"I believe so. Is that important?"

"I played football with Jason. Alfred's brother and the partner in his business. Based upon my remembrance of Jason and his family, there's nothing hinky going on. Please continue."

"The parents went to sleep and when they woke up, they found a note that said, 'Going hiking. We'll meet you at Mom's favorite inn before nightfall.' They were nervous but they drove to Len Foote Hike Inn."

"The kids were a no-show." It wasn't a question, Robert started thinking through all the times the park rangers called on him. "Did the parents try to find the kids?"

"When the sun came up, Alfred set Ellaine to let the rangers know what happened while he went back to their campground from the previous night to find their tracks."

"He knows better, he lived in the shadow of the mountain for long enough to know he could obscure the tracks... never mind," Robert cut off his torment. "Ok, did the dogs make it out?"

"Pack's dogs are in Chillicothe, OH at an annual contest."

"And Weaver's?"

"Weaver's dog died three years ago," Delta replied.

"Seriously?"

"Yes, Robert, you've been living under the influence of the mountain for quite a while."

"Ok, where were they camping?"

"Somewhere off Flat Creek Loop…"

"And they thought they could make it all the way to Dawsonville by nightfall? From Flat Creek Loop, I'm guessing I could make it in 12 hours, but kids? Even kids from Georgia, no way. Get the coordinates of their camp and I'll meet Alfred there at first light."

"Sent to your email address. Thanks, Robert. Delta, out."

"50-Out, shutting down." Moments later, the insects started filling the camp with native songs. In the distance, wolves started communicating with each other. "Yeah, yeah. How does a park ranger turned survivalist trainer, turned hillbilly reject, keep getting called to save idiotic people?" The pack kept howling as he secured his camp, making certain the fire he just lit was extinguished safely.

The hike was more annoying than dangerous, though the wolves did seem to be closer than he liked, and he fired a couple of warning shots from the .45 Redhawk he carried open in the Doc Holiday position. By the time dawn was breaking, he was less than a mile from the location Delta had sent to him. When he walked up on the campsite, Alfred was sitting on a lawn chair sleeping, the remnants of a fire smoldering in front of him. "How far did you walk down the trail?" Robert's deep voice came off as an explosion in the silence of the woods.

"What the…" The lawn chair crumbled as the big man jostled awake, in less than a peaceful manner.

"I said, how far down the trail did you go?"

"Maybe five miles." He stood, dusting himself off.

"Really? You tracked them for five miles? As I recall, you weren't that much of an outdoors kinda guy. That's impressive if it's true."

"If? They're my kids, why would I…"

"Yes, if. I don't believe you. I'm here to find the three children. I don't care if they are yours or some Buckingham Palace-looking butler-head-motherfucker's kids. I want the truth. How far?"

"Not far, a quarter of a mile maybe before I lost their trail." Alfred looked at the ground and closed his eyes. "They said they were going to…"

"I'm in the loop on where they said they were going. But did they really know, 'A', which direction Dawsonville was and, 'B', were they actually that good in the travailing the mountain trails? I don't see it. Why…" The howl of a wolf in the distance garnered his attention. "The sun rose several hours ago."

"I'm sorry?" Alfred sat up.

"The wolves, they're up late." Like a bullet from a gun, Robert shot toward the misplaced howling. Ignoring the obvious paths which would have several jigs and jags, and the call for him to slow to allow Alfred to catch up, his pace increased. For three-quarters of a mile, he danced around boughs and endured low hanging withes smacking him as he ducked under the trees before closing in on the sound. Pulling a loaded moon-clip from his waist pack, Robert reloaded the revolver, knowing the importance of entering an unclear situation with a fully loaded gun.

After 10 minutes, he broke through a final bramble, finding a pack of wolves facing off against, three mountain lions, a contest to earn the spoils, the three prone children. "Don't move. For God's sake don't fucking move." His first shot took the largest lion in the head. Gathering the attention of the remaining on himself, Robert ignored them all, turning first to the left and then to the right he searched.

"What are you looking for?" the boy — David, if his recollection was correct — asked.

"The alpha, he won't be in the direct attack." There, 25 yards behind the mountain lions, he spotted the large black wolf was closing quickly. Bang! His first shot missed as the dark creature danced to the left as the mountain lion in its sights, and nearest the children, decided Robert wasn't as easy a prey as the smaller humans were. The third shot took the undeterred lion in the head, the large frame dropped feet from the children. The fourth flash from the gun found the alpha between its golden eyes, the carcass crashed hard into the tallest girl, taking her out at the knees.

"Aww shit, my leg!" she screamed.

"Cate!" Alfred yelled, finally reaching the party. "Ass, did you shoot my daughter?"

"Stop, you idiot!" Too late, the much larger man crashed into him sending Robert's body tumbling end over end. Planting his foot, hoping it wouldn't break his leg, he stood, disentangling himself from the father of the children he was here to help. When the larger man crashed into the pack of wolves, disorienting them, it gave Robert time to shoot the last lion and the wolf approaching David. Like any respectable gunman, he thumbed the release, swinging open the cylinder and removing the brass cartridges held together in the moon-clip. Pulling another full one from his case, it was loaded and slapped into place in time to shoot the leaping wolf before it could bite him, though it landed heavily upon his shoulder.

"Help!" Alfred found himself in the middle of five growling canines. With no other course of action, he dropped into a tuck.

Shrugging off the impact of the leaping wolf, Robert squeezed the fastest five shots of his life, each bullet dropping three and killing two wolves. Walking up, he loaded the partial moon-clip from earlier and stopped the suffering of the other three pack hunters. "Fuck me, I hate killing these creatures."

"It was kinda necessary," the small girl said with her hands on her hips.

"Yeah, Cate, it was, but it doesn't mean he has to like it. Thank you, by the way," the tall girl who must be Jasmine rebuked her friend.

"Yeah, sure. Alfred, there's your kids. Do you

know how to get back to your car?" Robert loaded his Redhawk and holstered it.

"That was amazing shooting." David walked up, proffering a hand out to the stranger.

"Thank you." He shook the hand, still looking at the boy's father.

"I do, I just need to follow the trail you made. I imagine the animals will be far from us at this point."

"Well, getcha gone then." Robert pointed the way up the mountain.

"A man of few words?" Cate commented as she started back in the direction of his arm.

"Can't you escort us?" David asked.

"If I leave these dead animals here like this, a bunch of hikers will get into serious trouble."

"Why?" Jasmine cocked an eyebrow.

"Scavengers will think this area is a smorgasbord, and when they don't find food..." Robert started.

"Problems will ensue," Alfred finished.

"How is it you only made it this far in 24 hours?" He cocked an eyebrow.

"We were doing good when we had a cellphone, but when it died, I think we were walking in circles," David replied.

"No thinking about it, I counted that big boulder 12 times," Jasmine pointed.

"It's a nice boulder," Robert did his best donkey impersonation, to no reaction from those he just saved.

"I'm sorry, what?" Cate asked.

"Pop culture isn't her strong suit," Alfred laughed as the four headed up the mountain.

Chapter 7
It is the Truth, its Actual

Holding on to the edge of a southside building, the figure of a stout man craned his neck just far enough to look through the seventh-floor window. Freezing in that position for more than two minutes, eventually, the object of his investigation turned the light on in the room adjacent. Pulling his head back, he activated the remote trigger for the recording device attached to his sleeve. Trying to stay as still as possible, needing good video evidence for his client.

"Oh, Roger, I love it," a female voice, mere feet from him, voiced her pleasure to a gift of some kind.

"Of course, you do," a less than masculine voice squeaked back. "I have amazing taste." He laughed, a harsh barking expulsion of less than mirth.

"Can we go to the theatre now?" she asked. The question made the eavesdropping stranger, unobserved by anyone, roll his eyes knowing what was coming next.

"Sure, let me get the tickets," his voice trailed away and the window on the other side of him came into relief as the light came on. "Dora, can you come in here? I can't find the tickets, maybe you can lend a hand."

"Oh dear, you can't find the tickets?" her voice took the same path as Roger's. "That's terrible, do you think someone could have stolen them?"

"God help the stupid," the anonymous figure mocked as he pulled himself to the sill above. Once securely on the roof, he balled his hands several times, getting the blood flowing again. After they felt normal, and the couple below had several minutes to search for the missing tickets, he started to creep gently along the edge of the building. Stopping when he was just to the left of the window below, he pulled the lanyard hanging around his neck from inside his shirt. "Well, let's see if this works." Touching the camera to the pendant swinging on the end of the lanyard, 'click' the magnet found purchase. "Hmm, nice," he said, trying and failing to shake the camera from the plate. Lowering the lanyard over the ledge until it was well beyond the top of the window, he waited.

"You there! What are you doing?" the same squeaky voice asked.

"Fuck!" He pulled the lanyard up and slid it over his neck.

"Roger, there's a man lying on the roof. Do you think he's hurt?"

"Dora, this is obviously the thief of my concert tickets," he replied.

"Theatre," the correction came from the eavesdropper.

"What?" Roger asked.

"The tickets were for the theatre," he turned, standing, his hands opened and raised to shoulder height. When seeing they were both unarmed, he dropped his hands.

"Fine, fine. Who are you? Why are you on the roof of my apartment?"

"Well, that's a bit sticky. You see, I was hired by your wife to — "

"Wife? Roger?" Dora smacked the ticketless man across the face.

"Ooh that stung. Miss, should I finish answering him?"

"I don't care, I'm leaving." She stepped around him and walked down the stairs.

"Ok, Roger, my name is Private Detective Truth, and as I started to say — "

"My wife hired you, I get it. Now give me that camera and I'll let you leave." Roger gracefully rolled his arm, indicating the stairs as if he had just turned a letter. "You'll find I'm rather congenial, if you work with me." Roger crossed his arms, waiting.

"Thing is, you can't imagine how difficult it was for me to get these shots, so I'm just not gonna take the stairs." The private detective turned, and without a single breath, he leaped into empty air.

"What the hell?" Roger ran to the ledge, seeing the stranger stop his fall momentarily by grabbing a window sill on the building across the alley. Shaking his head as he watched the man release and freefall to the floor below, where he grabbed another ledge, once again stopping his fall. Miraculously, the man repeated the process five more times before landing on the ground. Turning, the man looked up and flipped off his stunned target, giving a guffaw before walking away.

"Asshat." The Private detective put his hands in his pockets.

"Mister." Dora's heels clippity-clopped up behind him, "Hey, mister, wait."

"Yes?" He spun around but continued his progress, walking carefully backwards.

"Can I please have the tickets? I really was looking forward to the theatre."

"There never were any tickets. Roger was lying to you to get under your skirt."

"But he said you stole them." She cocked her head like a confused puppy.

"He said I stole the concert tickets, the slob forgot his own lie."

"Roger? A slob? You got him all wrong, mister, Roger is very dapper." Dora gave a dreamy smile, making him turn and continue to gain distance, "Hey, mister, how did you get down to the alley before me?"

"I jumped. Now, if you don't mind, I have an entire file of rules I live by, and one of them is not to talk to the mark."

"Mark? No, no, mister, I'm Dora."

"Thank you for the clarification." His eyes were stuck in an endless eye-roll. The dark alley was a perfect place for him to step in a puddle before making it to his car. "Fuck, I hope that was water."

"It wasn't," a gravelly voice in the deeper shadows beside his ride said.

"Thanks for keeping an eye on her, Dag."

"No problem, Clear." The shadow transformed into a seven-foot-tall albino black man.

"Here's your cut." He held out 200 standard

gold.

"I'm fine with one of those, I wasn't the one hanging from the side of a building."

"Take them both. Next time, you may have the harder gig."

"Fair." The giant took the bills, immediately rolling them into tubes and tucking them into the barrel of his Kimber 1911, which he had pulled from his shoulder holster.

"If you ever need to shoot that thing, you're gonna lose a shit load of money."

"If I ever need to shoot it, I'm more than fucked as I got no bullets in it." Holstering the pistol, he walked off.

"You know I can give you some bullets, right?"

"Can't shoot anyhow, just like the way it feels. Besides, it was my grandad's, makes me feel closer to him to carry it." Dag's silhouette stayed just as large as he walked away.

"If you run into a stupid girl down there, ask her if she needs a ride home." Clear opened the driver's door and got into his 1969 Marauder. Closing the door, he flipped on the switch to open the headlight buckets before starting the car — a little trick he put in to make certain no one could hotwire the car if they got past Dag. He laughed as he started the 48-point turn to get this enormous car out of the alley.

Finally free, he thought about the stupid woman, Dora. Maybe he should have offered her a ride, "Truth's rules are always Clear," he laughed at his stupid pun. Thinking back, until the age of six, everyone thought his name was Clarence Joseph Truth. A truth that changed on his first day of school. The teacher, while calling attendance, was the first to notice that his correct name was actually Clearance.

The school corrected what they thought was a typo, but after doing a bit of research, his parents discovered the teacher had been correct, he really was Clearance Joseph Truth. Although, becoming a private detective having a name like Clear Truth wasn't such a bad thing. When a boy grows up with a name like Clearance, it's good to live by rules such as, 'Don't let stupid get under your skin'. Every person works their way through their lives with rules, most don't actually define them, or even know what theirs are, while others beat them into their brains like a mantra. He happened to be in the latter group. Truth's rules are what he started calling his guiding mantras.

The moment he returned from his daydream, he found himself in a traffic jam pulling on one of the aforementioned rules, 'Keep your nose out of other people's business, unless you're getting paid.' As the man in the SUV in front of him hit the woman in the passenger seat once, and then again, Clear forgot all about rules. Throwing his door open, he walked up and opened the passenger door of the SUV.

"I know CPR, can I help?" remembering the little certification card never quite fitting into his wallet.

"What? Shut my door and go back to your car!" the man barked.

"No, really, I think you're doing the Heimlich maneuver wrong. I can help." Taking the woman's elbow and guiding her from the vehicle, Clear whispered, "Are you ok?"

Before she could answer, the man stomped around the car. "I don't know what you're playing at but I'm gonna rip your damn head off."

When the man reached him, he turned, looking straight into the other man's chest, 'Of Course!' echoed in his head. "No, seriously, let me show you." Guiding the behemoth's body into position. "Here, stand around the back of the choking victim and reach your arms around her. Now, make a fist with one hand while placing your other hand flat against the back of it. Perfect, great, now you're going to put your balled fist three fingers below her xiphoid."

"She's not even ch—" the man started.

"Breathing," Clear raised his voice in panic. "She's not breathing? Oh my, quickly, now place your balled fist three fingers... well, you have fat fingers so maybe two... yeah, two fingers, below her xiphoid. No, wait, here let me show you." Spinning him around so they were face to face, "Right here at the bottom of the sternum is a floating bone," he said, placing his index and middle fingers against the center of his barrel chest.

"I don't know what your game is, ya lunatic! Robyn, get in the damn car, you stupid witch, the traffic jam is starting to break up." He gave the woman a push, directing her back to the open car door. When she stumbled and fell, he reached up, grabbing Clear's fingers.

"Exactly, right there's your xiphoid. It seems kinda useless but it indirectly attaches the costal cartilage to the sternum. When you're doing CPR or the Heimlich, you need to be careful of this little guy because—" halting the statement, he pulled his fingers out of the monster's grasp. Using this momentum to increase the force of the punch which landed at the base of his sternum, sending him crumbling to the expressway like over-watered concrete in a slump test.

"Bastard!" he moaned from the ground.

"Ma'am, if this man is someone you'd like to ditch, and I suggest you do, this'd be the time." Clear held a hand out to her.

Brushing it aside, she rushed over to the fallen louse. "Herbie." The first word she spoke was a squeaky, nasally whine. She bent over, helping him up, but while she did, her eyes looked the private detective up and down. "Asshat!"

Walking back to the Marauder, Clear pulled around them and drove off as she helped Herbie into the passenger seat. Another Truth's rule popped into his head, 'Some people don't know enough to be rescued.' Looking at himself in the rearview mirror, he said, "Can't blame her for checking you out though. You, my man, are pretty damn good-looking, for a short, bulky, greying bastard. But an asshat, really? Oh give it up, she's right, I'm fairly certain, we've been called that a time or a dozen." Laughing, he continued to drive, eyes sweeping the highway and then up to the rearview mirror, checking out the cars still sitting in the traffic jam. Many now having their doors opened, their drivers striding to the SUV offering their help. "Moron," he bitched at himself. "This is gonna get ugly, save yourself some aggravation, next time you want to ignore one of Truth's rules, just sit on a fucking cactus." He winked at himself and turned on the radio. A podcast about personal improvement shared a new positive affirmation prayer, which Truth memorized as he drove to his office.

When the sight of the Clear Truth Detective Agency sign came into view, a flash memory of all the skeevy PIs he worked under to earn that shingle raced through his mind. The office was in a building that used to be a pharmacy in a less than hospitable part of Boston, but at least it's close to the bars and seriously good pizza. Inside the office, Truth had set up a nice little gym in the back, mostly old-school free weights. At some point, when people started hitting truck tires with sledgehammers, Clear felt like giving it a try, so there were a few giant tires in the corner for sledging and flipping.

Clear knew he was kinda stupid that way; trying new and trendy shit. This workout really seemed to help him with traceur though, he refused to call it parkour. Clearance Joseph Truth started free-running more than 20 years ago when a gymnastics coach who had been in the French military got him hooked. Only the French could invent a way of retreating so fashionably.

His addictive personality typically burned through addictions rather quickly, not so with traceur. Being so into it, he removed a portion of the second floor of his building, setting up bars for practice. A few years ago, he even had an invitational jam here, and although he never competed in outside events, suffice it to say, those in the know of traceur knew the truth about Truth.

Chapter 8

Dare to be…

The light intermittently filtering in through the window of the ambulance started getting reactions from the man the EMT team now knew to be one of the richest men on the planet. "Telly, can you see if you can block the street lights from buzzing his face?"

"Sure, but why?" she turned from their patient, looking for the tie holding the shades up.

"The light seems to be irritating him," Bret replied.

"Stop, Telly, leave it open. Bret, PERRLA him and let me know what you see," Captain Green ordered from behind the wheel of the ambulance.

"Yes, ma'am." Removing the pen light from his pocket, he shone the small light into the open eye. "His eyes roll back when I turn the light on. Quickly returning when the light is turned off."

"Roll back? That's not what I was expecting. Can you tell if the pupils themselves are reactive?"

"I couldn't really tell. Let me try to—" Bret started.

"Please, don't."

"Jesus! Fuck!" The pen light fell to the floor as the young man pulled back from the patient who held his eyes closed.

"The glare is terribly painful," the cultured voice stated amiably.

"Is that him?" The Captain began pulling the

ambulance off the highway.

"Yes, ma'am." Telly reached out to stop Mr. Dare from attempting to roll over and away from the light. "Sir, you need to sit still. We are taking you to the hospital for some tests."

"Which hospital?" He discontinued his attempt to roll from the gurney.

"St. Elmo's," Captain Green replied as she dropped the car into park.

"Good, good." Ananias breathed in deeply and lost consciousness again.

"Ma'am, you might as well stay up there," Bret yelled up to his Captain.

"Why?" She pulled the rear doors open.

"He's out again," Telly replied.

"That was really odd. He was perfectly lucid." Bret reached down, picking up his pen light again.

"Alright, secure him, looks like he loosened those straps." Closing the door, she returned to the driver's seat and they were off again. 25 minutes later, she radioed the emergency room at St. Elmo's, "Dispatch, in bound Slade Dixie 112 with mid-50-year-old male. Unknown reason for unconsciousness. Temporarily regained…"

"Slade Dixie 112, why are you in transport to our facility? There were no call-outs for emergency care from this location. Redirect to Brown Desert Homeland, there are no beds available…"

"We are transporting Ananias Dare at his direct request," Captain Green's smile was obvious in her voice. Stopping her transmission, she looked at the microphone in her hand, "Asshat."

"Very well, I have your location on our tracking. You appear to be 20 minutes out. Are there any preparations we need to have made?" Dispatch recanted the earlier rebuke.

"The request was just to get him there. As I started to say, he regained consciousness briefly, and was lucid and responsive before passing out again." A moment later, she added, "The lights were hurting his head, we can put a covering on his eyes, but the room you will put him in may need filtering."

"Thank you, we will make the proper accommodations. We have contacted his doctor, I believe your arrival may be a few moments prior to hers. Can you slow your transport to allow her seven minutes?"

"Of course, sir."

"Why the hell would we do that?" Telly stuck her head into the front seat.

"Why not? This is a weird night anyway. We could turn around and fix up some random bar fight victims, or we can enjoy the ride. Besides, I need gas, the old girl has used almost all the pre-charge power and secondary petrol charging."

"That'll take 15 minutes."

"What's the matter, Bret, afraid I will short charge her?" Green laughed. "Again."

"You do know that really is bad for the environment, right?"

"It is? I thought you were joking the last

thousand times you told me."

"You know she's doing what is right for the patient, right?" Telly turned to face Bret.

"Why can't she do it without ignoring the rest of the... stuff?" his arms flailed above them.

"I'll try to do better," she said, stopping next to the public vehicle fast-charging units. "Anyone need anything from the Repository Center?"

"I could use some Nico-Gum, having a rough day today."

"I'll see what they have. How about you, Bret?"

"Vega-treats, I'm pretty hungry. Thank you, ma'am."

"That's what I'm here for." She connected the adaptor, then walked to the other side connecting the petroleum to the backup tank. Six minutes later, the support connections were replaced, and the ambulance was pulling back onto the highway. "Telly, are you sure you're not addicted to that gum?"

"Well, I like nicotine, can't smoke anymore, can't even synth anymore."

"Considering synthing killed thousands of people, mayhaps that's a good thing," the man said from the gurney.

"You gotta stop doing that, geez you're gonna give me a heart attack," Bret said, picking himself off the floor.

"Sorry. Was I out long?" Mr. Dare asked.

"Not quite 40 minutes. Why?" Telly touched

his neck to see if his pulse was irregular.

"The periods of darkness will continue until the light defeats it in three minutes."

"I beg your pardon?" Bret asked.

"He's out again," Telly replied. "Sounds like he knows what's going on. Why do rich people have to be so fucking—"

"What?" Captain Green asked as the silence stretched for a while.

"I don't know…" He paused, "Have to be all that." He pointed at the black braid with the precious stones. "That decoration is worth more than we all will make in 20 years. And it's just there, sitting in his hair."

"Take it."

"Excuse me, ma'am?" Bret almost peed himself.

"He won't miss it, he won't know when he had it last," Captain Green replied, nonchalantly.

"I would never." Bret shook her head.

"Of course, you wouldn't, neither would Telly, nor I. And they know that."

"Not everyone is honest," Bret shot back.

"And yet we picked him up in the heart of the capital, a ridiculously scary area… where was his limo, or hell, even his chauffeur? The rich stay rich because they are protected, he didn't just walk into that building. Something here is odd and different." The ambulance exited the highway, "Dispatch St. Elmo's, this is Slade Dixie 112."

"Go ahead."

"We are four minutes out, are we trending proper with Mr. Dare's doctor?"

"Affirmative."

"Please let her know he woke again, but only briefly."

"Shall do." The dispatch signed off.

"There is a small amount of blood trickling from his fingernails," Bret reported.

"Both hands?"

"Yes, ma'am."

"Odd, well, we're here and they'll need to deal with it at this point." She turned off the flashers, pulling up under the covered unloading area. Beginning to back up to the double doors, "Dispatch, Slade Dixie 112 for unloading. We have additional information that will need to be communicated to his—" her words stalled at the sight of a tall woman in a surgical smock running up, smacking the rear of the ambulance, and then throwing the door open.

"What was the new piece of information?" the woman asked in a heavily accented voice.

"This, ma'am." Bret held the splayed fingers, showing the blood.

"Very well, very well. Can you please escort Mr. Dare into the hospital? The man at the front desk will tell you where to take him. When you arrive there, please communicate this to the doctor in the room," she indicated the fingernails.

"Of course, ma'am." Jumping up, releasing the

stretcher, Bret stepped from the ambulance as Telly helped him maneuver the gurney out.

"I'm going to need your assurance that this trip never took place," the woman said after walking around to meet Captain Green.

"Not a problem." She shrugged her shoulders, looking up at the extremely tall woman.

"Well, technically, it currently is. To make it not a problem," Looking at the name tag on her chest. "Captain, I will need you and your crew to sign these non-disclosure agreements. Your signature is worth four times your annual salary, each. Deletion of any and all records, which I will facilitate, is worth six times your salaries. And finally, your departure of this state is 20 times each. If you choose to leave for ASP... 100 times and documentation. These numbers compound upon each other. In other words, if you sign, delete your records and go to ASP, you will receive 130 times your salary."

"Hmm. But I like it here so much."

"Captain Green, these are real numbers, real money. No one can know that Mr. Dare took ill in any way. Is that clear?"

"A couple of things, first, I know who you are, and you aren't Mr. Dare's doctor. Second, Mr. Dare did not simply walk into a random building. That was a terrible cover story. And third, he said, 'The periods of darkness will continue until the light defeats it in three minutes.' I'll sign your papers and get my team to do the same. But you will tell me what is happening."

"There is a conglomeration of the world's most

influential people. This group meets four times a year. The only way you can leave the group is to submit yourself to a very particular electric shock, additionally, all the other members get shocked and branded for each who leave. That is what happened, that's all."

"The doctors haven't even examined him. How can you know…" Captain Green started.

"He informed me in advance of his decision to leave, and clarified what occurs when a person elects to discharge their position. The shock is not long-lasting, it will clear up when the spells stop taking longer than three minutes between waking moments." She held a clipboard out, "I have answered your questions, and please let me know what your final decisions will be."

"America Springs Politica for me. I will let the kids make their own decision, there is a 90% chance that they will be following me as I trained them both." She walked into the hospital, followed by the doctor.

"Leave the documents with the guard at the reception desk. All will be fulfilled in 24 hours. I will send your assistants to you presently." She passed the captain and pointed to the desk, she was dismissed. She continued her walk up the corridor until she came upon the two assistants. "Your supervisor has some paperwork for you to fill out. I want you to know two things, first, Mr. Dare's friends must have your acceptance of the terms of the paperwork you will be signing."

"Must?" Bret asked.

"Shut up, Bret." Telly grabbed his shoulder,

"You will, of course, get our acceptance. Which way do we go to find Captain Green?"

"Right back down that ramp. She's at the reception desk." The doctor who still had never introduced herself pointed.

"Thank you." They started walking in the direction of the unreasonably long finger. After walking about 10 steps, Bret turned, "What was the second thing?"

"Yes," she slowly tilted her head from side to side, taking in the young people in front of her. "We don't know how much you make, and to a certain extent, we don't care." She pivoted her hips and walked into the room where her boss lay. "Doctor Phashtal, is Mr. Dare ok to be taken to his private room?" Removing the doctor's smock, revealing a multi-colored blouse.

"It's just as you indicated, your Honor. He is fully stable and all vitals are reactive, I will have him taken up at once." She addressed the nearly seven-foot-tall woman looking down at the man on the stretcher.

"I will see him to his room, remember, no one is to know he is here." The Judge replied.

"Very well, when you are there, I will run his blood counts, determining whether he is looking or the quick recovery you believe he is in for."

"Miusnka, you are so adorable questioning the boss." Taking the handle of the gurney with a wink.

"Judge Morris, can I ask…"

"No, there will be no revels tonight. Tonight,

Ananias will leave all of our lives as he has indicated. I have little to no patience for questions. You personally know, I've loved this man for decades, and I am doing my part to allow him to abjure his responsibilities."

"To you?"

"I have never been so lucky. It's his responsibilities to every fucking person on this world that I'm remonstrating for, not me." Shaking out her arms, the sleeves of her gypsy top loosened as she kicked the release, allowing the gurney to begin its progress from the room.

"You have got to be the most interesting judge who has ever sat on the high court," Doctor Phashtal smiled at the svelte female walking from her.

"Perhaps later we could discuss that further." Her smile was accented with a wink as the door closed of its own accord.

"You have some serious issues," the voice from the gurney said softly.

"I have a simple reply… fuck you, Mr. Dare."

"Judge, you have nothing to fear from me after today."

"Of course not. I'm just a judge who has been bought and paid for by the last…"

"The important part of that statement—a judge who WAS bought and paid for. Look, I have but a measure of time before I will be off in search of my holy grail… whatever that may be."

"Ananias…" she squared her shoulders to his.

"Stop, I need you to know you will be free after this last, small trip is over. Additionally, you must know I have loved you more than you can fully understand, more to the point... that needs to die now as well."

"I will always dream a way that there would have been more." She bent, kissing his forehead.

"Can that simple gesture be it?" He leaned back into her as they entered the room. "I will always cherish what we had. And, Praiha, know you have always taken my breath away, in another time, we would have been the unafraid lovers." He reached up, taking her hand, kissing it softly. His eyes, softly lidded for a 50-year-old man, peered up, seeing the tears running down her cheek.

"I hate you."

"I'm most certain that is the case but, your honor, please grasp the words of Mark Twain, 'Two of the most important days in your life... The day you were born and the day you learned why...' Today will once again start the understanding of the latter." His time elapsed, and he gave into darkness again.

"I love you. Bastard." A tear fell on his forehead when she kissed him one last time. To be a bitch, she turned on the TV, knowing that would drive him insane, and left the room.

In the night, hours or minutes later, he woke to the torturous machine the judge turned on for his displeasure — the idiot box on the wall. A particularly annoying series of colors dominated the dark room, breaking into his peaceful slumber. Color after color dug into his very psyche, "For goodness sake." He patted down the rail on the bed, searching for the shut-off switch. His eyes focused on yellow, black, and green screens on the television above him. "Hmm, iamthetraveler? Ok, let's see what you think about me."

'To those who call themselves the Traveler,

My name is Ananias Dare, I would not deem my life to have been anything aside from cold, calculating, and selfish. I have never given a single iota for doing anything for anyone but myself. Early in life, it became apparent I was a gifted scholar and an extremely competent mathematician. My father began my training to become a strategic planner. The training that he put to use made our family obscenely rich. I have sat as the chair of the think tank I formed for 25 years, a position I recently stepped down from. And at 52 years of age, turning my life toward giving back to my country directly. Rather than from behind the closed curtain.

Yours humbly,

A. Dare'

Chapter 9
Demon of Demo

The morning came without an alarm, JaLen hadn't needed one of those from the day he decided football was the path in life he would pursue. "Rise-n-Shine." He slid his feet to the floor and waited for what depended on the day of the week it was... today being Tuesday, his mind would demand pancakes. Who could say why Tuesday was Pancake Day? It didn't matter, it always was. If he gave in, he would be jumping in his car looking for the nearest morning eatery. A roll of his head on his huge shoulders and an arching of his back lifted him off of the bed. A few steps and he was standing in front of the toilet, beginning his morning with a good long piss.

Tapping off, he turned the shower on all the way to hot. "Playing with fire today, need to be really clean." He smiled at his reflection and walked back to the bed stand, picking up the notepad. "What do you think, Victoria-Lynn? Why not, right?" He grabbed the tablet, forgotten in his travel bag. "Let's see who these people are."

Typing in the query page search bar, 'iamthetraveler'. Nothing. 'I am the traveler', only song lyrics and music videos came up. "Flibberty Jibitz. How about, 'who is the traveler?' Seriously nothing?" He gave up and went to his email account.

'To whom it may concern,

I have, for years, felt a pang of guilt for not fulfilling what I would call my duty to country. What is your television bulletin board all about?'

His auto-signature populated the end of the email, 'Rip and Spit – Demo Demon', as he hit send.

"Alright, don't know if that was wise. Maybe I should have sent it from an anonymous email." Walking back to the steaming shower, he grabbed his razor and started his morning with a slight tingle of refreshment, knowing he didn't want to be anonymous, he wanted to know what was up.

25 minutes later, JaLen walked from the hotel room with his tablet under his arm, thinking only of getting out to his truck. Completely ignoring the gym today, after all, he was playing with fire, he needed to be at his best. Even an easy workout may make for an accident from extra blood pumping. Fire didn't like to be taken less than seriously, especially when the Demo Demon called on it for destruction. Smiling, he pushed the yearning for the fire away with the mashing of the elevator button.

"Sir?" a tiny woman with huge eyes, attending the elevator, touched her face, more specifically, the mask under the plastic shield covering her face. The animated emoji on her mask was presenting a terrified face.

"Shit, sorry." He turned and headed back to his room. Opening the door, he grabbed the balaclava from the purification stand. *I wear my balaclava specifically because those bullshit animations pissed me off,* he thought. *Idiot, if this is the way you start a day as important as today… fire gonna fuck you up.* Pulling the red face covering over his head, he let the room's door close. "Get your head in the game, son." He pushed the elevator button, waiting once more.

"Thank you, sir." This time, the emoji smiled.

"Um-hmm." The hate for this woman was unreasonable, but truly there nonetheless. When the door opened, he stepped out without waiting to hear the typical verbal cue of 'Farewell', allowing him to refocus himself and face the day. Walking out to his rental car, his phone started to ring. "This is JaLen."

"I know it's JaLen, I called you," a jovial voice replied over the truck's stereo.

"Hey, stranger, what's got you calling so early on this Tuesday?"

"The reports on the post-tension beams in your garage, they used a cheaper grade of cable than we initially thought."

"Shit, if I attempt to clear them early, snap, pop, boom. Concrete missiles the size of garbage can lids will fall on the crews. At least we reinforced the ends so they wouldn't shoot out and kill the neighbors for nothing." JaLen shook his head as he pulled out into traffic. "Well, Stephan, do you have any good news?"

"If they would just let us have the neighborhood for one day."

"That's not helping." Exhaling through his nose deeply, he composed himself. "You know as well as I that they are not clearing for this implosion. The fall zones need to be more than secured. We planned on the high-grade cables that were in the building specs to assist in directing the fall."

"JaLen, we all understand that, but not even Boz would have attempted —" the caller started.

"Don't tell me what is clear, but look, if we don't get this done quickly, the mambie pambies next door are gonna find a lawyer to take their case. You know what that means," JaLen cut in.

"I get it. What's your plan?" Stephan cut through all the bullshit, asking the direct question.

"To avoid a sit-down, I need to get several high tinsel cables here and change my explosive placement, Get Wall to the site with his simulation."

"And?"

"Tell him to bring me 20 yards of that trial det-cord."

"Um, ok, but what are you cutting at?" Stephan's voice made it clear he was completely confused.

"I'm thinking that if I can hold three sides for the initial explosion, the det-cord will allow me to shear the cable and direct the fall with a secondary pop."

"Oh, kinda like the first job we did in Venezuela?"

"Exactly, though we were using the secondary explosion wave to control the direction of the dust cloud and the air over pressure. I'm thinking the way Boz and his buddies worked through in Sellafield, to contain any potential radioactive contamination." He stopped his car as he reached the site. "Stephan, you there?"

"Yeah, just finished an email to get you the det-cord. Where are you?"

"Just arriving at the site, why?"

"I wanted to remind you the world is a terrible place and everyone in it hates you."

"I know they do, duh. How in the heck did we just find out about the low-quality post-tension beams?"

"I think we need to add to our lessons learned page, 'testing of the cables in post-tension beams early on'. I'll talk to ya later," Stephan cut the connection. Only his oldest friend could get away with such a captain obvious statement knowing there was no rebuke to be handed out in the future.

"Ya think?" the Demo Demon put his phone into his chest pack as he walked from his rental car.

"JaLen!" three teams came rushing up to him.

"The world really is a terrible place," JaLen muttered to himself as he walked forward.

When the first of the three reached him, "JaLen we need to review the wiring, the plans are not right," a woman slightly taller than his belly button said.

"Georgia, I know there are several changes that need to be done because of the updates that will be coming out soon, but they're not out, so we need to — "

"JaLen," the second team leader cut him off. "We need to discuss the permitting changes that came out this morning.

"Barney, the permits were all approved, why would there be changes?" he asked, balling his fists.

"The county heard that several of the local celebrities are suing us," the fat man with tiny glasses on his nose explained.

"Since I haven't changed any of the plans..."

"It's the post-tension beams. Didn't you hear about the recent discovery?" Barney raised an eyebrow, pulling his head back to look up at JaLen.

"And? Why would over-doing our protection be an issue?"

"I didn't say that it was, it's a change in the explosive placement that will..."

"JaLen, the homeowner associations have all been blowing my phone up," a woman at least four inches taller and 50 lbs. heavier than JaLen stepped up last.

"Better yours than mine," he laughed, in spite of the situation. As he did, his phone rang. "Excuse me, please." He held the phone up to the three and turned away. "JaLen."

"Don't you mean, Demo Demon?" the man's voice on the other end of the phone was unfamiliar.

"Sure, why not? Who do I have the pleasure of speaking with?"

"Did you mean to God and Country?"

"Pardon?"

"In your email, you said you did not fulfill what you would call duty to country. I'm assuming you mean God and Country," the unknown voice said.

"I actually don't know, I thought about it at the

moment I was writing that, but yes. Duty to God and Country, neither were fulfilled. Look, I really do want to speak with you but I'm in the middle of a shit show."

"Say you'll join us for a conversation in two weeks and I can cut through all the red tape and let your implosion go, as soon as you solve the issue with the post-tension beams."

"Two things, I think I have a handle on that."

"Your hope about your trial det-cord. You'll need to increase the heat of the melt, to get the 'pop', you'll need to get the precision cut that is needed. Are you in?"

"Heat... yes, that is right, if I turn that up, I can..."

"JaLen, are you in?" the voice was cutting and to the point.

"What um... well, hell yes, absolutely, I'm in, Chief."

"Not chief, the Senior Helvetian, Commandant of the North American Honor Guard. Look for your invitation."

"I didn't catch all that but, North American Honor Guard? I never heard of it," he said as the phone clicked off with his question left unanswered.

"Sir, are you talking to us?" one of the three asked.

"No," he waved the question off with the flick of his hand. "Heat, I need to increase the exothermic reaction. I need to isolate the reactants we are using and multiply them when compared to products..." He smiled, turning to face his three little team leaders. "Ok, who was first?"

They all started at once. While he waited for them to sort it out, he reviewed the options for increasing heat, if a system at equilibrium is subjected to a constraint, the system behaves to change that… who's principle was that? "Damn, damn, damn…" he muttered.

"I'm sorry?" the three replied.

"Never mind, go on, continue." He twirled his hand, indicating for them to continue their argument. *Le Chateliers Principle!* He thought, mentally patting himself on the back. *If I figure out how to release a liquid nitrogen bath in strategic areas at a specific time, I wonder…* "Will that energize the explosion?" the question rolled off his tongue as he turned, starting to walk away, ignoring the calls from the team leaders.

Chapter 10
No Chance for Reprieve

Music played in the garage/workshop where Leif restored treasures of a golden age in American history. Items that, with all the new-age fuckery, had been made illegal—things that could actually get him arrested or worse. Today, his attention was focused on recreating a Gatling gun from a pile of parts. Through his initial assessment, the six barrels which made up the rotating apparatus appeared to have been mistakenly mounted to the central shaft from a much newer ten-barrel model. The timing would align for one or two shots before it would jam, or shoot and shatter the third barrel, maybe killing the fool that built the abomination. A knock at the door startled Leif.

"Coming," he yelled as he rolled the antique gun into a paint storage area, before pulling a fogged 8x8 sheet of 1/2-inch plexiglass over the door and rolling a motor on a stand in front of that.

"Leif, it's me, I need to come in, there are several local police officers on their way here."

"It's not locked, Terry. Hey! Constantine is loose so take your hat off."

"I'll never understand why your damn dog hates hats so much," he said after pulling his hat off and tucking it into his back pocket. "Hang on, how did you know I was wearing a hat?" The Neapolitan Mastiff sat and offered a paw.

"Sarge, you've loved those newsboy caps forever. If you could change the police uniform, you'd wear one at work too. Now, why are the locals coming here? And how the hell do you know about it?"

"We in the county sheriff's office hear things." He saw the dog with his paw up still, Terry reached over and pulled a treat from the bowl next to the door. "Here you go, Constantine, you handsome devil. We especially hear things when one of our best friend's names is being called out over the radio as a target for arrest."

"Their gonna arrest me? Why this time?"

"A certain German businessman has had an investigator looking into you. Apparently, he asked you to fix one of those relics you love tinkering on. I think they said it was a machine gun." Sgt. Terry Collins peered around the corner into the shop.

"Gatling gun, actually."

"Lower the car, if they are as stupid as I recall…"

"They'll miss the paint booth," Leif laughed.

"Don't laugh just yet." Terry walked over and took a seat on the couch, the huge dog stepped up, and flumped down on his lap. "Lord, dog, you must outweigh me by 50 lbs."

"75, unless you gained some," Leif said as he lowered the car. "Which you definitely don't look like you did. You've weighed 150 since high school." Walking over to the refrigerator, he took out a can of beer. "You want one?" opening it, he drained the entire thing in one drink.

"Rather have an energy drink." He smiled while ruffling the drooling jowls of the canine on his lap. "They're here." The lights outside the man cave quickly went out.

"Sedulous HouLeiff, open up," three quick raps on a loose windowpane made Constantine jump from the couch. "Open up, this is the police."

"Gentlemen, please take your hats off before coming in." Leif tossed the can in the trash.

The door opened, and two policemen with their front-brimmed uniform hats still in place entered. Bowing up, the dog began growling. "He said take off your hats! And if you reach for those guns, I will show you how quickly two rookies can have their heads blown off by an old sergeant," he said, his gun already out and aimed.

"Constantine, PLATZ!" Leif ordered as the two men removed their hats.

"Sir, please put down your gun," the policeman with a regulation mustache requested.

"Actually, you're both under arrest," his partner said.

"That'll be interesting." Leif crossed his arms, leaning against the bubble gum machine near the entrance to the workshop.

"Are you questioning whether we can arrest you?"

"Son, you're trying way too hard," Terry holstered his side arm. "He was saying you are not arresting your superior officer for stopping you from doing something incredibly stupid," he said, holding his shield so they could see it. "What can we do to help you?"

"We have credible testimony that Mr. HouLeiff has illegal weaponry on his property."

"Such as?" Leif asked.

"We have no need to explain what we're looking for," the mustached policeman replied.

"You are?" Terry asked.

"Officer Davis, sir."

"Well, Officer Davis, do you have a warrant?" Leif asked.

"Of course we do." His partner once again decided he was in charge.

"Could you please do me the courtesy of telling us your name, or should I just keep calling you son..."

"Officer Thaddeus Chesterton."

"Ok, son, may I see said warrant?" Terry walked across the room, extending his hand.

"Yes, sir," Officer Davis handed it over.

"There is no distinction of the weapons you are looking for. Most irregular, the term illegal weaponry."

"It would seem that whoever their credible testimony came from was rather vague, and the signatory on this warrant is throwing a hail Mary, with that term." Leif sat on the floor next to Constantine, petting him slowly. "Have at it, boys, I'll head into the house."

"The warrant is for both the garage and the house," Terry advised.

"Well, they're already in here, take a look around, boys. Can I get another beer and watch some TV?"

"If you are intoxicated, that may be an issue during the arrest," Mustache said.

"I'll chance it, I know I don't have any illegal weaponry here."

"I'll stay with them." Terry inclined his head to the officers, "Lead away."

"Fine, don't interfere with—" Thaddeus started.

"Just stop. I've been here a time or two. Get on with it," the gentle tone he had held until this moment slipped.

"Very well." They walked throughout the two-car section of the garage that they were currently in.

As they walked past the fridge, "Terry, toss me a cold one." Leif turned his head, staying on the floor with a hand up.

"Yupper." A perfect throw hit the extended hand, which closed, grabbing the beer like an orchestrated act. "Good catch."

"Better throw," Leif winked, popping the beer which started to foam over. Constantine all but smiled, lapping the spill up.

"Nothing here," Mustache said. "Tad," he turned and started to the segregated single-car garage. "You want to start in the house? I'll go through this room."

"No, we stay together." He walked into the separate room, rifling through the toolboxes. Bending into the car, he popped the trunk. "Nothing in here," he said a moment later.

"We good in here, to the house then?" Terry asked.

"Yes, sir." Mustache left the room.

The phone in the corner rang as soon as they closed the door. "Hello," Leif said after jogging across to the man cave.

"Turn your television to channel 107," a reverberated voice ordered. Click!

"Hmm, I didn't even know that was a channel." He grabbed the remote from the coffee table, "One... Zero... Seven..." he imitated the robotic voice, chuckling to himself. On the screen, a harsh yellow screen with black lettering appeared. 'Ever feel bad for electing to not serve your country?' The black letters expanded until the entire screen was empty. A moment later, red letters came into being, asking, 'Wish you could undo that decision?' The entire screen melted, becoming white. From certain points, green began blooming until all that was left of the white were letters 'Reach out and ask us how: iamthetraveler@outlook.com'. After around 30 seconds, the television changed back to the movie he had been watching.

The star of the movie turned his head to deliver a famous soliloquy, "Leif," he said, "Constantine can come with you." The TV shut off as the door opened.

"They found nothing, and they are in the process of radioing in for directions of how to proceed," Terry said.

"Well, duh, they were told to arrest me, they can't just return without a prisoner."

"I heard the phone ring a couple of times, anything important?"

"More interesting than impor—" he paused his statement as the car outside started and then backed out of the driveway.

"Hmm, I guess that's it for tonight. Get whatever you have in that paint booth out of here tonight. And don't put it in that underground conex you think I don't know about."

"I'll take care of it, I just have to send an email first." Leif grabbed Constantine's ears, rolling them in circles.

"You know how to use a computer?" Terry laughed, tossed a treat to the dog, and walked out.

Chapter 11
Duty Bound

Turning into the local police station, Blaire pulled into Sheriff Ernst's parking spot. After putting the car in park, he turned the key off and stepped out, rotating just in time to see the sheriff looking at the Fairlady longingly. "My goodness, Blaire, this is the coolest automobile I've ever driven, thank you."

"Not a problem, sir. I'm seriously glad you liked it. Should I lock your squad car?"

"No, few and far between are the days when a fool may break into one of the county units. Especially when they are parked here." The sheriff turned and locked the doors on the small vehicle. Jogging up to the man who was a few years his junior, he handed the keys to him. "Did you really log into the power control for the apartment to change the settings?"

"I can't say, as I have the right to remain silent." Blaire winked.

"Hypothetically, how and why would you have done that?"

"Sir, every morning when I leave for work, I turn off my air conditioning unit. Yet, I come home to an apartment that is 64 degrees, and the unit is set to zero. My electric bill has been more than 350 standard gold for the last two months. I installed a meter to alert me when my power consumption hits 100 standard gold, which is double what I was told the bills average around when I signed the lease."

"And?"

"Sheriff, tonight, when I turned the power off in my apartment, Janey's lost power, too. What the fuck is that? Aren't there some sort of laws that protect tenants from crazy landlords?"

"How long have you lived in that duplex?" the Sheriff asked.

"Six months. The inconsistencies didn't come until it got hot outside," Blaire explained, getting frustrated.

"Wow, that's a big word, is this a voting tabulation software type of inconsistency?"

"Ouch!"

"Ok, ok, you're indicating that the cost for electricity was 100 per month in the winter?"

"Yes, sir, 100 to 125 standard gold."

"What type of heat do you have? Natural Gas?" Sheriff Ernst held his hands out in an inquiring method.

"Actually, no, it is electric baseboard heat. AND it was a cold winter."

"Agreed, it really was." The Sheriff nodded his head, "But, Blaire, the heat from those mining rigs could have kept you good and warm, eh?"

"I'm sorry?"

"Blaire, did you really think the fact that you weren't found to be growing pot took the glare of suspicion off you?"

"Hmm, I really didn't worry about it, I knew I wasn't doing anything wrong. Why would I worry about the eyes of the damned?" he said, shrugging his shoulders and rolling his hands over to give the world a palms-up innocent position.

"Eyes of the…" Sheriff Ernst gave a mitigated laugh. "Damned, is that what you said?"

"Yes, sir. I don't give a fuck if I'm on their list."

"Their list?" For the first time, the sheriff was interested. "Who is 'their'?" With his interest, his gaunt features came into contrast with his authoritative position, making him look frail.

"Sheriff, is that a real question?"

"Blaire, this isn't a spy movie. I need you to understand…" he started.

"Do you know who Marici is?"

"No, but—" This time, the sheriff was cut off as a bolt of lightning danced in a clear sky. "But I—" the thunder following the flash ended the statement.

"Marici is a six-armed goddess that the world's most elite group of hackers use to test those who forget they are supposed to walk around looking down. She found me today because of this bullshit." Blaire looked up into the sky just as another bolt of lightning crackled to life. "Whatever you think you're gonna do to me, have at it, I'm already fucked. My bank accounts and my retirement accounts will be gone tomorrow, I'm 52, I've been doing nothing in life but saving my money, and oh yeah, I can even guarantee my credit, which is perfect today, will be absolute shit by next week, if not sooner. And by next month, my Crypto-Wallets will also be empty." Taking a deep breath, and shaking his head, Blaire panted.

"You're 52?"

"Seriously, that's what you took from what I said? Yes, I'm 52."

"I would have placed you somewhere around 35." The sheriff stepped back, looking closer at his prisoner.

"Sheriff!" a deputy said as he stuck his head out of the station entrance.

"Yes, Jones?"

"Apparently, there was a lightning strike down by Main Street. Several people were injured, the EMTs asked us to get there and settle the crowds."

"Go ahead and take off, I need to get this gentleman to the cells."

"Yes, sir." The deputy walked over to the squad car.

"Leave my car, I won't be long," he said, shooing the man to the older four-wheel drive they typically only use when they take the dogs out. "Sorry, Blaire. I do need to take you into the cells for at least tonight."

"Understood, but if you don't mind, before you leave, can you move my car behind the building, kinda out of sight?" He tossed the keys back to the older man.

"Not a problem. But I told you, stuff is safe here."

"I'm not worried about it getting stolen, I'm worried they will see I'm here alone."

"Marici?"

"Each of the six arms holds a different bladed weapon, defining the protection on six methods of egress." Blaire started walking toward the station.

"Egress?" Ernst followed, "Don't you mean ingress?"

"No, she doesn't care if you enter, but she never wants you to be able to leave."

"But if she blocks six exits, surely there must be more." Punching 1, 2, 3, 6, 5, 4 into the keypad next to the door, it clicked and he opened the door. Turning, he said, "Let's go." As he inclined his head, Blaire notified how incredibly shaped the man's nose was. Chiseled specifically to lend structure to the concaved cheeks, and guidance to the soulless eyes. "What?" noticing the attention, Ernst wiped his nose thinking there may be remnants from blowing his nose earlier.

"Sorry, you know your features are... you should be sculpted," his words tumbled out before refocusing. "I used the seventh exit today, that's when I lost my head and stopped walking with my eyes cast downward. I thought it was the red queen, a strategic AI used in many home defenses. I took it as a challenge that I, of course, won."

"Pride goeth before the fall," he laughed to himself. "You know my wife used to say the same thing, that I should be sculpted, I mean." He kissed the silver ring with a square white stone in it.

"That is a rather interesting ring. Is that alabaster gypsum?" Blaire, ever observant, noticed the dullness that surprisingly reflected the lights of the stationhouse.

"It actually is, my wife had it made for me as a 40th-anniversary gift." Opening the cell with the key on his belt, he asked, "You want the television on?" the cell door gave an imposing clang as it shut.

"Why not?" Blaire did the most stereotypical thing he could, grasping the bars

Pressing his face to the opening. "Are the sheets clean?"

"They are," was the last thing he heard before he was left alone in a jail cell.

"Fuckity-fuck-fuck!" he rattled the bars, turning to sit on the nasty cot-like bed. "52 years old, I've never been jailed, finger-printed, or even had a mug shot taken… and I change the fucking thermostat and end up here."

The television was just finishing up an episode of an old ghost and monster hunter show. Hoping he would be able to fall asleep to the somewhat known show, he laid his head back. The excitement of the day really must have taken it out of him because the next thing he knew, the sheriff asked him if he had to use the restroom before he left for the night.

"I guess I should. What time is it?" Blaire asked as the cell door opened.

"3:10 am," the sheriff said, opening the bathroom door.

"You work too much," Blaire said as he finished peeing and washing up. "There's no garbage in the bathroom and I didn't want to flush this paper towel down the toilet." He held up the wet towel.

"Since that's the only bathroom in this area,

and we don't want loved ones leaving 'things' for their jailed family or friends, we don't have a trash can in there."

"Never would have thought of that. Where should I…"

"Trash behind the desk right there." Ernst pointed over the cubical divider. "Here are your keys, I left a note for the duty guard to let you out at 7 am. That way, your bitch landlord will be off to work, she leaves like clockwork at seven every weekday."

"Stalker much?" Blaire laughed, stepping into the cell again.

"Goodnight, and remember, if a six-armed woman tries to stop you from leaving tomorrow, stab her with those keys."

"Smartass." Blaire laid his head down as the lights in the area went out. The TV was the only light, and it seemed to be on a message board of some sort with three main colored screens. The entire room would glow green and then yellow, however, they were separated by the entire room going dark. After a few minutes, he had timed it out as to when the colors would change by counting. After 15 minutes, there was no need to count it out. When he sat up, rubbing his eyes as the screen changed from green to yellow, he slid his feet off the cot. When he opened his eyes, and focused on the TV, the message to the regretful scrolled passed. The final screen, green with white lettering, gave him the who, he had been waiting for, 'Reach out and ask us how: iamthetraveler@outlook.com'.

"Interesting." He stood up, starting to pace

when he felt something underfoot. "Seriously? Curious and curiouser." Bending, he lifted his own tablet from the floor in his cell.

When he opened the cover, he found a sticky note with the letterhead, 'From the desk of Sheriff Ernst.' With a handwritten note below that simply said, 'Thought you may want to send an email. The station has a VPN if you are nervous about six-armed women.' The login for it was written below the joking comment.

After connecting to the secure connection, he went to a private email server, logging in. Typing a short message:

'I am reaching out to you for several reasons that really don't matter. The only thing that matters is that your message resonates with me. I truly feel had I gone into the military right out of high school, my life's path would have been given direction, as well as finding a more stable set core of values for a boy who had none. Even writing this makes me think back when I evaluated joining the reserves, but as a man well beyond 35 years of age, that consideration has died on the vine as well. If there is anything a patriot with a Ph.D. in computer science, a programmer, and a hacker known as Teutonic Knight can do for this cause, please count me in.'

Blaire hit send and walked back to the cot thingy, and fell asleep with a smile on his face.

Chapter 12
Art is in the Eye of the Beholder

The distant baying of police and ambulance sirens continued in the cool night air. Finishing his two-mile sprint, Mason reached his car, seeing Cary's brand-new Mercedes parked beside his 1972 Bronco, reminding him of the death of both he and Ryan, "Dumbasses." His absentminded nodding allowed him to start the hocking of a thick loogy to spit on it. An urge he restrained, knowing DNA was a thing, instead, he removed the tube he had slung over his neck. Pulling off the long-sleeved black t-shirt, he swung open the unlocked door, allowing him to pop the hood. The door remained ajar as he walked to the front of the precursor to the SUVs. A kick of his foot released the steps tucked under the front bumper. Watching them slowly lower and make their way to the ground where he climbed them, setting the tube between the top stair and his crotch. Reaching between the grill panels, he pulled a secondary release and lifted the hood with the other hand, exposing the immaculate engine compartment.

To keep his gloves clean, he used the shirt to remove the dipstick, wiping it on one of the sleeves, putting it in then pulling it out once more, he found the level of oil in the engine to be sufficient. Returning the dipstick, Mason used the other sleeve to open the filler cap on the valve cover, and after cleaning it completely, he replaced that as well. Reaching far into the compartment, he wiped all along the fire wall before tossing the shirt on the ground and attaching the tube securely below the recently upgraded electronic ignition. That achieved, he closed the hood, stepped down off the built-in platform, making certain to tread on and drag the punished garment to the door.

Bending, he picked it up, shaking off the excess dust, he then wiped his hands upon it, wadding and throwing it toward the back of the truck. The falsely-aged shirt landed next to the empty oil can he had placed there earlier and in the puddle made by the funnel. Removing his boots so that he could take off his pants, with a laugh at being in the middle of nowhere, standing buck naked in a parking lot. Reaching his arm in the pant leg, he turned them inside out, which, in reality, was the correct side. Still laughing, he put the jeans back on before slipping the penny loafers from under his front seat onto his bare feet. Taking the boots to the still exposed steps, he tied them to the middle stair, removed his gloves, cramming them into the toes before he activated the feature to hide the platform once again.

Putting on the newly pressed high-vis yellow polo shirt hanging from the passenger headrest, he stepped up into his pride and joy. The leather band with his Grandma's crucifix slid over his head before starting the Bronco. Instead of acting on another impulse, that of punching the accelerator and spitting rocks all over Cary's car, he slowly drove away thinking about the day Gramps gave this vehicle to him.

"Remember, when you overhaul her and I know you will..." his grandfather had started.

"Of course I will, Gramps." Young Mason laughed, looking at the nearly pristine Bronco.

"Her name is Olive O. The blue stripes on the front-end are there for a reason, don't change them."

"Olive Oil?"

Gramps let out a hoarse laugh and then replied, "No, Olive Oatman."

"Don't really know who that is," Mason cocked an eyebrow.

"Well, do some research, and let me know why it's there. If you get me the right answer in three days, I'll take you on a job."

"Deal." The date was November 08, and he had gone straight to the public library. Finding nothing of note, he then went to the University library near the state capital, where he found limited information on the girl who had, in some way, made an impression on his grandfather. The connection eluded him, why would a girl captured by the Mohave Indians resonate so vividly that Gramps wanted to make certain this Bronco continued to carry the tattoos that she was given by captors? Sitting outside on a folding chair, he held his grandmother's hand as the Gulf War Veterans walked by.

"It's so strange," his grandmother, from her wheelchair, mumbled. "Of all the holidays we have lost in the last 20 years. I would think observance of our veterans seems to be one that they would have taken away."

"I hadn't really thought about it, you're right, Gram." He looked at the bedraggled men and women walking by, each of them looking far worse for wear than their peers looking on and clapping. *The trauma,* he thought, *they had gone through, the hate they faced at home by those who eventually tore this country asunder.* The post-traumatic stress... his mind jumped. *The blue lines, Olive Oatman was the first known PTSD victim. She had a tattoo on her face to remind her, she even wanted to go back to the Mohave. Was there a difference? My father lost his life, gave it gladly to defend what many before him had built.*

Shaking his head and pulling himself back to today, he continued to drive. Getting onto the county route, making certain to vary his speed between one and three miles per hour over the speed limit, knowing cops may find suspicion in a person driving an older vehicle right on the speed limit. The road curved and split, he stayed the course heading toward the same location he and the other two thieves had just broken into. A mile later, he reached a roadblock.

"Hello, officer," Mason rolled down his window, greeting the policewoman.

"Hello. I'm sorry, you'll need to turn around, we had an incident at the dwelling ahead," she said amiably, though her eyes were puffy from crying.

"Ok, but is there anything I can do? I mean, whatever happened seems to have upset you. I have cold water in the back if you'd like. My Gramps used to tell my sister, if you don't drink water after a cry, you'll get a whale of a headache. Funny, I never saw Gramps cry, I wonder..." his words trailed off.

"That is very nice of you, sure. I'll take a water," she smiled.

Stepping from the car, he walked to the back of the truck, opening a cooler attached to the door on a small platform. "Well, they're not cold, the ice is all melted, I guess that makes them wet water." His grin, genuine and warm, made the policewoman relax as she took the bottle.

"Wet water, eh?"

"Sorry, I'm not used to coming up on a real-world roadblock, what happened? Or am I not supposed to ask questions about an open investigation?" he changed his voice to sound like a stereotypical TV cop.

"It's not clear, it looks like a robbery, but it may have been foiled. Two intruders are dead, and six police off..." her voice caught and she took a calming breath.

"That's terrible," he said.

"They'll be processing for days." Her mind was elsewhere.

"I really am sorry. If you don't mind, how do I get through to the highway?"

"You'll have quite a detour... you know what, I'll escort you through. Follow me." She moved the cones, waved him by, and replaced them. Driving slowly, she led him past the driveway and to the other roadblock. "Thank you again for the water and kind words," she said as she approached his car.

"My Gramps would haunt me if I didn't follow his teachings," he winked.

"No matter what happens, if you find someone in the next 10 miles, don't stop. Actually, if you do see someone, give me a call. If I don't answer, call the station. Both numbers are on there," she handed him a business card.

"Wow, I didn't know they made these anymore. Thank you, I'll call." He drove away, rolling up the window. "Nothing, they know nothing. I hope they aren't around that van in 20 minutes." He set the small detonating device in his mouth, biting it in half, driving on the opposite side of the road's shoulder, he threw the first piece out, holding the other until he reached the highway. Waiting several miles before he grabbed a burner phone from his glove box, he called the station house number from the business card.

After two rings, the phone was answered by a woman with a shrill voice. "Latentville Police Department."

"Listen very closely. I need you to contact the police at the Kenduix mansion. Tell them the vehicle left there by the home invaders will explode in 60 seconds. The explosion will take out anything within 100 yards in all directions. You have been warned, God help you if you ignore this call. 55 seconds." He hung up.

45 minutes later, the Bronco was pulling into the warehouse that the job was supposed to conclude. "You're late," a fat woman with green hair said.

"Really? I hadn't noticed. Where's Umberto?" Mason asked.

"He was called away, an hour after you were supposed to be here."

"Rachel, I don't have the time, nor the patience for this. Where is…"

"Wait a minute, where's Ryan?" She just

noticed Mason was alone.

"Dead, along with Cary. Although Ryan did kill Cary…"

"You mother fucker!" She pulled a huge gun from under her armpit.

"Rachel, put the gun down," a tall man with white hair approached from the front of the Bronco. His accent was off-putting.

"He killed — " she started.

"I didn't kill anyone. Ryan was killed by cops, though he killed six of them… no, actually, he killed four, the door killed the other two." Mason babbled.

"Put the fergin' gun down. Unless this storyteller doesn't have what he was sent for."

"Fergin', that's a new one on me."

"Shoot him."

"Oh yeah!" she raised the gun again.

"I have it! Dutch, I have it!"

"Negate the previous order and get away from the vehicle. Now, Rachel!" When she hesitated, he shot her, square in the temple. Her body melted under her, rather than falling.

"She could have shot me!"

"Her finger wasn't on the trigger, she was just fergin' with you. But she didn't listen, and since Ryan's dead, there is no reason to keep his wife around. Pull that truck forward, and get out."

"Fine." Following orders, he pulled forward far enough to clear the body, and after grabbing a pair of latex gloves from the glove box, he pulled them on before stepping up, making certain to not step in any blood. As he approached, Dutch, not worrying about the blood, held up the fat woman. "What do you need?"

"Help her shoot herself with that cannon. Make certain to hit the same bullet path that I made, but it doesn't have to be perfect."

"Whatever floats your shipping container." Mason grabbed the gun, wiping it free of blood on her sleeve before pressing it into her hand, putting her finger on the trigger and pulling it. Blam! The old bullet track was erased.

"That was a big bitch. I'm winded." Dutch walked away, thumbs in the small of his back, catching his breath. "Get me the delivery, let's get this done."

Two minutes later, Mason had traded the latex gloves for the work gloves in his boots, removed the tube from under the hood, and taken it to the door Dutch had gone through.

"The fact that you put that under the hood of your car is so stupid!" Dutch scolded, much like Gramps had done when he went off-script the first few times.

"The tube is insulated to 1000 degrees, says so on the inside, my engine doesn't run that hot," he laughed.

"How did you get it out?"

"I don't know what you're talking about, I was given this to deliver," Mason said.

"Smart boy."

"I'm not quite a boy, sir. I do need payment so that I can complete this transaction."

"You'll need to wait, I need to make certain the payment was received."

"You sold it? I thought... Nuenen..."

"No, I did not sell it. I need to know that Daravan received my payment. You did leave it, yes?" Dutch lifted an eyebrow.

"I was told that there was something left on a desk, but I didn't..."

"Smart boy, it will be at least four hours before my friend will get back to me. Have a drink, take a nap."

"How about I bring this back in the morning and..." Mason turned and started back to his truck.

"My dear friend... you are not leaving here with that painting. I won't take a chance that you will be caught, and I lose both my payment and the painting. However, you are welcome to get in that truck of yours and leave, I may not be here when you return."

"Dutch, understand one thing." He stopped walking. "If I chose to leave, I would find you, no matter where you think you're gonna hide. Don't think I'm missing the fact that you're aiming a gun at me right now. You, however, missed that I am aiming a gun of my own, and if I hear you cock your single action, I'm gonna piss all over this piece of art."

Dutch looked over, finding that Mason's penis

was in the tube with the painting. "That is the craziest thing, I've ever seen someone do."

"Yeah, and I really have to piss. And when I start, there is no stopping it."

"Fine, fine, you take it to a hotel somewhere nearby and come back in the morning." Dutch's gun went back into its holster, just as Mason's did.

"Be back a seven." He tossed the tube on the passenger seat and drove off into the night. When he was safely away, he said to himself, "There's no fucking way I'm gonna stay in a local hotel."

25 minutes later, he found a property with an 'open house tomorrow' sign on the front lawn. On the sign, it read: 'Immediate occupancy available'. Breaking into the lockbox on the front door, he walked through the house finding it free of habitants, just as he thought. Running outside again, he pulled Olive O into the garage. As he parked, the lights of the old Bronco showed a small television sitting on the workbench, shutting her off, Mason got out and immediately turned on the TV, finding a folding chair next to the bench, he set it up and quickly fell asleep.

In what felt like minutes later, a news brief was finishing on the TV, he knew there was nothing about him on it, so he tried to ignore it. Reclining the seat as far as it would go, he dozed off again. Again, waking as the noise of the garage TV was replaced by a different type of loudness… Silence and bright colors, a person couldn't be screamed at less subtly. Yellow, black, green. He clapped his hands, hoping the garage was powering the television with a clapper. No such luck, he knew he wasn't going to get anymore sleep with the stupid loud colors. Stepping out of the Bronco, he read the screens as they scrolled past.

'Ever feel bad for electing to not serve your country?' was followed by, 'Wish you could undo that decision?' and finally, 'Reach out and ask us how: iamthetraveler@outlook.com'. Mesmerized, he read the screens two more times, Yellow, black, green. Yellow, black, green.

"Well, Gramps, you always said, 'A coincidence is not the world's imagination at work, because the world has no imagination. Take all things at face value.' It feels like this is a message to me." Mason looked at the tube with the painting that had gotten at least nine people killed in the last 24 hours, returning his gaze back at the green screen. "I'm probably an ass for this." He grabbed a new set of latex gloves and walked through the garage and back to the house. Turning on the old-fashioned desktop computer, he attempted to connect to the WEB. "Still works," he chuckled to himself as he went into an off-world server and selected share connection. Connecting his tablet to the desktop, he had blind access to his VPN, which would add another level of security to log into his email account.

'Login: Username: teslagreybear@gmail.com. PW: Bulld0gBr1g4d3'. He sat back and waited. Faster than he expected, he came to a web page that long ago he had customized, showing only the emails in the last 24 hours, and the 'write new email' button, which he selected.

'To whom it may concern,

I happened to see your banner on after-hours

television. I believe I fall into the group of people you were reaching out to. I would like to hear what your group stands for.'

Hitting send, he shut down the computer and returned to the garage. Walking up, turning off the television, and then pushing the garage door open. He jumped into Olive O as the door opened, driving until he was clear of the garage door where he stopped and ran back in. After folding the chair and double-checking everything was in place, he hit the close button and jogged out again, making certain not to trip the laser as he left. Leaving the driveway, he saw the picture on the 'For Sale' sign was a familiar face—the green-haired dead woman at the warehouse. "This is going to be the worst open house in the history of open houses."

A minute or two from the warehouse, his phone started to ring. Answering it, Mason waited. "Did you realize that you didn't sign your email?" A robotic, reverberated voice said.

"I'm sorry?"

"I believe I fall into the group… yadda yadda."

"Well, I didn't think a 'yours truly' was really appropriate." Mason's mind was a blur, *how had anyone gotten this burner cell phone's number?*

"First, had you not called and warned all the police officers to clear the area, this call would not have happened. Second, you need to head to the airport, take your helicopter, fly over the warehouse you are about to pull into, and drop the tube with the painting from it…" the robotic voice ordered.

"If I —"

"I will let him know that he has a special delivery."

"Sounds like a plan, captain," thinking he was being cute, Mason replied, a moment before driving past the warehouse, heading to the hanger where his personal helicopter was waiting.

"Not captain, Senior Helvetian, Commandant of the North American Honor Guard." The robotic voice became a deep baritone, "Once you *deliver* the painting, and have got that gorilla off your back, I will text you the location you are to head to."

"Alright, it may take a while, I need to—"

"The helicopter is prepped and papers are filed."

"Well, ok then. What happens if the guy named Dutch decides to shoot?"

"You did mean what you said in your email, even if you didn't sign it, yes?" the deep voice asked.

"I did."

"Then if he tries to remove a gun from his holster, we will remove the problem. Understood?"

"Without a doubt."

"Then, Mason, get a move on."

"I'm moving, sir, I'm moving." Mason released a breath, grabbed his grandmother's crucifix from around his neck, and gave it a kiss.

Chapter 13

Forest Fires from Parties

The radio barked to life, "Base one to any in the range of this transmission. Base one in need of immediate help."

"Are you fucking kidding me?" Robert opened his eyes.

"Jesus Christ, I'm doing my job. We just got a call for a lost hiker!" Delta's voice was panicked.

"Put the microphone down," an unknown voice broadcast over the CB.

"What the hell?" Robert slid his pants on and then pushed his bare feet into his well-worn Red Wing cowboy boots. After putting his Bond Backup into his boot, he pushed the pant leg down.

"Fine, take it. I don't know what your goals here are anyway. It's not like 50 out of 1000 people are concerned about what a small mountain ranger station broadcasts. Whether we are overrun by terrorists or whatever the hell you are," Delta was reaching out to him in a make-shift code.

The night was cool, but his waist-length Harley hoodie was perfect, allowing access to his Redhawk with the moon-clip case. Deciding to add his Kimber Ultra Raptor II into the small of his back, and the sling with eight throwing knives, "As if a bandolier is gonna stop terrorists," Robert poked at himself as he continued preparing. Loading his 12-gauge Shockwave with 10 mini slugs, and then sliding it into a small leather sheath, which, he attached to his backpack. Opening the pack, he filled it with around

200 12-gauge mini shells full of buckshot. Tossing the backpack on one shoulder, he started running through his plans. "What the fuck are you gonna do to take back a ranger station? Start with distant firing…" he spoke as he headed into the tent where he pulled the foot locker vault from under his cot, flipping it open, and grabbing his 700.

"If I have to divert to close combat, I'd potentially leave the hostages as fodder for these animals?" Slowing himself down, a game plan started to form. "This is a bolt action. Idiot, if we need to go for some long shots, it'll need to be quick firing." Grabbing instead his MCX, threading the suppressor in place, checking the green dot, and then taking off his backpack again. Adding the 12 preloaded magazines, each with 30 rounds of 300 blackout into his pack before zipping it and throwing it across his back again. Lastly, he put on his old biker legpack, securing it around his waist and right leg before dropping all the .45 long colt he had into it. Loading five moon-clips with .45 ACP adding those, before putting 24 magazines filled with the same rounds for his Kimber. Feeling too loaded down he put 16 of the magazines into his backpack, while taking 10 minishells from it, and adding them to his legpack. "That's better," he said after zipping it up. "That should be enough… even if I get in a real shoot out." Robert's thoughts wandered to his father's instructions. Following his childhood training, he double checked the back pack, and then put it on. He then slung the MCX around his head and shoulder, laying it across his chest. The old lessons to make certain his weapon was easily accessible echoed through his memory, punctuated with his old man's barks.

The jog would be too far, so he jumped on his Quadrunner. Opening the counsel, he removed a pair of night vision goggles, placing them on his head, then started the machine. Without the light on, he proceeded down the mountain, spooking all types of animals, but when he came across a bear, he realized too much speed could really be a bad thing. 25 minutes later, he shut down the Quadrunner and started making his way silently for the final quarter-mile. The pack was beginning to weigh him down prior to arriving. "You're getting old," he chuckled before taking a knee, removing the night vision and lining his scope, trying to see through the window. The first thing he spotted were three of the rangers, the terrorists had placed them in front of each of the windows.

"Pretty smart," he muttered. Replacing the night vision, he looked around the grounds and up onto the roof. Finding they had each of the three windows guarded with a man on the ground and one above them. "How many of you are there?" he asked the still night air.

"At least one more than you can see down there," the voice was pompous and feet from his left side, the first throwing knife was unsheathed, thrown, and entered the man's throat before the dumbass had the brains to draw his gun. Robert drew a second knife, which he drove high on the man's thigh, trying to hit either the exterior iliac or the femoral artery, as he grabbed the one in his throat, driving it still deeper. "You need to be about it, not just talk about it, putz."

He removed the blades, wiping them on the dead man's jacket, taking in his short blonde hair and dark tan.

"Radio check…" the small voice sounded.

"Fuck." Robert grabbed the earpiece from the prone figure. Jamming it into his ear, he heard several call backs.

"Dabber, you ok? Dabber?"

"Dude, I'm pissing," Robert pushed the call button, and replied trying to sound as pompous as the dead guy had.

"Any issues out on the periphery?"

"Yes, I'm still pissin'. Can I finish now?"

"Take this shit seriously, we need to secure this base and make ready for the senator's family visit."

"I'm not brain dead, I'm also not the one sharing the plan over the airwaves, secured or not, get your head in the game." Robert gambled that the pompous ass was more than a lacky. Taking a knee once again, he began looking through the scope, seeing the young man speaking into the radio, he was just as tan as the dead Dabber.

"You're right, my mistake." The young man inside clipped the microphone on his body armor.

"What the fuck, frat-boy terrorists?" He started removing the body armor from the dead boy. "This armor makes a center mass attack useless." Pulling off Dabber's vest, he inspected it, finding a 3a rating with front and back plate inserts. "Guess I will need to gut or headshot all you bastards." Removing his backpack, Robert put on the body armor, adjusting it to fit.

"There's a car coming up the park pathway," the radio crackled to life.

"Derick, don't shoot unless you need to," the same frat-boy ordered.

"You got it, Jimmy." The headlights were just coming into view.

The terrorist named Derick is up the road… How many more of you are there? he thought through it as he watched the three men on the roof all shifting their positions to the side by the on-coming car. Flipping his MCX off safety, he made ready to return fire on those preparing to shoot at the car. He began the slow creep down toward the outpost.

"The car isn't slowing, Jimmy, what should I do?"

"Let it pass, we'll need to take care of it down here. Roof team, make ready."

"Check," teams one through three replied.

"Ground team, keep your eyes on any coming from the opposite side."

"Check," teams four through six signed off.

"Dabber, you still good out here?"

"All good here." Robert took cover behind a fallen tree, lining his first shot on the roof team farthest from him. Knowing his only shot, based upon the body armor the actual Dabber had been wearing, was a liver shot or a more difficult headshot.

As the men lined up on the incoming vehicle, Robert touched under his arm, "No side inserts." Life may have gotten easier. He stepped through the sequence of events that would follow, knowing his first shot would be a headshot, and if the other two were untrained, or had fallen into a battlefield tunnel vision, he would repeat the same headshot again, if the target didn't present, he would aim for the side, possibly clipping their heart. His plan was simple — take out the three on the roof before focusing on those at ground level.

"Don't let that car make it here, boys," Jimmy said in the headset. "Fire, now, fire." The guns began firing.

Before any of them had fired twice, the furthest shooter's head jerked to the right. His body fell from the roof. Taking a breath, Robert focused and fired again, dropping the second shooter.

"Car disabled, Jimmy," the remaining figure on the roof reported, "What the fuck, Troy, Eddie, where the hell are you?" As he spun in place looking for his two compatriots, Robert realigned his shot. When his target was sideways, he fired three rounds in succession, hitting the remaining shooter all three times. Pulling himself back behind the fallen tree just as bullets started to fly, a couple slapping his cover. "Fuck! I'm hit, Jimmy, someone shot me."

"What? I thought you said the car was immobilized?"

"It... iiissss." Robert looked up just in time to see the final member of the roof team member fall to the ground.

"Dabber? What's going on out there?" Jimmy asked, his voice showing signs that he was freaking out.

Robert tucked his MCX under the tree trunk before beginning to dog crawl, heading to the stump. After reaching the new cover, he released the clasp on the holster holding his Redhawk. Before drawing it, he pulled the Kimber from the small of his back. Propping himself against the stump, sitting on his shins, he waited, listening to Jimmy yelling at the ground crew to scan the area. Removing the earpiece, he let it dangle, trying to hear anyone closing on his position.

Finally drawing the Redhawk, he held a gun in each hand crossing his chest. While he knew it was a terrible shooting position, he also knew he had no choice — any other position would reveal his location to anyone searching him out.

"Derick," one of the ground team to Robert's left was speaking way too loud, giving a good cover to cock both his guns. "Derick, get back here, it's just the three of us against an unknown number of shooters."

"Sebastian, what the fuck is wrong with you, announcing our numbers?" Jimmy's voice could be heard without the headset.

Hearing no others in the area, Robert released the hammer on the revolver, holstering it, drawing instead another throwing knife. As the barrel of the gun passed by without clearing the area properly, Robert almost felt bad for what was about to happen to this untrained frat-boy. "Derick, how close are you?" Sebastian had one hand to the transmit button as a blur to his right leaped up from the ground. There was a quick pressure on his neck and then the earpiece was pulled off his head. "Who are you?" was the question in his eyes, but only a series of gurgling air released from his neck. When he turned to look at the person standing beside him, the newly illuminated floodlights from the outpost reflected off the metal in the stranger's hand as it flashed toward him.

Robert laid the young man down before removing his goggles. *Fucking morons, what cause are you dying for, here tonight?* he thought. Clipping the holster over his revolver, releasing the hammer on the Kimber, and holstering, Robert made ready for what he knew he had to do next. Before he acted, he put the earpiece in again.

"Derick, close on Sebastian's location quickly," Jimmy was shouting.

"100 yards and closing," the response sparked Robert to drop to his knees. Mistakenly, he did this too quickly which allowed the sheath with his Shockwave to smack on the ground, disconnecting it from the backpack.

"Idiot, take your time." He crawled forward, finding the still warm barrel of his MCX, closing his fingers around it, he kicked himself into action, 'Go time, go, go, go.' Standing, he pulled on his instincts, placing the Shockwave strap around his head and sprinted back into the woods to fight from the higher ground. A few steps later, the error of not securing the strap on the MCX became apparent when it found purchase on a bramble and was jerked from his hand, causing him to trip, which earned him a hard rap on the head from the partially secured Shockwave.

"Over here!" two voices called out.

"Fuck it," Robert grabbed the Raptor grip of the Shockwave, the trucker's special withdrew easy, and he pumped three shots low into the silhouette closing on him. Two bullets impacted on his backpack, Robert dropped as he spun, firing carelessly in the general direction the bullets had come from. *Seven shots left*, he thought, holding the shotgun grip with one hand, attempting to untangle the strap on the MCX with the other. *Shoulda put the buckshot in.* Chastising himself, he pulled a knife from his bandolier and sliced wildly, finding the strap in the shadows and cutting it.

"You asshole!" Another silhouette bounced across the ground, the laser on the gun giving away his position. He considered throwing the knife in his hand toward the laser, but knowing it was a waste of time, instead, he put it back where it came from. Regripping the shotgun, understanding the risk of being found thumbed on his green point laser and unloading all seven shots into the oncoming figure. Bending, he leaned the Shockwave against the tree trunk, grabbing the freed MCX, he scrambled in the direction he had come from. "You think you can just shoot people and hide!" the obviously hurt voice said as he started firing on the location of the green laser. Eventually, his slide locked back. "Hope you enjoyed that." Laughing, the shooter walked up finding just a gun. "No!" he turned, giving a full-body image.

Robert, having laid in wait up on the hill, did not waste the opportunity, and a headshot closed the chapter of this fool's life. "One outside, and an unknown number inside," he whispered.

"Derick, we just lost the base support. Where are you?" Jimmy yelled into his headset.

"Shut up, Jimmy," the voice that came back was whispered.

While Robert strained to hear where the voice in the woods came from, too many gunshots had been fired, and his ears were ringing. Finding a large enough tree to hide behind, Robert caught his breath, removing the heavy backpack, tying a knot in the strap, he slipped the MCX around his head. Quickly scaling the tree, he found purchase on the third layer of branches. Unslinging his rifle, he sighted on the building trying to see if there was a clear shot to free Delta and the rangers. Finding each of the windows were still being blocked by the rangers, he thought, *there must be more than one gunman inside there or the rangers would have rushed him.* The ringing was reducing enough now that ambient sounds were coming back.

"Jimmy, shut off the floodlights, you're making it impossible for me to use my night vision."

"One second, Derick. You, go over and shut down the lights," he ordered.

Watching to see which of the rangers would leave their window. Surprisingly, the frat-boy told the ranger at the window closest to the action to turn off the lights. Jimmy pushed Delta in front of him, protecting himself fully. Robert remember Jimmy had been speaking into a microphone, still clipped on his vest. *He doesn't have an earpiece.* Lining up the shot, and waiting for the lights to go off, "Delta, go limp!" he said into the microphone. All at once, she dropped to the floor, the lights went out, and Robert fired off five quick shots. The muzzle flashes had given away his position, and as return fire came in, the MCX fell from his grip.

"Shame, you don't have your gun anymore. Oh, and look here, I have a backpack that looks to have all your other weapons," Derrick said from below.

Upon hearing the comment, Robert shifted his body to the opposite side of the tree to where he knew he dropped his backpack. "Your invasion or whatever this was to kill the senator has been thwarted. Just take your remaining friends, and you're injured, and get the fuck out of here."

The resulting gunshots peppered the old branches. "I'm gonna skin you alive. Dabber and I have been planning and drafting people for this... AHHH!" Derrick yelled as the floodlights came back up. Reaching up, he grabbed the night vision goggles to pull them from his eyes. The moment of pain had made him take a step back.

The gunman crouched down, dropping the goggles, and when he stood back up, Robert unloaded the Redhawk's six shots into the group's leader. Releasing the cylinder, the spent moon-clip dropped, so he loaded a fresh one in and closed it. "Delta, can you talk? Are you ok in there?" he asked, hoping the fact that the floodlights had come back on meant there were no more terrorists inside.

"We're clear in here, the rangers are getting

arms and coming out to help."

After jumping from the tree, Robert kicked the gun away from the fallen gunman. Taking his radio and goggles, adding them to the inventory in his backpack. "Pretty sure we're clear out here. Call the senator, let him know to call off his trip."

"I'll call HER right now," Delta chuckled as she emphasized 'her'.

Chapter 14

Superpowers Suck

The rest of the drive was uneventful, yet as Clear turned onto the street of his office, seeing the 'Clear Truth Detective Agency' sign, he thought, *something feels amiss. Amiss is a word private detectives use instead of hinky, because hinky doesn't sound as tough.* Spotting as he got closer, a car was parked in his private parking spot. "Since when do cops drive black sedans?" he muttered to the steering wheel. *Interesting, the car doesn't have any license plates, nor markings of any kind. Hmm, amiss and nor? My inner dialogue must be set to old-school.* He laughed, deciding to double-park as close to the driver's door as possible, "Let's see you get out now, asshat."

Inside the building, a movement caught his eye, throwing open the door, he made a B-Line for the stairs leading to the front entry. "2, 4, 6." Reciting as he climbed the stairs, not even knowing why he did it. For years, he counted every step as he touched it. He seriously pissed off some people when he did the stair-climbing event at the First Wisconsin Center. Clear refused to call it any of the new names, a building should stay the name of what it was called at construction, it just should.

Peering through the windows by the door, he could definitely tell someone was inside, but Evgeniya, his secretary, wasn't due back for two days. Reaching for the doorknob, "Damn it," chastising himself after remembering he left the keys dangling from the ignition. Leaping down all six steps, "1," bending a little on impact, he glanced across the street, seeing Evgeniya's pistachio green-colored Mini Cooper parked, "That ain't even your spot," he muttered, knowing the real question was, *why is she back early?* Removing his cell phone from the side pocket on his carpenter pants, he pressed and held down the '5' to quick-call Evgeniya's number.

'No Coverage' showed on the display.

"That makes less than no sense; there's a repeater on the roof." Completely confused, he opened the car door, removing the keychain and reversed course. Pressing the indent on the key fob to lock his car as he reached the steps, taking them three at a time, "3, 6." The key had no sooner touched the tumblers when everything went black.

Waking when the toe of a well-polished, rubber-bottomed shoe nudged his shoulder, "Hey, buddy, this ain't no place for a nap."

"Sorry, officer, I wasn't sleeping, I was simply waiting for a chance to make you feel important." He could already feel the throbbing from the bump on his head. Deciding the bump probably wasn't as bad as he thought, the throbbing in his head was because he was laying on the steps, and while not completely upside down, his head was several inches below his feet. "Lucky I didn't just slide all the way down."

"Aren't you's cute, get up before I bust ya for being drunk in public," the man addressing him was a cop. *Called it.*

"I haven't been drinking." Still lying on his back, he rather stupidly attempted to do a sit-up. Unluckily for him, his bulky upper body outweighed his short legs, and because Newton was an asshole, he slid down the remaining steps. Resting on the sidewalk, street level, Clear opened one eye, seeing the smiling face of the cop who had been busting his balls.

"No, no, you's weren't drinking, I know. You's were accosting some poor schlub out on da highway," the cop's heavy Jersey accent was borderline ridiculous.

"He filed a report with you guys?" Clear asked, slowly standing, brushing himself off while looking around the sidewalk.

"What are you's looking for?"

"My keys, I was trying to open my office when—stop!" he yelled to the cop who had climbed up the steps. Too late, he already reached up and grabbed the keys from the door. Zap! The policeman twitched for a quick moment before he performed the same sliding down the step trick Clear had done moments earlier, coming to rest at street level, next to Detective Truth's feet.

"What da fuck just happened?" he asked from the sidewalk.

"I think those rubber soles on your shoes just saved you from a nap. How's your hand?" Clear reached down, helping him up by the crook of his arm.

"Thanks," he said and then looked at his hand. "It burns, but fuck, my back's already stoaving up." He reached his hand into his jacket, removing some folded pieces of paper. "Anyways, I got this 'Hold for questioning order', but I ain't in no fit state to be dragging anyone anywhere right now." Allowing the document to open, Clear saw his picture staring back at him.

"Best thing I heard all night," he gave the cop his best lopsided grin. "Can I see your nightstick?"

"Um, sure. What are you's planning to do with it?"

"Violate city ordinance." He walked back up the steps to his office, "2, 4, 6." With a crash, the pane of glass next to the door shattered. After clearing out the loose shards, he poked his head through the opening. "That's different," he said, finding the door handle was encased by a small green pulsating orb.

"What is?" the question came out on the street.

"There's a —" Smacking the orb with the nightstick, what any normal person would expect to happen didn't, instead the orb snatched the baton from his hand, and before his eyes, it dissolved into ash. "Holy, Jesus fuck!" Jumping back, completely pulling the casement out of the door frame.

"Did you drop my nightstick?" the cop asked as he attempted to extricate himself from the wooden frame.

"Drop it? No, definitely didn't drop it. Fed it to a goddamn character from a video game? That may have just happened. Yeah, let's stick with that, yes."

"Shit. I liked that night —" he started, but the foolish statement was cut off when the green orb flew out from the broken window, disappearing into the night sky. "Ok, seriously, what the fuck was that?"

"If it walks like a duck and quacks like a duck, it's a duck. If it pulses with green light and flies into the sky, then it's definitely not a duck." With the spots from the dazzling ball of light fading from his eyes and his need for giving smartass answers out of the way, Clear grabbed the keys hanging from the door and stepped through the newly created opening. "Evgeniya, are you in here?" Getting no answer, he tentatively touched the doorknob into the main office with the back of his hand. Feeling not even a tickle, he unlocked and opened the inner door. The brass bell over the door rang as the door opened.

"You's know, having a 'not-duck' experience together and all, perhaps it's time for introductions; I'm Vito Sebastianelli," he proffered a hand, which Truth shook. Vito had a firm workingman's grip.

"Private Detective Clear Truth." For the first time, he really looked at the cop, 45 years old or so, standing around six-foot-two and had a bad case of Dunlop's disease, but it was his smile that grabbed Truth's attention, it was genuine in the way only an innocent idiot could achieve. "If this was a more formal setting, I'd insist you call me Mr. Truth, but in lieu of the situation, just call me Clear." Together, they walked into the room looking at the immaculate space.

"So, what did you's do to piss off the little green men?"

"Don't know that I've met any green ones to piss off."

"Fair. Who's Evengaga?" Vito asked.

"Evgeniya Souza, she's my personal assistant." Seeing the suspicious look on his face, he said, "Nothing all too personal about it actually, she's into the waif male model types. Odd thing, she's supposed to be on vacation with her sister, Fainah."

"Why was you's yelling for her if she's vacationing?"

"I'll save my witty retorts for another time, her car is across the street. It's the little green one." Clear walked through the office, "I ain't gonna find her here, but something is most definitely hinky. Er, I mean, amiss."

"Are you shu-er about her car?" he pronounced 'sure' like it was two separate words, making Clear think of an old soccer coach he had.

"Yeah. Why?"

"Maybe it turned into an orb and attacked us," he laughed at his own joke.

Standing stoically, Clear didn't join until Vito gave a little snort, and started laughing even harder. The silliness of a huge man snorting with laughter tickled him and he joined the laughing. "You finished giggling, little school girl?"

"Funny, funny." He wiped the tear that came from his eye on the third snort. Together, they searched a bit longer, finding her work area was the only one that had been disturbed. Nothing in the rest of the office or the break areas were even moved. "Apparently, they were looking for something that she had, not you's."

"Do you have a slim-jim?"

"To eat, or for breaking into cars?" Vito asked. "I'm a beat cop, where would I carry one?" he said, turning around with his hands out to his sides.

"Not a problem, I think I can find one." Clear walked outside, jumped up on the handrail, grinding his way down on his shins like a skateboarder would on their board. As he slid, he popped the trunk with the remote.

"How did you's open the trunk? That car has gotta be older than you's."

"Modifications, this car is a tank and it will last forever so I've tinkered around with her quite a bit." He pictured the shop in the rear of his office, which used to be a delivery dock. "Besides, if anything breaks on Anne Bonny, I try to fix her with more up-to-date parts."

"Anne who?" Vito looked like a confused puppy, head cocked to one side.

"Bonny, Anne Bonny, she was a pirate, this is a Marauder."

"Um, yeah, but..."

"I must insist you put that chain together yourself." Clear shook his head.

"Why did you's park so stupid? Never learn to parallel park that boat?"

"What are you talking about? I was—" his words faltered, noticing the unmarked black sedan was gone.

"What? You's was what?"

"I was blocking in an asshole that was parked in my private parking spot."

"Didn't do a great job of it." Vito looked at the empty area.

"This is just fucked up. My car's still blocking the spot sufficiently enough that I can barely fit through to get in here. If they pulled onto the sidewalk, my sign would've been toast." Reaching inside the open trunk lid, he removed a tool taped to the lid itself.

"Did you hit your head a bit when you fell? I'm a cop, put that away," Vito chided.

"Vito, we need to see what's in her car — gas receipts, food wrappers, anything that can tell us what she's up to," he explained.

"Clear, I understand what you's is planning. Problem is, there ain't no green Mini on the block." He swept his arm, showing, as he said, the street was sans any little green vehicles at all.

"It was here. I swear."

"Let's go in and — " Vito started.

"And check the surveillance footage. Great idea," Clear interrupted.

"I was gonna say get some ice for you's head and my back, but hey that's a better idea. Maybe I should take that for safe-keeping, would hate to have to arrest you's for breaking into a motor vehicle that doesn't belong to you's."

"That's the single longest statement I've heard from you." He ignored his comment, taping the slim-jim back to the trunk lid for safe-keeping. Then they proceeded back to the office to review the recording for the last few hours.

"I thought you's said there were surveillance cameras? I didn't see any."

"They're hidden in the second-floor planter boxes." Walking over and pushing down on the handle of the liquor cabinet; making the top rise up, revealing the monitors. "See, that's a live shot." The four flat screens showed amazingly sharp pictures of both the front and the back of the building.

"Now dat's a nice setup, these must be retarded expensive," Vito's mouth fell open.

"They definitely were, but not as much as this thing," Clear said, sitting behind his desk. "The base is made out of the springs from a Model A, they're sitting on stainless steel orbs. The top's mahogany with a leather inlaid blotter, with stainless steel towers that, as you can see, end in mahogany orbs on the floor. Here's my favorite part," he turned the knob on the faux front drawer. The two towers as well as the parapet between them started to rise, synchronized with the top of the desk sliding back three inches. When the movement had stopped, a large monitor was positioned between the towers and the front lip of the desk had rolled over, leaving the leather blotter lining up with the front of the desk.

"That's really cool, but what is it?" Vito asked.

"My computer."

"Can't be a computer, you's need a keyboard and mouse to work a freakin' computer."

"Nanny, monitor on." The monitor sprang to life. "Nanny, surveillance system, Northeast camera only." The monitor now showed only the view where his car was currently parked. "Surveillance, roll back four hours, and then forward at double time." When the picture changed, the cars that were next to his parking spot were different. "Pause video." The black sedan pulled into the parking spot, and across the street, a pistachio green Mini parked at the same time.

"I'll be damned. Can I try?"

"Actually, I had to do a voice stamp to make it work for me. No one else can use it."

"Fuckin' aye?" Vito used the profanity as a question.

"Fuckin' aye. Surveillance forward normal speed." The image started to move, Evgeniya stepped out of her car and walked across the street.

"You can't park there," her Russian dialect coming through on the two stainless steel tower speakers.

"Sound too?"

"Fuckin' aye." The doors on the black sedan flew open at the same time, but as the figures started from the car, the picture went to static.

"What the hell?" Vito asked.

"Never saw it do that before. Surveillance, forward until picture returns."

"Clear," a British female voice said. "There is audio in the section you will be skipping."

"Thank you, Nanny. Please return to five seconds prior to static image." The cars were parked, and Evgeniya was getting out of hers.

"You can't park there," Evgeniya as before said, then the doors opened and the picture went out.

"You don't get it yet, we can pretty much do whatever we want. We're the government, and we're here to help," a male voice said, followed by the sound of the car doors shutting.

"I still don't understand what you're looking for," she replied.

"Look, we gave you the opportunity to do the right thing and you blew it," a different male voice said.

"I've told you and told you, I didn't see anything." The sound of the bell on the front door tinkled as Evgeniya opened it.

"Nanny, continue playback, change to inner camera." The image of his office came up, Evgeniya was walking backwards, her arms giving emphasis to her statements. As a leg in dark pants entered the frame again, the picture broke into static.

"And we believe you. But there had to be a reason you were there," one of the men said.

"At that specific time, and why you didn't just listen to instructions?" the other said.

"I am, bitch, I listen to no man," Evgeniya said defiantly.

"Your words, not mine. Now sit there and shut up while we look through your records." The sound of shuffling papers and drawers opening and closing. "Now see, I knew we'd find something."

"This time, you ride in the back of my car, and Seven will drive yours." The sound of footsteps, and then the tinkling bell again. "Get the door."

"Shall do," the second voice replied.

"Clear, oh God, what happened to him?" The Russian beauty's voice was full of concern.

"Surveillance, continue playback Northeast camera again," Clear said. The video briefly showed his car double-parked in front of the sedan before returning to static. The sound of Evgeniya's cursing in Russian could be heard right up until the car door slammed. According to the time stamp, five seconds later, the video came back, and the Marauder was sitting awkwardly across the parking spot, which was empty.

"What do you's suppose they found?"

"I know she's clean, they couldn't have found anything—" his words were cut off by the sound of the phone ringing. "Clear Truth Detective Agency."

"Is this Mr. Truth?" the Russian woman's voice on the other end of the phone was so scarred from cigarettes, the smell of them could be imagined as she spoke over the telephone lines.

"Yes, it is. How can I help you?"

"This is Fainah Souza, my sister, Evgeniya, works for you, yes?"

"I thought you were with her on vacation?" Truth inquired, ignoring the question.

"Why yes, we're in Martha's vineyard, well, at least I am, my sister left last night to go for a walk and—" she started.

"I don't think we should talk over the phone. Did you two end up staying at the place I recommended?"

"I'm assuming so, yes. The owner told us all about the alabaster—"

"Swell, I'll see you there tonight." Clear hung up the phone.

"Her sister?" Vito asked.

"Yeah, she doesn't know where Evgeniya is. I'm going to head there to meet her."

"I tell you's what, I'm gonna send out a statewide BOLO for that green car. Do you happen to know the license number?"

"Surveillance, replay same sequence showing Northwest camera." The picture popped up, showing the front of the building again, across the street her little green car sat. He placed his thumb and index finger from each hand on the blotter, drawing them apart. The picture zoomed in.

"That's a touchpad?"

"And a keyboard."

"Fuckin' aye?" Vito asked.

"Fuckin' aye," he typed, the text appearing across the top of the monitor. "Nanny, please print current image." A moment later, a piece of paper with a black and white picture of the Mini slid onto his desk.

With the license plate number in hand, Vito headed off to do whatever beat cops do. As Clear drove, he wondered how a boy from New Jersey ended up walking a beat in Boston. It was an easy trip, traffic from I-93 South loosened up at the Mid-Cape Connector as a podcast about self-improvement played over the stereo system.

When he reached and drove through Woods Hole, following Crane St. as it turned into Cowdry Rd.

A song from The Greatest Showman played as he reached a barricade with a sign announcing the Ferry was not running. Truth pushed pause on the music, and hit the steering wheel, "Fuck. They have it set up easy enough to turn around but one of Truth's rules caused him to put the car in park and walk up to the ferry.

Truth's rule: If you don't know, then fucking ask. Don't be a stereotypical male about useless shit.

"Hey, buddy," Clear waved at one of the men on the pier. "Why no ferry runs?"

"The island's closed to the public. Hell, for that matter, this area is closed and you shouldn't—" his words were overshadowed by two behemoths in sport coats and dark glasses.

"The ferry is closed to the public, get behind the barricade, Mr. Truth."

"How do you—" he started.

"That wasn't a request, Clearance," the larger of the two men cut him off.

Clear turned and began the short walk to his car, "Three-hour ride for nothing," he muttered just loud enough, knowing they were still watching. Getting back in the Marauder, he backed casually onto Jupiter Point Rd. and proceeded to drive away. Already knowing his new destination, Nobska Lighthouse, from there it was only a seven-mile swim in the frigid waters to Martha's Vineyard. That's why he always had a wetsuit on hand, he may not have been a boy scout, but he did learn from the fine example they set.

Driving to the southernmost point on the peninsula, the lighthouse parking. "God, I hope Anne Bonny's 18-foot-long frame fits into those small parking spaces," finding a spot at the end of the row and without curb stops, he parked. Proceeding to the rear of the trunk area, he unpacked his gear.

He dropped his wallet, keys, and cellphone into a plastic zip bag which he put into a duffle. Clear stripped out of his shoes, socks, and shirt, getting ready for the swim. Retrieving a spring-suit — an old friend from his surfing days. It had half-legs and full-length arms. After it was on and the back cord was pulled, he put on his surf shoes and it was time to hit the waves. To make certain he looked like a happy vacationer, he grabbed flip flops and a tank top, placing them in the duffle as well. Before zipping it up, he threw a couple of bottles of water along with two empty gallon milk jugs in as well. Their purpose was to help him float on breaks.

Walking across the street to the rocks that made up the beach, he placed the duffle on his back and got into the water. Happy it wasn't as cold as he thought it'd be, he got his bearings and headed out.

Two hours into the swim, he offered himself words of encouragement, "What the fuck were you thinking? Ok, ok... keep moving, we'll get there eventually. One of these days, your arrogance is gonna kill us, but not today." After the three-hour mark, he saw lights swaying along the beach.

At about the three-and-a-half-hour mark, he realized the swaying lights were flashlights. "Fuck.

There's security walking the beach. Just great, I need a plan." He floated for a while, the current took him to the western side of the island without wasting energy. Drinking water as he floated, not wanting to dehydrate while being surrounded by water. He formulated a plan, which after another two hours, he determined was completely wrong; having thought the Nashaquitsa would take him to the ocean. He found himself, walking through people's yards in the dark. "I'm so gonna get shot. I don't even think this pink and baby-blue wetsuit will get me out of this one."

By the time he reached the wildlife refuge at Long Point, the sun had still not made its presence known, "It's not like I don't have skills, I mean, shit, I just swam the Vineyard Sound to reach a non-paying client. I don't just have skills; I have a superpower. Sucks that my superpower is being a fucking idiot, but at least I have one." Another two and a half hours later, he reached the eastern side of the Deep Bottom Cove. From there, making it to Fainah to find out what happened to her sister was a matter of changing his clothes.

As he reached the house adjacent to the preserve, more flashlights could be seen, *These idiots are everywhere. Thank goodness the grass is long next to the preserve.* He laid down and began belly-crawling much further than any grown man should have to. After 10 minutes that felt like an hour, he reached the rear of the house. Tip-toeing his way onto the back deck, he looked through the kitchen door. The lights were on and Fainah, looking pissed, sat at the table where the same two men from the transport ship were glowering down at her. "Listen, lady, we know he's on his way to see you, and that you called him." The first man pointed a pistol at her face.

"Yes, I called him to make certain he knew Evgeniya wasn't going to make it back when she was supposed to.' Fainah's voice was more heavily accented than her sister, being older, she obviously spent more time getting indurated into her vocal styling.

She could be a pretty woman, with a serious emphasis on could. Her years of smoking have given her a permanent set of bitch lips. Shame really. Clear's overly tired mind thought, watching the events unfold inside.

"Oh, and what did you tell him?" the other man asked.

"That she was too busy getting her ass fucked to come back to work." Her expression was cold and dead.

I don't think poker against her would be winnable.

"Aren't you cute..." the same man started.

"No. I haven't been cute in 35 years. When will my sister be back?"

"When she tells us all she knows," the first man shot back.

"She's only been with mamby pamby boys her whole life. I'm sure she knows, not so much." The words barely finished as the gun smacked her in the cheek. The blood running freely down her cheek and onto her lips caused Clear to do something really stupid.

"Hey, honey, I'm home, what's for dinner?" The casual entrance through the back door confused the men, giving him enough time to walk up to the one who had hit Fainah, lift a frying pan sitting on the counter, and smack him in the head. The larger of the two reached down, grabbing Clear around the throat, backing him into the wall. As his feet started to lift from the floor, 'Fwap, fwap, fwap,' the grip loosened and the big man fell, letting Truth see Evgeniya, holding the suppressed pistol.

"Him too," Fainah used her chin to point to the man her sister had taken the gun from.

Without hesitation, 'fwap, fwap.' She then walked over and gave Clear a big kiss, tongue and all. "Thank you."

"Well, that just happened." He chuckled and untied the other woman. "I don't even want to know what's going on, or how you got back here. I just want to know if you have a way to get off the island?"

"Of course not. The President is here. He has a meeting with—" Fainah started.

"Aliens?" Clear cut in.

"What? No, several donors." Evgeniya put her hands on her hips. "That stupid orb was not an alien, it was a modified drone the agents of New Roanoke used."

"You offered to help them, then what is all this about?" he indicated the dead men. *Great, I'm standing next to what could be dead agents,* he thought.

"I told you before, the 'Semena'. My name is still associated with them."

"And I told you we'll get to the bottom of that very soon."

"Putz, it's too late, Evya was being targeted by agents of New Roanoke for being a member of this group," Fainah replied.

"Oh, shit, sorry. Tell me what Semena is again," he used his disarming dumb guy approach.

"Seeds, they plant Russian seeds in North America and call on them when they need something. After you're activated, and perform the requested action, you must make your way back to the homeland."

"Ok, so the seeds are a type of sleeper cell, yes?" Clear asked.

"Da, that is correct," they both said together.

"I'm a fuckin' idiot." He nodded his head absent-mindedly, thinking to himself, *Superpowers activate. I'm in a room with members of a Russian sleeper cell, surrounded by dead agents of New Roanoke. Absolutely brilliant!*

Chapter 15
Shall You Cast That All Aside?

Ananias Dare's eyes opened after another round of passing out. Taking a look at the stopwatch app on his phone, he gave a smile when he saw the timer read three minutes and 50 seconds. Happy he had decided to start the app as the tell-tale signs of the blacking out process reached its crescendo. In short order, the effects would leave him forever and he could check to see if he received a reply to the email he had sent.

"Mr. Dare," a doctor unknown to him walked into the room.

"I'm sorry, I didn't hear you walk in. Must be a bit preoccupied," he said, pushing himself into a sitting position, and then holding the button to raise the bed to support himself.

"It would appear, your aliment has almost worked its way out of your system. Is it ok if I close the door and ask you two questions?"

"Of course, Doctoooorrrr..." he rolled his hand, drawing the word doctor out, prompting him to fill in the blank with his name.

"I am not of the mindset to lie, therefore, I will ignore that inquiry," the tall man said as he closed the door.

"Hmm, ok then," Ananias muttered.

"Do you really feel yourself cold, calculating, and selfish?"

"Before I answer you, may I have a name? It's so much easier to talk to someone when you have a name."

"The Senior Helvetian, Commandant of the North American Honor Guard."

"All that, huh? How about Commandaaannnttt..." again, he rolled his arm, trying to get more personal information.

"Let's stick with the Senior Helvetian," the chiseled features on the man may have smiled yet it looked like a sneer.

"Ok, Senior Helvetian, sir. Yes, I do consider myself cold, calculating, and selfish. I have watched too many, with far more redeeming qualities than I, fall beneath my footsteps. More than just being a man of single-mindedness, after a round of individual reflection, I redefined myself conniving."

"If you joined our ranks, you will be just that — a member of our ranks. Not king dick of a think tank," he waited, not turning the statement into a question. The delay was a ploy on two sides, the first being he, requested permission to ask two questions, and the second, testing to see if this man had an issue with silence. After a count of 30, he inclined his head with a slight nod. "What if I told you that you could not keep your wealth?"

"I wouldn't care. I could always donate it to the widows and orphans fund," Ananias rotated his hands, turning his palms facing up.

"That is a very respectable reply. However, please don't do that. Your money will aid in the cleaning process for the governmental funds that I will need to pass through the new world. With that in mind, we'll need you to set up a new company. In order to employ a couple of others who will be joining us, we'll also need a plane, oh, your pilot's license needs to be renewed. It expired yesterday."

"Sir, yes, sir."

"Understand this, you are not in the military. With that, no haircuts..." The Senior Helvetian started.

"Thank goodness, do you know how..." Ananias started.

"As I was saying," he said through a laugh. "No haircuts, and no, 'Sir, yes, sir!' we need you trained but not conditioned. Those in the actual military are obvious to those who care to look."

"I look forward to learning more," Ananias nodded his head.

"This is all still coming together, and the important part of all this is that those coming into this must not have any connection to the military. As I said, you will learn more about that later, for now, there needs to be a meeting between you and those in my office," he chuckled again. "I'll have my people call your people," he tossed a burner phone on Ananias' lap. "There will be two calls. The first will take place within three weeks, be ready at a moment's notice to do as directed."

"Should I have something set up first?"

"Call number one will aid you with creating the proper account, the second to take out stakes in specific coins."

"You do know that you don't take stakes in crypto?"

"It will become apparent as we progress, the person you will be speaking with is a gifted scholar and a more than extremely competent mathematician," he turned and walked from the room.

"I can live with that," the smile that touched his eyes was foreign to Ananias Dare. "The plane? Should I start looking for a specific type of plane?"

"If it makes you happy to do things like that, of course. Please don't purchase anything until the new company is formed."

"Understood."

"I have to say, I expected you to give more... 'I know', or 'Duh' type of comments. Thank you for proving me wrong," the Senior Helvetian winked at the man across the room.

"One more thing if I may before I blackout again... did you say North American Honor Guard?"

"I did, more to come on that as well," he left as Ananias started to slide down into the bed.

"See you soon, sir," he didn't reach for his phone to start the timer, he knew this was the last of the pseudo-seizures. The room fell away.

Leaving the bed, he hastened to his private bathroom, finding a toiletry kit waiting, he grabbed it and stepped into the shower.

"Mr. Dare, why are you getting dressed?" the tiny Asian nurse asked half an hour later.

"I didn't feel like laying around in my own filth after I showered and shaved," he winked.

"But, sir, you could pass out again at any moment."

"Nurse…" Ananias paused and looked at the name tag above her left breast pocket, "Cratchit? Is that seriously your name?"

"No, sir, there was a ridiculously good-looking man leaving your room earlier. It was he who asked me to wear it." This time, it was she who gave a wink.

"Marvelous. Now, I will take my leave. Be assured, I have liv'd my life, and which I have done, may thou within himself make pure! If thou shouldn't never see my face again, pray for my soul," he inclined his head and started to walk from the room.

"More things are wrought by prayer than this world dreams of. Wherefore, let thy voice rise like a fountain for me night and day. For what are men better than sheep or goats that nourish a blind life within the brain, if, knowing God, they lift not hands of prayer both for themselves and those who call them friend?" the nurse replied behind him.

"You, young lady, most definitely did Lord Tennyson proud there," Ananias smiled broadly.

"Thank you. Arthur's last request has always been my favorite scene, in his works," she gently touched his back. "However, I must hold my wishes for your best, and instead, wonder in the midst of so much absurdity and turbulence in the world, are you a patrician serving the intelligentsia of New Roanoke, or an impecunious of the Battle Born ASP?"

"Hmm," he started walking from the room

before pulling up. "Your question is framed in such a manner to leave me with no choice but to be embarrassed with the answer I would give." Without turning, he said, "In good faith, I still forward you well wishes, along with love and strength to your family through said absurdity and turbulence in the world," he took another step and a high-pitched sound garnered his attention. As he turned to look at the nurse, the world faded away.

Waking on a marble floor, he got up, dusting off his suit before realizing he was in a completely new location, truly not knowing where or when he was… In the shadows of his mind, he remembered the establishment he was last in had been in a warmer climate. However, outside his current window was snow. "If I had the counsel of Merlin, and Sir Melliagaunce stood before me, I would have understood the level of his treachery. Yet here I wake in this new dungeon," he touched the marble floor and started walking through the opulent halls of his new location, taking in many details from the diverse floral arrangements in each branch corridor. Finally finding a stairway, he began walking down, understanding that he was leaving a teal floor. Continuing down, he passed oxblood, magnolia, and sage before reaching the white level. Instead of thinking himself into a stalemate, he walked straight to the desk. "I will be needing a mode of transportation."

"Dear boy, I don't believe you've brought your alibi. Little time left for those like you to survive. Draw deep, find a solution to the problem facing you," the woman fell into static.

"A deep fake, so wonderful. Can I ask a question before you wink out fully?"

A barely perceptible face floated absently in free air. "Darling, there can be none but he who has earned the right to…"

"You, away," Ananias pulled his fingers together, resting his thumbs against his chest briefly. With a flick of his wrists, his hands came apart, fingers fanning outward.

In front of him, the apparition of the attendant greeting him shattered into a million points of light before forming a knife and entering his shoulder. At that, a new face formed. "Identify yourself, sacrifice."

"Sacrifice, eh? It seems we have reached the end of this inspiring saga if I am that, but what will this glorious hecatomb be to?"

"I was mistaken, you are the blood, not the…" The floating face became that of a woman — unsmooth and unfinished.

"You want blood? Fine… here you go," he pulled a blade from his front pocket, running it along his left shoulder, allowing the points of light to leave.

"Wasteful… You can only wish it were that simple! You are the blood and we will carry you in our veins even if you die!"

"I have always felt I was the king of the obscure. Yet in this, I am lost," Ananias pulled his hair back from his face.

"There can be no simple answer to this. Just know that the moon, the night, and even the very soul of the world beats within your veins."

"I told you, I don't follow..." He was beginning to get frustrated with the riddles.

"No?" The laughter that erupted from the incorporeal being made Ananias step back absently. "Should you actually ever begin to recall what you encouraged, and moreover, what you prevented. It's disturbing to us that the elephant wanted to forget. Even us."

"Disturbing? Understand this and tell them all, I never wanted to forget anything, that would have made all those years wasted. I will remember, and when I do, they need only look behind them. I'll be there and I'm never going to allow the likes of you to come to be," he stood back, arguing with the creature of artificial intelligence he had stopped the world from inventing for many years. "But if need be, I'll face you whenever you'd like."

"What if you already have?" the unformed face defined itself into a nurse.

"For so the whole round earth is every way bound by gold chains about the feet of God," Ananias completed King Arthur's statement that Nurse Cratchit had begun in what couldn't have been more than a few minutes earlier. "Though, you are not she. Are you Judge?"

The tiny Asian woman reformed into the seven-foot-tall love of his life. "How, Ananias? How did you know it was me?" she asked.

"It's not what we know that defines us, but how we adapt to what we don't know that fulfills that role," Ananias closed his eyes, allowing whatever event he was experiencing to lapse. "Fuck, I hope I remember whatever I just said later... it was epic."

"Mr. Dare, you need to wake up," a voice seemed to come into the room and spiral around his head before dying away. "Mr. Dare! I seriously need you to wake up! How did you get in here?"

Time started again, along with the questioning voice, the smell of coconut filled his nostrils. Opening his eyes gingerly against the bright light, Ananias scanned the room searching for the origination point of the pleasant odor. Finding he was on the floor of the hospital bathroom, he couldn't find the smell. He began the process of sitting up, finding his left shoulder burned slightly. He turned his head, looking for the cut he had given himself to disturb his blood. Finding, instead, a plastic film that smelled strongly of coconut. "Don't touch it, sir. Let's get you up." Strong hands under his armpits helped him to his feet and back to the edge of his bed. "I need to wash your hands, you don't want an infection."

"Of course, of course. May I sit back?"

"Yes, sir, here, let me raise the head of the bed so you don't fall flat," the voice was that of a male nurse, not the young woman from last night.

"Thank you, Nurse..." Ananias read the name tag. "Sturluson. Interesting, would your first name be Snorri?"

"I don't understand, is that actually a name?" the nurse looked confused.

"Nothing, never mind," he smiled again.

"If you don't mind a question..."

"Of course not, go ahead."

"What made you get a tattoo while you were lying in a hospital bed? Hospitals aren't exactly the safest place for open wounds like that."

"Tattoo? I didn't..." Ananias looked down at his shoulder, having to brush his long hair back to see the blurred image under the plastic. A tattered American flag, forming a bald eagle. He could see one wing went onto his chest, ending above his pectoral. Not being able to see, but he could feel the other wing traveled onto his shoulder blade in the back.

"You didn't..." he started.

"Ignore me, I wasn't really thinking."

"You do know that the symbol of the old flag could get you in trouble, right?" The nurse asked.

"Can I assume you won't tell on me?" Ananias looked at him.

"Of course not, sir. I am so proud that you, of all people, are looking back to know how we can move forward."

"There is also that pesky confidentiality agreement you signed. Thusly, if you said anything about what may have been an illegal tattoo..." Ananias winked. "You could potentially end up far worse than you are today."

"That too," Nurse Sturluson replied.

Chapter 16
Digging into the Basics

The phone began to ring 20 minutes after JaLen's head hit the pillow. Seeing 'Blocked Number' on the screen, he dismissed the call. Three times this went on until, on the fourth call, the blocked number changed to the controls engineer on the project. *Odd, why would she block her number?*

"Georgia, I told everyone, no calls! I've been up for two days straight, and I need a few hours of sleep."

"I'm sorry, JaLen, I couldn't get you to answer so I had to spoof a number that I figured you would."

"Hello, Senior Helvetian," he said, keeping the anger and surprise from his voice.

"Hello, Demo Demon. Congratulations on another successful implosion."

"Thank you. And thank you for that little bit of insight," he said, sliding up and sitting against the headboard.

"That did not come from me."

"Well, pass it along, please. What can I do for you on this early morning?" JaLen asked.

"As our call ended, you asked a question, and I thought I'd answer now that the concern of your project has passed."

"The North American Honor Guard question?"

"There are two answers to that. The larger and

full story will need to be answered after you have met with us and made a full commitment. The shorter explanation may satisfy your immediate confusion."

"That would be good. I really don't want to be lined up in front of a firing brigade."

"Smart of you. Yet, I don't know that anyone can guarantee you of that. When the country was sectioned into three, it was to quell the widespread anger and stop the start of Civil War II. My opinion is that the desire was nothing more than appeasement 2.0... When Chamberlain didn't crush Germany before they advanced their technologies, he allowed several million people to die. The Parting stopped a potential war here but it allowed the Chinese to start their global supremacy. And again, millions have died, most of them were allies of the United States of America..." The Senior Helvetian, Commandant of the North American Honor Guard, paused to allow questions.

"No disagreement," JaLen filled the dead air.

"When the Parting took place, the shadow government that so many conspiracy nuts spoke about..."

"The shadow conspiracy," he gave a small laugh.

"That's precisely what they were called, but let me assure you, they did, er... ah, do exist. Made up of top leaders from all three branches of the Constitutional Government. But because they had no power, they became more like the Social Media Influencers of pre-2020. It has helped the original three lands, now two, to form new governments, establish laws, and more importantly, they manage most of the military. Do you understand what the Arch-Base is?"

"Yes, sir. Sorry, it's a grandmother thing, I can't not call you sir."

"Understood. Let's hear it, explain to me what you believe the Arch-Base is,"

"The centralized hub of military, controlled by a Congress of Governors, or the COG of the three countries."

"And when the three became two?" the Senior Helvetian asked.

"The total number of governors was cut to keep them equal," JaLen replied.

"Correct, it was also the first time, even during the Parting, that the leaders of the military generally went nuts," hearing no reaction from JaLen. "I take it you didn't know that, eh? It was actually very scary for those that knew. Because the keys and launch codes had always been coordinated through the COG, those holding the keys for the disbanded country went rogue."

"Wouldn't they only have half of the codes?"

"Ah, but do you know who held the footballs outside the military?"

"The leader of each of the three."

"And…" one could almost imagine the man on the other end of the phone to be rolling his hands to encourage the other person to continue.

"The President of the NWO was kidnapped a

week before they joined New Roanoke."

"Yes, and in all the negotiations and drama with the kidnappers in the midst of the merging of 2/3 of the United States, the concern for the launch codes actually fell off the table."

"The nuclear launch codes went missing? I'm glad I didn't know," JaLen felt his stomach turn a summersault.

"Over the course of 48 hours, the New World Order disbanded, and the leader of the NWO was recovered... Well, pieces of him."

"Wait. are you telling me the parts they kept were enough to verify his end of the launch codes?"

"You're every bit as sharp as I thought you were," the Senior Helvetian said.

"But, sir, why didn't they just change the codes?" JaLen, now fully awake, stepped from the bed.

"They surprisingly couldn't be."

"That doesn't make sense. If the entirety of the military complex and all the COG were in place, how could something as important as the nuclear launch codes be hijacked?"

"Suffice it to say there were seven bad actors. And those seven caused so much confusion that the codes and the missile silos were functionally lost. They used our own safeguards to establish the new firewalls." The Senior Helvetian explained.

"To what end? Did they not want the NWO to disband? Did they not want the military leaders to lose their seat at the table?"

"If you don't mind me saying, you're asking all the right questions, but if you were either of those parties, would it make sense to get involved at this level?"

"The military leaders, no. It would be too obvious. But the people in leadership of the NWO, they would be losing if the New World Order actually dissolved. They were the people who were demanding their own nation when the 2024 election went the way it did. So, yes, I could see them doing something like this. The larger question would have to be how they did it, which, to me, would lead straight to China. Were they just sowing seeds of discontent, to make it easier to take ... Actually, no, it wouldn't have been China—" he cut himself off abruptly. "If it was them, why wouldn't they have just supported the NWO's continuation."

"Keep going…"

"I love to watch action movies and cop shows. When they wanted to solve crimes, they would 'Follow the money', or they would check to see 'Who most benefits' from the crime. That would take me to either ASP or New Roanoke, but it could have been a combination of the two."

"Hmm, interesting jump. Let's leave it there."

"Wait, what?" JaLen almost dropped his phone.

"The North American Honor Guard was formed in the midst of these issues. We have representation, in the case of any emergency, from all countries on the North American continent."

"Including Canada and Mexico?"

"And all the others beyond Mexico."

"You shitting me? Isn't there like 24, including the two remaining United States?"

"You must not have gone to public school."

For the first time, JaLen knew the Senior Helvetian was smiling on the other end of the miles. "No, I did not sir."

"There's a journey that's about to start. Are you going to be ready?"

"What is the next step?" JaLen asked, sitting back on the bed, his curiosity having gotten the better of him.

"Say yes or say no, and you will see."

"I believe I did say yes already once, but to clarify, yes, I am all in, Senior Helvetian."

"If you came to us now, you would be bringing three things; your past, the present, and all our futures. I need only two of those. Time to settle with your past," the words had only finished coming from the phone when a clear tone took its place. The world faded away.

"Luv me if you caine. Boomity boom if you caint," a pretty voice sang, with a terrible pretend hillbilly twang, next to him in bed.

"You know..." he opened an eye, seeing the freckles on her cheeks, and one of her twinkling blue eyes, singing to the song on his iPod. Knowing she couldn't hear him, he rolled onto his side and pulled the cord on the earbud. "It says love me if you can, shut up if… never mind," he kissed the back of her hand.

"I was trying to let you sleep."

"Is that why you were yoddling?" JaLen smiled up at her.

"Oh, hush you…" she ran his hand over his left shoulder, leaving a blood trail in his mocha skin, "Shit, I cut you!"

"It's fine, it's fine. What are you doing here, Victoria-Lynn? You haven't visited my dreams in quite a while. Are you worried about the decisions I'm making?"

"Not even a little, I guess I've known you'd never move past what happened." His long-dead wife clasped his hand tightly.

"That is not only 100% true, it's also 100% justifiable. How could any person move beyond a sin that caused them to lose everything they held dear?" JaLen again kissed her hand, his tears running freely down his cheeks coming to rest on it.

"You're a good person, good people make mistakes. My reaction to the mistake you made shouldn't be yours to carry around," Victoria-Lynn let her tears fall, mixing with his.

"I know that's how you feel, each time you've visited my dreams, you said as much. I live each day to make certain I see you again."

"I need you to know that will come on its own. What you are planning to do right now requires you to live in each and every minute. Second-guessing the past won't help." She reached her other hand across and touched his shoulder again, another trail of blood appeared.

"Shit, girl, that time it hurt," JaLen laughed.

"Sorry, but it's necessary, you need to understand I won't be visiting you again. You've got this, big guy, and don't forget to buy a tube of coconut oil."

"JaLen? What are you doing in here, and why are you naked?" a female voice asked.

"Here, where?" he asked, feeling something land on his midriff.

"You're in the job trailer. More specifically, you're in the job trailer laying naked on the conference room table, moron," Georgia said. "It's a good thing I got in early, not like I haven't seen you like this a few dozen times. Do you still keep a to-go bag in your rental car?" the door closed at the other end of the trailer.

"Yeah, but I don't think that POS is out there," swinging his legs off the table, he muttered to himself, and then pulled the safety vest she had tossed to him around his waist.

"Got it," she burst out laughing seeing the mesh skirt he made out of the vest. "That actually makes it worse. Moron." Handing the duffle bag she had gotten out of his truck to him, the shiny bandage on his shoulder became apparent. "Did you get a tattoo last night?"

"What? No, of course not…" He looked down

at his arm. "Get a tube of coconut oil…" he mused.

"I beg your pardon?" Georgia lifted an eyebrow.

"Never mind." Opening the bag, JaLen smiled, thinking about the odd dream. Pulling out a pair of jeans, he put them on.

"Cowboy, eh?" raising her eyebrows together this time. "Hubba hubba. What is it?"

"What's what?"

"That tattoo, how many times am I allowed to call you moron in one day?"

"Six. I told you I didn't get a tattoo."

"Moron, take the wrapping off. You don't really need it, they put them on to protect from blood-borne pathogens," she laughed as he struggled to remove the tape behind his back. "Let me, you look like a damn dog chasing its tail. It's an American eagle made out of a flag. Dude, that's so fucking illegal. Get a shirt on," she looked around as if the cops were going to spring from the closet.

Pulling on his cowboy work boots, he walked over to the unusable bathroom, looking in the mirror. "Why do they put bathrooms in job trailers?" he mused as he looked at the ink, it was indeed an illegal as fuck American Eagle, made out of stars and stripes.

"Where did you find a tattoo artist to do that? I actually love it," she asked, tossing his shirt to him. "Put it on, Moron."

Chapter 17
Man's Best Friend

Leif opened the email app on his phone, typing 'Iamthetraveler@outlook.com'. he hit enter twice, ignoring the subject line.

'Mr. Traveler… That was a neat trick telling me that my dog is welcome to join me in whatever adventure you are advertising for. As it turns out, yes, I do feel bad about not joining the military. I never really thought the authority and regimentation of the armed forces would mix well with my devil may care attitude. If there has ever been a time for fixing the sins of the past, this would be a great time for it. We've lost our country, and our fore-fathers must be completely ashamed of who we've become. What can Constantine and I do to help?'

As he went to hit send, he decided a signature may be appropriate.

'The one and only never-ending pursuit.'

Then he hit send.

"What do you think, puppy, you feel like fighting the world's bad guys?"

"Woof!"

"Atta boy!" Leif tossed him a treat and headed for the concealed room. "First, we better get rid of this project." Pushing the motor and then the plexiglass out of the way, "How the fuck did he know about my conex?" he asked Constantine as he pulled the Gatling gun from the paint storage area. "I buried it under the canopy of the trees next to the river, so no aerial photos. And I buried it at night so I would know if someone came by."

"He knew the guy you bought it from," the baritone voice startled Leif, but not for too long.

In the blink of an eye, he had his black on black Vaquero out from his shoulder holster, cocked and aiming at the newcomer. "Are you the Traveler?"

"You could say that. Can I ask you a question? You can keep that aimed at me if you'd like."

"Didn't plan on putting it down, go ahead with your question."

"Why no subject line?" The man's features were chiseled, most women would melt just looking at him.

"Didn't really plan that, just happened," Leif lowered the gun and controlled the hammer return.

"Do you know how to use that, or do you just spend a bunch of time drawing it?"

"Best not get cute, or I'll show you," he smiled. "Do I call you Mr. Traveler, or something else?"

"Senior Helvetian works. How is it that the cops didn't see that gun? It's not like it's small, and you are rail thin."

"Beer, Senior Helvetian?" Leif indicated the refrigerator with his chin.

"I'll pass," he replied, leaving the earlier question floating in the silence.

"They didn't see it because they suck at their jobs. Simple as that... shit, they didn't even see this closet."

"To be fair, you hid it pretty well. Is that a flammable storage cabinet?"

"Yup, it's even ventilated to the outside. Christ, all they had to do was walk around the building. I have no patience for those who go half-assed through life. Why did you come to visit?"

"Before I get into that, do you need me to dispose of any 'weaponry' while I'm here? We have fantastic places to make things mysteriously vanish. We call them the sock drawers."

"If you were here to arrest me, you already have me dead to rights. I have this and a couple of other articles of concern if they were to send someone competent out here," Leif nodded his head. "What type of vehicle do you have?" He pushed the cart with the parts of the antique gun toward the garage door. "Push that button next to you, please."

"I have a truck," he reached up, pushing the garage door opener and followed his potential recruit outside.

"Good, we'll need to drive it back to the exterior storage cabinet," Leif watched as the other man lowered the gate, showing the bed was about eight inches higher than the bottom of the tail gate. Reaching to the side, the Senior Helvetian touched his palm to some type of reader. After a moment, the hidden drawer began to open. "No shit."

"Handy for all types of things." the two of them loaded the Gatling gun into the drawer.

"This is nice, how much weight will it hold?" Leif started looking at the mechanism holding the drawer.

"I was told not to put more than 500 lbs. in it, but I don't know what the actual capacity is."

"How do you close it?"

"There are two buttons under the lip of the drawer, you have to push them both. Like so," he reached both hands under the drawer which started closing. "I love this part, if it senses something is hindering the closure, it releases pressure rather than reopening."

"That's good. I hate that my garage door does that," he lifted up the tailgate, closing it.

"Alright, let's go pick up the rest of the concerning items. Jump in."

"One second, let me close the garage door and stick my traitor dog inside," Leif started walking. "Come on, you, what kinda watch dog are you, letting a complete stranger walk right up on me?" Once inside, he pushed the button to close the garage door. "You stay in here and think about what you did," he laughed to himself as he jumped into the pickup.

"Traitor dog?"

"Funny that he didn't bark at you, hell, surprising he didn't bite your head off, walking in uninvited and all."

"Where am I driving to?" The Senior Helvetian asked.

"Just drive toward the pontoon boat, back by the tree line," Leif pointed. "Have you been here before, maybe when I wasn't around?"

"Word of a good Samaritan saving a girl by

facing down a man actively shooting at him with a laser pointer. Stories like that fly in the face of the shit hole this country has become."

"I'd like to think that is — " Leif started.

"Hold up, then I did a little more digging. Turns out, you drive around that highway and help people very often and rarely get paid. What gives?"

"It's simple. My mother broke down on the highway and ended up getting killed. I set up a small fund to pay for gas and repairs on my tow truck to go help people. It's not my job, I do it on my own time."

"And nobody knows?"

"What do you mean by nobody? My buddies in the force know I'm out there, things don't typically get all fucked up as they did with that German jackass. Now, stay to the left of the boat, there's a space between the trees, you won't see it until you're right on it."

"That German businessman is the one that tipped off the cops to the illegal weaponry. Why didn't your buddies shut him down? Damn, this is an amazing hidden access."

"I know right, if the boat wasn't there, I'd miss it myself. My buddies work in the county and the state police. The locals are assholes, and easily bought and paid for, they don't care about common sense. Go on with your story, get to the part where Constantine didn't kill you."

"After the crazy shit with the laser pointer, I decided to pay you a visit, you weren't here. I may have let myself in. I also may have used your entire box of treats to pacify your beast."

"Ha! I knew I wasn't losing my mind about having to buy extra dog treats," Leif laughed. "Ok, stop just before the river. Here, good."

They got out of the truck, "I was surprised at what a fix-it mother fucker you are, I did a bunch of background checks and decided to get serious about a conversation. You see that bulletin board posting you saw on channel 107? It has been seen by several thousand people. And we're going to be starting a freshman class as it were. I need you, I need a fixer with a heart of gold."

"It's not like I'm the best mechanic…"

"That isn't actually the point, a laser pointer to save a damsel in distress, balls of steel. I need you, and I don't say that often. You are the only one I am personally pursuing for this freshman class. My team are looking into some others, and the rest will come on their own…" He stopped talking as Leif kicked some debris away, exposing two doors leading into the ground.

"Welcome to my back 40 storage."

"I don't think even a competent investigator would find this," they walked down a dozen steps. "You even have lights. Solar?"

"Yes and no, battery-powered with a solar charger up the tree." Walking deeper into the conex, passed pallets of food storage, water, and ammunition. "These are the questionable weaponry."

"Jesus, fuck, is this a blunderbuss? These look like repeater crossbows. Shit, fuck damn, these are actual Tommy-guns…"

"26 of them and 450 loaded magazines," Leif held up a round magazine.

"What the hell are these?" he picked up several small boxes.

"Tattooing machines, just pissed me off that they made tattoos illegal, so I started collecting them."

"Huh. that's interesting," the Senior Helvetian sighed under his breath.

"What is?" Leif leaded his head back, for the first time attempting to make eye contact, "Damn, you're taller than I thought."

"You need to get a tattoo if you say yes and join."

"I have tattoos, no big deal getting another."

"This one is a purging as it were. The tattoo is given in conjunction with a hypnotic tone, it drives you into a very deep sleep. It reaches into your mind and snatches whatever is holding you to your past so that you can move into our future."

"That's better than being awake for the tattoo, they suck."

"Let's get these Tommy guns out of here. The rest of this stuff isn't actually illegal, they may question the quantity, but a decent lawyer can deal with that."

"I don't actually have a lawyer."

"Good thing I do," he gave a smile that made his eyes look human.

After loading all the guns, they started to drive

out of the canopy of trees, only to be stopped by two glaring lights. "Get out of the truck with your hands up."

"Good thing they won't find anything," Leif started to open the door.

"You may want to toss that beautiful quick draw pistol under the seat," the Senior Helvetian said as he stepped from the car with his hands up.

"Good plan," Leif followed the suggestion and slipped the gun from the holster and tucked it under the passenger seat.

"Hands up," the familiar voice ordered. Officer Thadius stepped up to Leif with his gun drawn.

"My hands don't go any further up, I'm old, you dum—"

"Sir, if I may reach into my pocket, I have an ID that you may want to see."

"Two fingers only!" regulation mustache said. "And hand it straight to me."

"Of course," the Senior Helvetian did as requested and then held out his ID.

"This isn't even a real Identification, there's no such thing as the North American—" Mustache commented.

"Honor Guard, and yes there is. Take one of my business cards and call."

"Shut up, you pompous ass," Thadius barked. "We don't have time for your bullshit."

"Mr. HouLeiff, what were you doing in the

woods?" Mustache ignored his partner.

"I was showing him where the best place in the state is to catch trout."

"Sir, I don't mean to doubt you, but I don't see any fishing poles."

"Trout are out of season, and as he is passing through, I wanted him to know in case he comes back when it is legal to fish for them and I'm not around," Leif smiled.

"Fuck this, you're coming with us this time, HouLeiff," the asshole cop started forward.

"Leif, are you in? I mean it, this is commitment time."

"Of course I'm in," he looked over at the man who sought him out to join some fucked up adventure with his dog. As his eyes focused, the tall stranger pulled on a white stainless Vaquero, a mirror image to Leif's black on black. In less time than it took for him to have sex the first time, both cops were on the ground. "Drag that clown out of the way, we need to leave."

After dragging the asshat who had threatened one too many people out of the way, Leif climbed back in the pickup. "That is a sweet gun. I think I could take ya though." He sat back into the seat.

"When I saw the one you drew on me, I knew I made the right choice. Oh, and, Leif…"

As he turned his head to look at the man who just killed the two idiot cops, the world faded away.

"Leif, wake up. Why are you and Constantine

sleeping in my driveway?" Sergeant Terry Collins' voice was somewhere in the distance.

"Terry?"

"Woof!" Constantine's bark compressed his chest.

"Jesus, puppy, don't do that," Leif opened his eyes gingerly against the light. "How the fuck did we get here, pup?"

"Woof."

"You don't say," Leif laughed.

Tap-tap-tap!

The knocking on the windshield made him focus. "Leif, why are you hiding here?"

"Hiding? What are you babbling about?"

"You killed…"

"I didn't kill anyone, it was that recruiter. The guy that called me when the cops were at my place."

"Listen, the bullets came from your gun."

"No, he has the same pistol I do,"

"Leif, we took a sample of your bullets because of the incident with the shooting two doors down from you. Remember?"

"Fuck you, Terry, of course I remember. I didn't do this."

"Well, come with me and we'll figure it out," he opened the door and grabbed Leif from his left underarm.

"Ouch, what the hell?" When Leif reacted, Constantine bowed up, looking like a hell hound. "I'm ok, puppy," he gave him a snuggle. "I better go, he may rip your head off."

"Turn yourself in."

"Not gonna happen," he drove, rolling his shoulder. "What the fuck!" He stopped the car, seeing the neighbor two doors down who had died in a shoot-out three years earlier. He parked the car and ran over as she mowed her lawn. "Dana, you're dead, I saw you die…"

"I didn't die. It was part of the long game, they needed to get your bullets on file."

"No, your face was blown off,"

"Don't be silly, my face is fine," she turned her head to face him, the eye on the left side of her face hung limply in a fractured mess of pulp where the three bullets exited her face. Just like the day he had gone to give first aid.

"Oh, God, how can you be here?"

"Leif, sugar, neither of us are here, but my husband is, and he thinks you and I are sleeping together."

"We never."

"Don't you think I know that? It's him you need to convince," she pointed over Leif's shoulder just as the first bullet tore into it. "David, stop!" she yelled.

"Woof!" the dogs both barked.

"Constantine, Fausta, attack!" Leif pointed to the man just as he pulled the trigger, shooting him in the shoulder again.

"You mother fuc—" David's words were drawn out as Constantine jumped, biting his shooting arm. Bang! The gun fired, followed by yipping. With a second bang, there was no more yipping. "Get off me, you fucking mutt."

"NOOOOO!" the six bullets were out of Leif's gun as David aimed at Constantine. Each of the six bullets found home. "Fausta, baby girl!" Leif got to the dying dog as it took its last breath.

"Leif!" Dana yelled, he didn't look up from his beautiful puppy. "You should get some A&D Ointment for that shoulder."

"What?"

'Tap-tap-tap.' Knocking on the windshield. "Leif, what are you doing in my driveway?" He opened his eyes, looking through the window of his tow truck at Terry.

Turning his head, he saw a sticky note on his rearview mirror, 'You don't really think you're faster, do you?' Below that was, 'PS - tell Constantine, I'm sorry about Fausta.'

"Well?" Terry asked.

Leif looked at his friend, and then back at the drooling dog next to him. "Dude, I'm so sorry I didn't save Fausta."

"I miss her too."

"You know you're all jacked up! Balling like a baby, hugging your dog, and you don't even have a bandage on that boss tattoo. But yeah, I miss your baby girl too," Leif looked over as his best friend and the toughest cop he ever met, crying over the dog that had died three years earlier.

Chapter 18
Can She Really Do That?

Walking from the police station, he ceremoniously looked up to the sky, seeing an extremely haphazard flying helicopter passing in the sky above him. "Idiot, that is such an easy way of getting the authorities after you," he walked out to his Fairlady, thinking over the last few hours. Looking down at the tablet in his hand after it vibrated a few times, he ignored it and set it on the lid of his trunk as he fished for his keys.

"You may want to check that," a deep voice said walking up behind him.

"That was impressive, almost like you appeared out of nowhere," Blaire smiled as he turned and faced the newcomer. "What makes you think I need to check that message?"

"It's from my group telling you I will be following up on that email."

"Interesting, did you race their email to me?" His smile faltered.

"I wanted to meet you in person. How did you end up here? There's no record of an arrest."

"I didn't really do anything to be arrested for, the Sheriff knows that my landlord is trouble, so he obliged her. Wa-la, I spent the night in a cell."

"How did you like it?"

"Sorry?"

"Sleeping in a prison cell... actually, a jail cell. How did you like it?" the tall man asked.

"I didn't, it felt like a serious step in the wrong direction of my life."

"Is that why you reached out?"

"Not specifically, no."

"Blaire, you've given me no reason that you are doing this. Let me make this clear, I need to understand who I am giving the nod to."

"Before I reply to you, please tell me who you are," Blaire stood up straighter.

"My apologies, I am the Senior Helvetian, Commandant of the North American Honor Guard. If you wish to address me, Senior Helvetian is fine."

"When I was in high school, I enlisted and was ready to go into the Marines. My mother and my grandmother begged me not to. I reached out to the recruiter and I was informed that, if I came in with a letter establishing that I would be a full-time student, I could step away from my commitment to the Marines. I did this for the matriarchy in my family. It was a mistake, I truly feel anger toward both my mother and even my grandmother for it. Though I understood Grandma lost a brother to the great war, which drove her to not want me to go in. It still rattles me that I wasn't man enough to just do it."

"That says it all. Let me tell you, honoring family wishes doesn't make you unmanly. Are there any other reasons?"

"Yes, sir. My knowledge, my drive is more today than even then, I know I can make a difference, I can bring to the table that which isn't there because no one has it to bring but me." His excitement showed well enough in what he was saying that the Senior Helvetian allowed a large grin to openly display. "What?"

"That was the answer I needed to see in your eyes," he turned and started heading away. Stopping again, he turned, "Oh, and, Blaire…" a high-pitched noise filled the morning and all went black.

"Blaire," Janey's voice came from behind him.

"Where am I?" His head was swimming as he pushed up off the driveway.

"Blaire!" she repeated.

"Yes, ma'am?"

"Don't yes ma'am me, you son of a bitch! I'm being arrested because of you!"

He stood, finding indeed his landlord was in cuffs and being led to the station by a woman police officer. "Because of me?"

"Yes, you useless twit! How else would anyone know about the power wiring in your apartment?" she yelled.

"You know you have the right to remain silent, right?" Blaire yelled, following her around the corner. The last thing he saw was the lady cop winking at him. "Fucking awesome," he considered doing a little Irish Jig, instead, his mind started replaying the previous 10 seconds… The two arms holding and leading Janey by the shoulders, while a hand was shackled to Janey's right arm and another was chained to her left. Uncertain, but there may have also been two other hands on her hips. *Marici?* Turning, he ran back to the police station to find a closed door. Reaching to the right side of the door, Blaire punched in 1, 2, 3, 4, 5, 6. All the lights flashed and three tones echoed red in the darkness. "Wait, when the fuck did it get dark?" he turned in a circle, finding that the stars and moon were in the sky. "Strange. I remember the code." This time, he punched in 1, 2, 3, 6, 5, 4. The door clicked, taking a deep breath before pulling it open, Blaire ran into the station. "Hello there!"

"Foolish boy," said the female police officer. With a loud 'sching', each of the six arms had a weapon in it. Hanging from two of the arms still wearing handcuffs, still holding Janey's arms. On the ground, the armless landlord was sitting on the floor in shock, a soundless scream on her face.

"Marici, what do you want of me?"

"With you, nothing. You are the one coming for me, I merely wanted to welcome you to the gates of hell. Can you live through losing everything again? After that feckless broom rider sued you for palimony, and breach of contract, driving you into bankruptcy…"

"I never went bankrupt," Blaire steeled himself for whatever bullshit was going to be thrown at him.

"While that is true, you did, in fact, lose everything. Even that cute little car you drive around, she made you pay her three times its value to get it back… and it was your grandmother's car," the severed arms bounced as Marici laughed at his pain.

"I got it back though," he sneered.

"You didn't see, it had a boot on it before you came after me. The ASP Intelligence Agency has a seizure order on it," she laughed some more. "Apparently, it was used in a drive-by shooting, to kill a feckless —"

"You killed Lidia?" Blaire took a step forward.

"I? Foolish boy. Wait, I used that one already, how about, moronic jackass. Yes, that feels right. I didn't have anyone killed, even this slumlord. She came to sign papers against you, and you killed her. Then while attempting to cover it up, the sheriff came in, speaking of moronic jackasses," she muttered aside. "When he tried to stop you, there was no alternative, you had to take his gun and shoot him three times," As all the blades pointed into the cell, Blaire saw that the sheriff was indeed lying dead on the floor.

"Without any GSR on my hands, how would they tie that to me?"

"Are you really asking me that? We control entire countries, tying a murder to you would be as simple as turning on a shower."

"Of course, it would. Well, I came in here to try and save her, so since she's dead. And my car is impounded..." Blaire walked into the cell, checking to see if Sheriff Ernst really was dead, taking the handcuffs from his belt, tucking them into his pocket. Standing, he pulled the pistol from his holster. "Tell me the truth," he said, pulling the hammer back on the revolver. "Were the court records during that bullshit trial altered by anyone in association with your organization?"

"GSR, remember."

"Just answer," the gun fired, she swatted the bullet, and like a bat to a baseball, it flew back, catching him in the left shoulder.

"Fine, pedantic child. Yes, you were gaining too much too fast. We deep faked the shit out of you to her. That insecure girl never even questioned it. When you took that lie detector, we spoofed it. Even after that, Lidia almost took you back, did you know that? She went to that diner, you remember when she found you with Denise, she had no choice but to believe the evidence."

"I wasn't there WITH Denise!"

"Of course, you weren't, we had her fired so that she would cry on your shoulder," her grin made Blaire shoot the gun once again.

The bullet rebounded from the sword, finding his left shoulder again. "Fuck, shit! Fuck you!"

"Such profanity. Poor little fuck wit. You lost everything, yet you refused to join us the first time we reached out."

"What? You never…" pausing as his mind was bombarded with the memory of the only time he could have been contacted. "The job in Alaska?"

"Ah, he does remember. Yes, that pipeline job was nothing more than grade level systems architecture."

"Hardware-based hacking. Had you just come forward," again, he paused. "You wouldn't want someone who jumped at the call. You knew they would be too easily corrupted by what they are doing.

You need real people who could be swayed to the dark side."

"Dark side? Seriously, you geek. No, Blaire, that is a romanticized version of what you want us to be. The truth is much simpler," she raised her hands up 'shick' the weapons all disappeared. The six arms began to merge into two, and her blue skin turned a light brown.

"Lidia? No fucking way, you... you're a luddite," he almost toppled over.

"Was I? Or did you just project that on me, perhaps?" the voice was the heavenly alto of the woman who left him homeless seven years earlier.

"I never..." visions of their life together danced through his memory. "Meant to do anything to hold you back." A step forward, then another. "What we had..." two more steps and he reached out his right hand. Quicker than a blink of an eye, the five hands grabbed ahold of his arm. The sixth held a 16-inch kukri to his throat.

"Is there a chance that you really are that stupid?" Lidia now spoke with the raspy anger of Marici.

"Let him go!" Sheriff Ernst did not wait, the bullet struck her in the temple. As she fell, the kukri ran along Blaire's left shoulder, slicing deep.

"No!" he dropped to his knees. His tablet skipped under his car.

"I don't think it broke," said a policewoman escorting his landlord into the police station.

"What, oh yeah, I hope not." Grabbing the

tablet, he stood, his tablet began sending a continuous on and off vibration sequence of various lengths. He tossed the tablet through the open window, onto the front seat, "What the... Why is this window open?" he mused.

"In for one night and you got a prison tatt?" Janey mocked. "What an asshole!"

"Enough out of you, ma'am," the police officer jostled the handcuffs.

"Only one set of arms. Jig time!" He started in at the chorus of the Irish dance, spread his legs apart, crossing his left foot in front of his right, then spreading them apart before bringing them together again.

After two rounds of heel toe, heel home, his phone started ringing. "Answer," His voice command connected the call.

"Don't do that again," the baritone voice of the Senior Helvetian came over the speakers in his car. "Do you really think that a Teutonic Knight would actually do that?"

"Well, maybe not after the first victory, but yeah, I could see a badass knight doing a jig after a full-on massive victory."

"And you feel that was a massive victory?" he paused. "Not important, remember the helicopter that flew over before you blacked out?"

"I do."

"It is waiting for you, take your grandmother's car to the helicopter pad next to the hospital in town. There, you will be greeted by a man named Jeremy.

Give him your keys so the Fairlady can be looked after while you're otherwise disposed of. I promise that vehicle will be in better shape when you get her back than she is in right now."

"Yes, sir, I'll find this Jeremy."

"Try not to call me sir, it gives the wrong impression."

"I'll do my best, but Gram raised me right, so I may slip now and again."

"That's fine, it's genuine, doesn't actually feel military the way you say it. After you turn the keys over to Jeremy, wake the helicopter pilot, his name is Mason."

"I can do that," Blaire got into the car, smiling as he saw the bag of sour gummy worms. "Thanks for the gummies, but, sir, what is the tub of A&D Ointment for?"

"For the prison tatt you got on your left shoulder." The line clicked off.

"Prison…" He felt his left shoulder, unable to see much. "Ok then…" he opened the tub and applied some lotion to the new ink. "I wonder who this Mason is, and why he's sleeping on a helicopter?" he asked no one as he started the Fairlady.

Chapter 19
The One Who Flew Over…

Dutch stood outside as the helicopter approached. "What a fucking waste." Mason held the chopper in place, waiting for confirmation.

"Not at all," the voice over the headset replied. "Desecration of a corpse is a serious crime, which, of course, is the lesser charge, you see, he says you killed her. He delivered all the video files that he took."

"And you believe him?"

"Drop the painting."

"Fine," Mason slid the window next to him open and dropped the drafting tube. "It's on its way."

"Bank hard, right NOW!" The Senior Helvetian ordered.

Mason reacted without thinking, upon hearing the order. The hole in his windshield appeared, its trajectory put it inches from his left ear. "What the fuck!"

"You're clear. You have earned your place, that was the reaction that jet fighter pilots train for years to achieve, you literally dodged a bullet."

"Thank you, sir, credit has to go to my gramps," he laughed.

"I need you to head to the coordinates I am sending you. Before you ask, I've got you the proper clearance."

"Headed there now. Ok if I let loose with a little Robert Johnson?"

"I tell you what, put on Justin Johnson instead, JJ's blues kicks some serious dick!"

"Sir?" he laughed. "Ok, Senior Helvetian." When no further comment came, Mason addressed his virtual assistant, "Bam-Bam, play Justin Johnson Blues."

"Would you like the one-hour live?"

"That sounds perfect. Bam-Bam, if we're still flying, play my Robert Johnson mix."

"Yes, sir," the virtual assistant replied.

The music started, a slide guitar began to fill his Mason's headset with memories of his Gramps and all the lessons he gave. The plans he had for him, helping to end the life. 'Boy you need to listen to me, the place in which you end is most likely dependent on where you start. But I'm telling you it doesn't have to be. Love those who love you. Like those who like you, and forgive those who hate you. Now, walk away and think about that.' The very last words Gramps said to him. "Bam-Bam, let's switch it up," he said after two hours of flying.

"What would you like to listen to, sir?"

"Give me some sing-a-long pop bullshit."

"Very well, sir." A series of music that, in reality, he hated, played, but the ability to sing loudly gave him the extra boost to keep him flying the final 10 minutes. As he was arriving at the designated location, the bullet hole in the glass in front of him started to annoy him. "What kind of scum bag is this Dutch guy? And exactly how the fuck did I get caught up in a job that went so wrong?"

"Mainly because..." The Senior Helvetian's voice scared the hell out of him.

"Holy shit!" The helicopter banked on its own. "You almost killed me," he had to turn around and go back, having flown a bit past the landing spot, trying to stabilize the aircraft.

"Nice recovery that..." a small laugh accented his comment.

"Well, I'm nothing if not a good chopper pilot," Mason chuckled as he landed at the designated location, 100 yards away from the hospital's pad. Powering down the helicopter, he sat back as the rotors began slowing.

"To finish answering your earlier question, you got caught up with Dutch because you ignored what your grandfather told you."

"Wait, how do you know that?" Mason asked, now really confused.

"Young man, you truly don't understand who we are yet. Soon, you will," a high-pitched whistle brought the darkness.

"So few people even care to understand what the world lost when the United States collapsed," Gramps was wrenching on the chopper motor. "Hand me two of the three-quarter-inch box wrenches out of my box in the office."

"Yes, sir," Mason jogged to the toolbox. "Here you go."

"Nice hustle," Gramps chuckled.

"I'm not as quick as I was when I was in my twenties."

"You're not as quick as you were in your 30s," Gram rolled into the hangar.

"Ouch, I just turned 40 today,"

"Point stands, mate," Gramps struggled to loosen the bolt.

"Get up there and take those wrenches before that old codger breaks his shit."

"Gram!"

"Well, look at him, he's purple."

"I'm always purple, I wanted to be a prince, remember? Fine, fine," he gave in after looking at her stern visage. Offering the wrenches back to Mason, "After you get those…"

He held his hands, waving them off. "Any reason not to use your impact drill?"

"Flippin' platypus eggs, I forgot about that thing. Sure, go get it, and a —"

"three-quarter-inch impact socket," he cut in.

"So, why didn't you offer the impact until you had to do it?" Gramps asked.

"I think me offering you the easy way out was… coaxed out of me during my training," he jogged to the office again. Returning with a shallow socket in one hand and the impact drill deep socket already attached in the other.

"Tired already?" Gram smiled at her grandson.

"I had an issue getting the old battery to settle

on the charger."

"I hate that thing. So, what do you miss the most about the pre-separation?"

"Rich people who thought their security was top-notch," Mason's comment made Gramps snort. "Now the rich people really do have top-notch security, and dogs, and death rays."

"Death rays?" Gram's eyes shot from man to man.

"He's joking, dear."

"Sorry, Gram, it was a bad joke. But yeah, jobs have changed now that there are few rich people. Now that we need to travel abroad to—" Mason started.

"Enough!" This time, it was Gramp's turn to cut him off. "Never know when ears are finding their way in."

"Sad but true." Even here on the boat. "I had a couple of job offers back home, I didn't really know the players."

"Well, you need to remember, the days of trusting people are definitely behind us. If you don't know everyone you're going into business with, and what their ACTUAL motivation for the business is, you'll find out at the most inopportune time. Take that to heart, never ignore that piece of your training."

"Training, training, and more training," Gram laughed. "At what point are you going to take that stigma off the boy?"

"The day he stops training him… duh!" A man

in a black suit, black shirt, and a black on black geographic patterned tie walked in. He ran his left hand down his long red beard, pulling it into point.

"Angus, the fact that you're here, and I heard no entrant vehicle can't be good," Mason climbed the ladder nonchalantly.

"Look, I offered you both a chance to join me. Hell, I even tried to get her to talk you into it," the pointed beard jutted out at Gram.

"Did you hear what I was telling Mason? Or did you just come in during the training comment?"

"I heard enough," Angus walked in, staring at Mason untrustingly as he operated the impact drill, loosening the bolt.

"Got it."

"Good. Give me the nut, and use this to push out the bolt," Gramps climbed the first two steps of the ladder, trading items with his grandson, dropping another item into his jacket pocket. Stepping back down, he said, "Then you know why we couldn't join you on that job."

"No, I really don't understand that at all. Don't think I missed that sleight of hand, what did you give him?"

"A punch."

"No, what did you put in his pocket," Angus pulled a gun from under his shoulder, cocking it.

"You ginger fuck, a hammer, see, a hammer," Mason held up the hammer in one hand and the punch in the other.

"Sorry, been a bad week," he allowed the

hammer to release. "What was your reason for turning down the job? It's important," the gun stayed in his hand.

"You didn't tell us the whole truth. Why did that job need to be done when you specifically said it did?" Gramps replied.

"The tenants were out of town for three days and two nights. It isn't rocket science," the flush in his cheeks was obvious against the beard and long hair.

"Angus, why are you here now?" Mason asked.

"That isn't the right question, more to the point would be me asking you why you're here."

"We're on a sightseeing trip, but the helicopter had an issue," Gram said.

"Come on, you maintain that thing better than the military care for their choppers," Angus shook his head.

"That's true, but the pitch change bearing doesn't feel like it's transferring the blade shear and bending to the yoke like it should. I'm not putting my girl in a helicopter over rocky cliffs if I am not 100% confident."

"And what is it you're doing? I don't see new bearings out here, just a pile of bolts."

"Seriously?" Mason tried to understand why Angus cared.

"The bolts are being changed to lend additional support to the bearing lugs. I'm hoping to get better recovery and some of the torsional bend back by changing them."

"Angus, you haven't told us the reason for your dropping by," Gram commented. "Can I get you something to drink? Why has your week been so rough?"

"Why are you asking about my week?" He once again cocked the pistol, aiming it at her.

"Sweetie, you just apologized for overreacting because you've had a bad week," she started to turn her wheelchair back to the mess area.

"Where are you going."

"Getting you a glass of iced tea," she continued to roll away.

"Stop, damn it, I'm in charge here!"

"You are?" Gramps shook his head. "Why do you think you need to be in charge? You're among friends, aren't you? Look, just tell us what's up and tell us the truth."

"Shut up," Angus looked at his lapel, and then made his best imploring face. "Why are you here? What are you up to?"

"Fine, we had to get into international waters because Mason had a tax issue," Gramps said, still looking away.

"Issue? The taxation agency of the NWO decided he was a resident of that country, and he needed to pay the minimum Caucasian tax rate for a resident of five years. As we were in California at the time, the only way for us to leave was our boat," Gram chimed in.

"How did you get stuck with a residency in the

New World Order?"

"I didn't relocate after the five-year grace period ended. But to be fair, it was 10 years until it wasn't."

"Alright, we told you, what do you need from us? The games have gone on enough, we have work to do," Gramps' patience was waning.

"I told you, Chuck, I'm not here to answer your questions. What do we need to do to get the chopper ready to go?"

"By we, the man in a suit means, get to work while I watch," Gramps said. "Don't call me Chuck, you asshatted ginger bitch."

"Gramps," Mason laughed and got back to the removing the bear cover off so he could change the lugs out. Two hours later, the impact drill was tightening the cover back in place. Angus was sitting at the small corner table drinking iced tea, laughing with Gram.

"Almost ready, good to go," Gramps started the hydraulic pumps that were used to raise the platform and open the ceiling. "Mason, put the tools away when the fluids come up to temperature."

"Yes, sir," he said, taking the remaining tools back to the office area. As he stepped into the office, the door slammed behind him. A rough water bolt was slid into place, effectively locking him in. "What the fuck! Let me out!" Opening the toolboxes, he found a one-inch drill, putting it in the drill. He then pulled the Sawzall out, putting a metal cutting blade in it. Mason waited for what he knew would happen next. As if on cue, the grinding of the gears to open the ceiling started. Using the noise to mask his actions, he estimated the position of the bar and drilled a hole. Finding his estimate was too good, the drill rammed into the metal bar. "Fuck," he took a moment to look through the hole. Seeing nothing, he drilled another hole coming out just at the top of the bar. "Perfect," the opening noise was still going on, so he grabbed the saw and started cutting. "I'm not gonna make it," Mason knew he couldn't get it done before the deck finished sliding back, and that he would have to wait for the noise of the lifts for the helicopter pad to start again.

The first gunshot came after the grinding stopped. "No!" Gramps yelled. "Shoot me too, you mother fucker! I can't start the copter without raising it up first."

Too? Mason peered through the hole, seeing the empty wheelchair. "Let me out of here!"

"We don't have time, Chuck. Shut up in there. I'd hate to kill my leverage!" Angus yelled back.

"Mason, listen to me, stay where you are," Gramps said calmly. "Stay out of my desk."

Opening Gramps' desk, he found the loaded Derringer, Mason tucked it into his waistband. When the rotor started turning, he knew there wasn't going to be another chance, Mason took the saw and finished cutting through the bar, then kicked the door open. Walking around the corner, he ignored his fallen grandmother. As he rushed to the chopper, the wind from the rotor attempting to take off from inside this enclosed space slowed him tremendously.

"Stay back, Mason!" Angus' words couldn't be heard but his actions were easy enough to read as he held the gun out of the sliding window, aiming it at him. When he didn't stop, he fired, hitting him in the left shoulder. He pulled the small pistol from his waistband, with his right hand shifting his body, catching a second round in his left shoulder. Gramps grabbed Angus' arms, distracting him.

"Fuck you!" he shot Angus through the windshield as the two men in the helicopter struggled over the pistol. The small caliber did not kill Angus. Mason pulled the hammer, and engaging the manual safety release, he shot again, just as Angus shot Gramps.

"No!" Mason sat up in the seat of the helicopter, scaring the man who was about to knock on the glass, making him take a step back. "Who the fuck are you!"

"I'm Blaire, I was told to come here."

Chapter 20
Can't Roll a Meatball up a Mountain

"Robert, who was in that car?" Delta's voice was unbelievably calm.

"I couldn't tell you. But I plan on finding out after I get all my gear back together," he pulled his backpack from the clutches of the jackass who apparently set this entire thing up. "Your dead ass should be happy that the investigation into who the hell you are, and what the hell made you think you could come on my mountain and piss on my friends. I would make your entire family pay, I may find out anyway so I can kill the dumb bitch that birthed you, or I may take your head with me to let her know you're never too old to be an abortion," he kicked the dead man for good measure.

"Robert…" the yell came from the cabin.

"What?" he said into the microphone, the crack at the end of his statement made him realize why Delta had yelled through the woods. "I was broadcasting wasn't I?"

"Yes, and while I appreciate your sentiment… maybe internal dialogue is more appropriate."

"Gotcha," he finished collecting his weapons, and possibly some equipment from the well-geared dead men. Placing the single-eyed night vision on his forehead, he walked up to the car, smashed against a tree with steam escaping from the radiator. Robert aimed his Redhawk into the window. When he found no one inside, he instantly dropped to his ass, the sound of three suppressed shots sang out. "What the fuck! I'm the one who stopped the shooters."

"I couldn't give a fuck, you approached my car with your gun drawn!" the voice in the nearby trees said.

"Yeah, but only one of them."

The laughter from the same location made him feel better, "Who are you?"

"I'm just the dude the rangers called for help."

"But?"

"I don't really have a but…"

"Then how do you take a shit?" the same laughter echoed.

"How long have you been waiting to use that?" Robert laughed, much quieter than the other, and pulled the night vision over his eye. Seeing the second figure creeping through the woods, trying to get behind him. "By the way, that gun I aimed into the car isn't the one I'm currently aiming at the moron trying to get position on me," he shot the Shockwave into a tree in front of the 'sneaking' person. "Walk to me with your hands up. Don't make me kill again tonight, although…" he paused his statement. "It has been a while since my death toll reached into the double digits in one night," he racked another shell into the Mossberg.

"Ok, sorry!" The person he had just shot at was a woman.

"Enough, drop that gun and start walking to me. And, Funnyman, if you start heading this way to ambush me, I will put two rounds in her before I turn it on you. Trust me, this may be a compact weapon, but it will kill you just as dead as my revolver."

"Fine I'm unarmed, heading to you. Tricia had my gun, just in case,"

"Tricia, you need to hold that gun with two fingers off to the side as you walk up to me." After the two kids joined him at the sedan, he said, "Seriously, give me the gun, and let's head into the ranger's Station. What were you two driving into the woods at night for?" He looked between them and mumbled a, "Never mind, I don't really want to know."

"No, ew, nothing like that," Tricia said and then began placating the guy. "Justin, you know I didn't mean ew like er… ah. Look, mister, I have a girlfriend, I don't like boys."

"I get it, I get it. What are you doing out here?" Robert asked as he led them to the cabin.

"We were at lunch on campus and we heard that there was gonna be an attack on the ranger station," Justin said. "My brother works here, and we couldn't get him or anyone on the phone, so we drove up after our last class."

"Are you fucking kidding me? Why the hell didn't you call the police?"

"Sir, how long have you been under a rock? There are no 'police' to call," Tricia glared at him.

Remembering all the 'defund the police' rallies back in the day. "That never took, after the crime rose to a point where the lawmakers were in real danger, they dropped it."

"Ok, so the answer is about three years," Justin

mocked. "All police agencies were privatized and I don't have money to call U'Per." When he saw Rob's blank face, he explained, "It's the rental cop agency, you can call them but you need to either have an account, or you need to have a credit card with at least 10,000.00 standard gold on it. You do know what standard gold is, yes?"

"Head in, smartass," he opened the door to the ranger's station, saving his remaining street cred because he had no idea what standard gold was. When he followed Tricia into the cabin, he saw Justin hugging a tall fat ranger. "Thumb, is that your kin?"

"Yeah, Robert, thanks for saving him."

"Anything for you, I still owe you for helping get that solar generator up the mountain."

"It was easier than rolling a meatball up there," the ranger said.

"You can do that?" Robert and the big guy laughed at some odd inside joke. "Alright, alright. What the hell happened here?"

"We were playing our weekly poker game when these psychos busted in, holding several guns on us," Delta said. "That asshat who was in here with us was babbling about the senator's family needing to pay. I called her, by the way, she's stopping her trip."

"Cool, thank you," he said absently as he pressed a couple of shells into the shotgun before putting it in the leather sheath, then putting it on his back.

"You're gonna be cleaning those for a while, eh?" Thumb asked.

"Long while, yeah. Go on, Delta."

"You're Delta?" Justin leaned back, taking in the muscular ranger.

"Don't start, Puppy!" his big brother flicked him on the back of the head.

"Any who," Delta raised an eyebrow, looking between the brothers. "I did have to call in the cops, and the County Coroner, so, Robert, you may want to take your stuff for cleaning into the basement and get some rest. I know between saving those kids earlier today, and saving us tonight, you must be very tired."

"Surprisingly, yes I am. That adrenaline rush didn't last very long at all," he grabbed his gear and headed down to the cot he'd slept on a few times over the years. Turning on the small television, he walked to the coffee table next to the cot, using it to break down and clean the weapons. After field stripping and cleaning the weapons, he wiped down the new equipment with alcohol swabs and packed them in individual compartments in his backpack. Before he could lay down the random show that was playing as background noise, the room started scrolling through colors, but it was when the room went black that he looked up at the screen. *IamtheTraveler@outlook.com? Interesting pitch, maybe I'm a fit.* Robert walked to the old desktop computer in the corner on a roll-top desk.

After a 15-minute boot sequence, he logged into his personal email account and sent an email to the Traveler, laughing to himself, he thought he may be sending an email to Robert E. Lee's horse, although as he recalled, the horse had two L's in its name.

'Dear Traveler, I find that after reading your

public service announcement, I needed to throw my lot in with you. I am a survivalist that lends his unique skillset to save people in the mountains, and as you may hear in the next 24 hours, thwarting attacks on certain senators. I think this may be a perfect win-win. Regards, 50-Out'.

He hit send and shut down the computer, then walked back to the cot and lay down. When his eyelids closed, the world signed off, 50-Out.

Sometime later in the night, yelling woke him, and he started to sit up. "Just stay there," a deep voice instructed. "This night vision monocular is badass. Did you borrow them from one of the dead men outside? Don't answer, I really couldn't give a fuck. This question I do need an honest answer to, did you really kill them all, alone?" he stopped speaking and waited.

"Do I have the right to remain silent, or no?" Robert asked.

"You are most definitely not under arrest, at least not from me. I'm here to answer your email. Let's start with what does 50-Out mean?"

"When I figured out the fools in charge couldn't get anything right, and the world kept letting me down, I was 50. That year, I packed everything and moved up to the mountains. I was a disillusioned conservative, watching the Gipper's party take a 'walk softly and leave their stick at home' candyass attitude. Reagan would roll over and spit if he saw these bitches in action."

"Why not get involved?" the deep voice asked from the darkness.

"Members of Congress are reelected with a 1% approval rating, once you're in… the system is rigged. Not worth exposing myself to that brand of evil," Robert lay his head back.

"I think you are a good fit for us, but I may steal your name for the team I personally will be in charge of. If you're in it, you'll need a new one."

"That sucks. But ok."

A high-pitch caught his attention, overriding the yelling from upstairs, then all went black.

"Stop " the yelling from the side of the stage caught his attention. Two women were rushing the stage. The Bubble Gum rock band's lead singer kept singing as he turned to welcome his two fans. "Get to him!" the other bodyguard/roadie, Wade, yelled. A glint of metal in the hands of both girls made him take notice and begin his sprint toward his charge.

"Sedric, to me!" he yelled to no avail, he only saw the fans he wanted to see. At the instant of impact, he arrived, grabbing the singer, throwing him into the crowd, leaving his own left shoulder exposed to the two girls.

"Die!" they screamed as their knives found purchase, driving deeply into his shoulder. His eyes kept contact on his charge as Robert plowed forward into the assassins, bowing them over, the impact snapping the fragile neck of one and causing the other to land on the blade of the first. The crowd, initially having caught the singer, quickly began passing him deeper into the auditorium, ripping his clothes off as they did. Robert jumped from the stage, knocking several fans to the ground as he ran on the backs of the seats, grabbing the torn clothing from the psycho fans. By the time he caught Sedric, he was completely naked. Pulling the singer against him to stop the photos, he then draped part of his shirt around the unconscious man to cover his buttocks. Changing course but still walking on the backs of the seats, he returned to the stage, stepping on the guard rail and then onto the stage.

"Is he alright?"

"Bring the stage lights down and the fucking house lights up. What the fuck are you waiting on? Protocols are there for a reason," Robert yelled as he took Sedric off stage.

"Protocols like protecting the band and not throwing them into the arms of insane teenagers," Wade replied.

"Seriously? If you had stopped those girls, none of this would have happened. Where did they even come from?" Robert played what happened back, Wade was out of position. When he was yelling, his pants were down at his knees. "Sex, you fucking bastard, you were having sex with—"

"Not sex, just a blowjob," he cut in.

"From a teenager, you sick bastard." Still holding Sedric in his right arm, the punch from his left caught Wade unawares and laid him out on the floor. Seeing the blood running down his arm, after slugging his coworker, he shook it off taking Sedric back to the dressing rooms.

20 feet from the door, the manager, Mr.

Derphume, walked up, "You know you're fired, right?"

"Am I?" Like a sack of potatoes, he flung the naked singer onto the concrete floor, head-first.

"You bastard," the manager yelled. "You might have killed him!"

"Actually, he was stabbed by one of the girls," he pointed to the two dead assassins. "Before he was carried away, when I reached him, he was naked and dead. I was trying to save his mother, who I know is backstage, from seeing this," he pointed to Sedric's dead body, right on cue, his mother ran from the dressing room.

"That's my son! That's my boy! My boy! Nooo!" falling to her knees, her gut-wrenching sobs echoed across the back-stage area.

"I would lock down the stadium so the other killer can't escape," Robert gave it one more chance.

"Other killer?" the manager asked.

"Yeah, the one who was blowing the guy you should be firing," he pointed at Wade.

"No call for this fucking place to be locked down! Besides, this is China, we have no authority to—"

"There's a fucking surprise, that's why I said you needed to spend the money for a full crew. Remember? Right AFTER I told you this was a really bad idea," he gave him the single gun salute and headed off.

"Can you at least get the rest of the band back home?" Derphume asked.

"Far be it from me to leave an innocent group of boys stranded in China, while assassins hunt them down," Robert shook his head and walked to the dressing room to get the rest of the band.

Waking in the basement, as the lights were barely illuminating the area. "Robert," it was Delta's voice and from the sound of it, she may have called him a few times.

"I'm up, I'm up," he babbled, finding the light on the headboard side box.

"Can I come down there?"

"Pretty sure nothing is stopping you."

"Robert, are you dressed?"

"What?" he said looking under the covers. "No, I'm not. But I am covered."

"Get dressed and get up here."

"Fine." Throwing the covers off, Robert started looking for his clothes, feeling a pulling in his shoulder. Glancing down absently seeing a bandage, the girls cutting his arm in the dream jumped into his mind. "Delta, did you bandage my arm after I passed out?" He pulled on his pants and shoes.

"If I had been down there, don't you think I'd know if you were naked?"

"Hmm, makes sense. I can't find my shirt."

"Just get up here. I don't care if you don't have a shirt on. We have sweatshirts in the closet up here for people who get lost. I'll grab one for you."

"Ok, ok," he checked his Kimber and clipped

the holster at the small of his back before running up the stairs, two at a time. "What's the big—" he cut himself off when he saw the reflection in the mirror at the top of the stairs, the ranger's cabin main floor full of state police.

"Here you go," Delta saw the bandage on his shoulder. "Put it on before you go in there," her stern face indicated the bandage.

"Yes, ma'am," Sliding the huge sweatshirt over his arms, he pretended he didn't see the others. "Man, is this Thumb's sweatshirt?" His head popped out as he rounded the corner, "Oh, hello."

"Hello, sir," the smallest person in the room said. "My name is Brenda Bearheart. Yes, that is my real name," she smiled, her deep brown eyes, jet black hair, and tan complexion lent itself to her native American name.

"Ma'am," he inclined his head. "Is this where you read me my rights?"

"You are most definitely not under arrest, at least not from me, er… ah, us. We're still trying to get an understanding of what occurred here last night. I have a few questions, are you ok with that?"

"If you could show me some ID," he waited, and she complied. "Secret Service? Perfect. Ask whatever you want, I have nothing to hide," he hopped up on the counter the rangers stand behind and issue permits to campers, turning his back, unconcerned, on the six men on the other side.

"First question, how many men did you arrive with?"

"With me?"

"Yes."

"Just me, ma'am,"

"So, you're saying you killed nine heavily armed men with—" she started.

"Yes, I—"

"Uh, uh, uh," she held up a finger. "Please allow me to finish. As I was saying, you killed nine heavily armed men with three different caliber weapons?" her raised index finger lowered, and her hand rolled, motioning for him to continue.

"Are you counting the shotgun shells as a caliber? Because if you are, there were four different calibers." He saw her eyes shoot to one of the men behind him to the right. "12 gauge, 300 blackout, 45 ACP, and 45 Long Colt."

"Ok, got it, we found no shells of LC."

"True, I started with Long Colt, I wasn't certain if I shot six, so I unloaded into my bag. I used moon-clips of ACP thereafter. Currently Reds loaded with LC again.'

"How many weapons did you arrive with?"

He sat for a moment, "I arrived with four."

"Why the delay in your reply?"

"I was making certain there wasn't a part B to that question," he kicked his feet like a kid sitting on a tall chair.

"What made you decide to take on an entire group holding this station under siege?"

"I ain't afraid to shed my blood for friends. I got a call on my radio, it sounded like there was an issue. When I arrived to see what was happening, I was attacked by their sentry, Dabber is what they called him. I killed him in self-defense, and at that point, I knew I had to take the fight to them."

"Robert... is it ok if I call you Robert?"

"Please."

"Excellent, while, Robert, I respect you came to the aid when called."

"Twice in one day," Delta interjected.

"Precisely, you're not the type of person to hide even if the odds are against you. We have no idea what the reason was that this group was going to kill the senator. Do you know why that is?"

"Because I erased the threat."

"Yes, because you used lethal force on all nine of them."

"So, while these baddins were trying to kill me and my friends, I was supposed to aim for their what, leg? Or maybe use a tranquilizer dart to subdue them while they were trying to X me out? Oh, wait, I didn't have a dart like that. I had bullets, and I X'd them out with said bullets rather than taking one prisoner, oops." His legs stopped kicking. He saw Delta's eyes get big a moment before they looked at Robert, imploring him not to do anything.

Feeling the person behind him get into his space, Robert slid from the countertop calmly, taking a step into the room, leaning against the wall next to the window he had shot the man through. "Enough,

Walters," Brenda glared at her subordinate. "Robert, you understand we are not your enemy, right?"

"Chuckles over there aside," he indicated Walters with his chin. "I didn't think you were. More importantly, Brenda… is it ok if I call you Brenda?"

"Please."

"More importantly, Brenda, I didn't shoot him for coming at me. Which means I am not insane, which is what you were really asking."

"Ha, too rich," Walters scoffed.

"Yup," pulling the Kimber from the small of his back. Bang! "Keep laughing, Chuckles," he holstered the gun.

"Stop!" Brenda stepped in front of Robert, waving off her men going for their weapons. "Get out, Walters!"

"Yes, ma'am," he said, cowed and realizing the man he was mocking could have just killed him and his entire group because he was an ass to a man that no one had checked for weapons.

"Robert, please turn over that gun," Delta held her hand out.

"Sure," he said, pulling it out again, releasing the magazine, racking the slide locking it back, ejecting the bullet in the chamber, which bounced around on the floor as he turned the gun over.

"What was that stupidity about?" Brenda asked.

"You're not really asking me that question, are you? Your team is sloppy, I walked in here armed, after killing nine people mind you, and no one bothered to even ask me if I was carrying. Your team is discourteous. In the last 24 hours, I've saved three children and five rangers' lives, and they mock me? My patience is wearing paper-thin, do you have any other questions for me or are we finished?" Robert crossed his arms.

"Fair. You have answered my questions well enough. But, Robert, you do understand killing people is against the law, right? We would be within the rights of the country to arrest you. With that in mind, where can we reach you if we have more questions?"

"Here. I live about five miles that way," he pointed.

Brenda looked at Delta. "I can usually reach him by radio," she said as she nodded her head and the agents all left the cabin.

Stooping to pick up the magazine and the loose bullet, he asked, "Can I have my gun?"

"I can't believe you drew a gun on that agent."

"He's an ass and he's lucky I didn't pop him. Fuck, had I thought they were gonna arrest me, I would've popped him," he smiled with his hand out.

"That's not funny." She turned it over to him.

Chapter 21
The Days are Leading to What?

"Let me make certain I'm on the same page as you. The agents of New Roanoke made it apparent that you needed to work with them as they pursued the rest of the seeds. I follow that, but how did they find you?" Clear addressed Evgeniya.

"An advance team of the Secret Service arrived here at Martha's Vineyard to prep for a Presidential visit. The first thing they apparently do is to search all the properties. During this sweep, they found an activated Semena cell. The shootout that ensued caused the death of the Secret Service Team Leader, and three members of the cell," she replied.

"And then when they found Evya and I, speaking the way we do, they decided to call the Agency," Fainah added. "They found that she was a Semena."

"They threatened to lock me up if I didn't help them," she squinted her eyes. "I, of course, agreed, having separated from that evil group several years ago. They said first I needed to prove to them that I was innocent of whatever the Semena were plotting."

"How do you do that if you didn't even know they were plotting anything?" Clear shook his head. "Do they even understand how sleeper cells work?"

"From my brief interaction with those two," she pointed at the dead agents, "They didn't understand anything other than the fact that I have nice tits."

"I guess they weren't as stupid as I thought," Fainah added to Clear's discomfort.

"Give me that gun, then I want you to go change your clothes and wash your hands and arms with soap for a long time, in hot water. DO NOT wash your hair, wet hair would be a tip-off that you were cleaning up from something," he said.

"I have no blood on me. Why should I change my clothing? I like this blouse," Evgeniya crossed her arms.

"It's the residue from shooting a gun, you'll hear the agents call it GSR," Clear held out his hand, requesting the gun, making certain Evya didn't step into the puddling blood. "What the hell, this is my gun," surprised, he commented.

"I put it in my purse when they took me to the office," she gave a sad smile.

"Wipe my prints off the handle of the pan, grasp it in such a way to hit him like I did, and then toss it on the counter, upside down. Lastly, did he have a gun?"

"Da," Evya pointed to a gun next to the table.

"Put your hand inside your sleeve, grab the gun, set it next to his hand, and kick it away."

"What? Why?"

"Just do it, Evya," Fainah ordered.

"Fine!" the younger sister began to pull her sleeve down.

"Thank you," Clear winked at the older sister, then walked outside where he picked up the garbage can next to the deck, and placed it into the grass. That being done, he reached his arm into the can and fired the rest of the magazine into the bottom of the can.

"Why did you shoot the garbage can?" Fainah asked.

"I was making certain the ejected brass casings were caught, while getting the GSR on my hand. Is she doing what I asked?" he fished the empty shells from the bottom of the garbage can before placing it back where he found it. Kneeling in the grass, locating the holes created by the bullets, he forced the brass into them. Standing, he walked over the holes, crushing dirt into and effectively erasing each one.

Watching what he was doing, Fainah didn't answer right away, "Yes, she headed off to change. You do such strange things?"

"Not at all, my life is driven by a specific set of rules…"

"Truth's rules, Evya tried to explain this to me."

"That's cool," he flushed a bit. "Anyhow, take the situation we're in.

'Truth's rule: In a time, crunch situation, every action must be for a reason.'

"Our goal right now is to reverse the stage that was set, I shot the agents, and Evya hit the one with a pan. You need to make her believe that, as I'm making you believe it. The angles will be difficult to explain, but the gun I had her kick away is to address that. We stay within the bounds of this rule until we have addressed the situation."

"How do you know to do these things? Were

you in the military?" she asked from the deck, angling her head to take in everything he had done.

"No, ma'am," Clear replied. "I just think through how the police will react. Will they arrest or walk away, followed by whether the DA will bring charges or drop them. In this case, your black eye and Evya's busted open lip will play in our favor. Remember, we are trying to convince them I shot the men because I thought they meant you further harm."

"Should I call the police now?" Evgeniya asked from inside, still buttoning her blouse.

"I'll call. You two go sit in the front room, don't step in the blood," he waited until they were out of sight. Turning his body to be in full view, no matter which direction the police or whoever arrived from. Kneeling, he placed the call to 911.

"Emergency services, how can I help you?" a generic voice asked.

"There's been an incident at my location. I'm on the back deck, in a neutral position."

"We have agents feet from your—" a different voice started.

"No sir, you don't," Clear cut him off.

"I have two others approaching you now. Do not move from your position."

10 seconds later, two agents ran onto the deck from the waterfront, guns drawn. "Don't move a muscle," the older of the agents ordered.

"I have no plan to," he held his phone in both hands, up and over his head.

"What the fuck?" the younger agent said from

inside the house.

"There are two women in the front room," Clear said calmly. "If you need to handcuff me or whatever before you go talk to them…"

"Put your hands behind your back," the older agent cuffed Clean, positioning him to face away from the house. "What happened?"

"My receptionist was on vacation. Her sister called me and said they were in danger. I entered the house and saw one of the men hit Fainah, so I shot him. As I did, the other man started to rush me, Evya hit him with the pan, when he started to get up with a gun in his hand, I shot him twice."

"They were agents of New Roanoke," the agent explained.

"I had no way of knowing that until I was comforting the ladies."

"Stay out here, I'm gonna ask them for their stories," he walked into the house. "Walker, go outside and call this in."

"Yes, sir," the younger officer walked onto the deck.

"Oof," the kick in the center of Clear's back wasn't a surprise, he allowed it to force him onto his stomach.

"That was my fucking cousin, you bastard," he gave two kicks in the ribs of the downed prisoner.

"Walker, I said call in, I didn't say go uber-pwnataur on the prisoner!"

"Sorry, sir," Walker replied and walked off

toward the nature preserve. "We need CSI, and the Coroner at my location," he paused. "Yes, two agents down, ma'am." After replacing the phone into his belt holder, Clear, still lying on his stomach, watched him walk around to the deck. "You're so fucked, the boss is heading over here," he glared at the prisoner.

"Alright, Walker, that'll be enough of that. Sir, get up," the older agent ordered.

"Yes, sir." Clear got up, turning to lean against the railing to see inside the house.

"I need to know… how did you get on the island?"

"Well, agent…" he waited.

"Brilldor, Senior Agent Brilldor."

"Thank you. Well, Sr. Agent Brilldor, I swam."

"That was what the elder sister said, I didn't believe her."

"She was telling the truth. I swam, I had no choice. You see, the men at the peer said no transports were available."

"So, you swam?"

"I had my pink and baby blue wetsuit in my trunk. I threw my street clothes in my waterproof bag along with my phone, and swam. It kinda sucked," Clear said the last comment biting the inside of his lip to make certain he didn't smile.

"Didn't it make you wonder why the island was shut down?" Agent Walker asked.

"Not really my problem. I knew my friend was in danger, if God herself was the one torturing my friend, I would have come without a delay," Clear saw a tall Latina enter the house and walk past the sisters. "Brilldor, what the hell happened, and how did he get here?"

Turning abruptly, the senior agent was caught off guard. "Commander Cortez, sorry I didn't hear you arrive. This man, Mr. Clarence Truth, received a phone call from Fainah Souza indicating that her sister, Evgeniya, which is Mr. Truth's secretary, was in danger. He drove to the peer to take a transport and travel to the island. When he arrived, he found the transports were not running. At that point he took it on himself to swim to the island."

"Seriously?" she glared at him.

"Actually, no ma'am," he did his best to divert his eyes, but it wasn't in him. "My name is Clarence."

"No, I was asking about swimming did you swim to the island? Clearance is that even a name?"

"Yes I did swim, and its a name unique to one person."

"Go on," she scowled and turned her attention back to her agent.

"Arriving at the rental property, Mr. Truth found an active altercation, that's when the shooting commenced."

"You're saying that you walked in and shot two agents of New Roanoke?" Commander Cortez asked.

"Mr. Truth claims that they didn't identify themselves as such," Walker replied, shaking his head disbelievingly.

"What, Walker?" she inquired.

"Mr. Truth also said that the women knew they were agents. Regulations state if you've identified yourself, you place your identification around your neck. Pete was big on following regulations," his eyes flicked to his dead cousin.

"Shouldn't be hard to verify, go take some pictures of the scene and then roll him over," Clear replied.

"Enough, you. Stop, Walker," the commander ordered the junior officer to stand his ground. "That is the CSI's job, let the process work itself out."

"Yes, ma'am," Walker stepped back off the deck. Clear noticed he was pacing back and forth over the spot he shot the ground, smiling internally.

"For what it's worth, sir, I am sorry about your cousin."

"Like you really give a fuck."

"I care enough to take my lumps," Clear cocked his head, letting both the men know he had no intention of spilling the beans on his bruised ribs. Also, letting them know they owe him their jobs. An hour later, the commander had interviewed the women, the CSI team confirmed the agents were not wearing their badges in a visible location, and Clear's handcuffs were removed. "Thank you," he rubbed his wrists. As she removed the cuffs, her phone started to ring, causing her to walk off to take the call.

After a five-minute conversation, Commander Cortez returned to him, "Last pieces of info I need from you before you're free to go, how did you get the gun here?"

"Same as I did my clothing, I put them all in my dive bag, it's waterproof."

"That would lead me to believe that the gun and suppressor are registered to you?"

"Yes, ma'am, they are."

"I need to see both your concealed carry license, and BATF stamp for that suppressor."

"Not a problem," he reached around to his back pocket. Finding his wallet missing.

"Issue?" she cocked an eyebrow.

"My wallet, I don't seem to have it," Clear tried to think back to when he last had it. When he was on the peer, he was ready to pay for transport. Did he separate it from his pants when he put them in the bag?

"Sir, that is a serious problem."

"It is probably in my bag."

"Which is where, sir?"

"I, um…" Clear's mind raced.

"Take him into custody, we'll figure that out tomorrow. I need to get back to Coyote," she headed back through the house.

Clear put his hands behind his back, "Evya, I just changed out of my wetsuit over there," Clear pointed his chin toward the nature preserve as Walker walked up to him.

"No cuffs, I know you're cool."

"Thanks," he gave the younger agent a nod.

"Clear, where do we stay? I can't sleep with dead men and blood everywhere," Evgeniya rushed up to him.

"Call Tux. He will take care of you," he replied, the younger officer had waited for him to give an answer. "But I need you to look for my bag."

"We will, I promise," Fainah said from behind her sister.

"Sir, we need to get a move on," Walker said, moving him out the front door. Walking along the road, "Why didn't you narc me out? Striking a bound person is sacrosanct. I would have been fired period, do not pass go."

"I told you, I really do feel bad. Besides, I've lost people under extreme situations, and beating the asshat that did it was therapeutic."

Walker laughed but said nothing further. About a quarter of a mile later, he said, "How do you know Tux?"

"I saved his wife and daughter when they were kidnapped," Clear replied.

"You're that guy? I thought you were a private detective."

"I am, I'd show you my ID but it's kinda missing," he gave a chuff.

"Did you really jump off the roof of a building, through the window of an adjacent building?"

"The halls were guarded rather heavily, how else would I have gotten in?" Clear asked straight-faced.

"I can truly say that wouldn't have been the

option I would have gone with," Walker shook his head. "How many floors up were you?"

"I was even with the 12th floor of the building the wife was in, she was on the 11th."

"Wow, I remember Cortez giving us a debrief, none of us believed it. I even spoke to Tux at the pub and he had no idea what really went down."

"He wasn't there, how could he? He did pay the deductible for my hospital bills, so that was cool." They arrived at the car and Clear opened the back door, then jumped in. "Where are we off to today, Hoke?"

"What a smartass," Walker stepped on the gas and they took off. A few minutes later, the car pulled into the Edgartown Police Station. "After I cage you securely, I'll head off to help the ladies look for your bag, and make certain they have somewhere to sleep."

"Be careful with those women, they will suck your eyes out and tandem skull fuck you," he stayed completely dead-pan walking into the station.

"Deputy Skully, could you please take this man back to a private cell?" Walker requested.

"Sir, that's all we have around here. The Secret Service emptied out all of them," she took Clear and started walking away.

"Hold up," Clear requested. "Walker, I'm serious about the sisters, careful, there."

"I'll take that into account," he left as Deputy Skully led Truth to the cell.

"Any chance I can pass the time with a book or

magazine?"

"No, but I'll turn on the television," she did exactly that as she left.

"Christ on a crutch, I fucking hate the TV," Clear bitched as he sat down. "I really hope Walker puts my comment to the test," he said, laughing to himself as he lay down on the strange plastic cot. The long night and the even longer swim caused Clearance Joseph Truth to fall into a deep dreamless sleep.

Yellow, black, green. Yellow, black, green. "What the hell? Deputy?" He tried ignoring it, turning his head, he realized he had reached the point that he was drooling in his sleep. "Oh, for fuck sake," he wiped the drool off his cheek. Yellow, black, green. "Seriously, what the hell is causing that?" he looked around seeing the flashing screen.

'Ever feel bad for electing to not serve your country?' The text was written in black, on a yellow screen. The room went dark, 'Wish you could undo that decision?' Red letters asked on the black screen. 'Reach out and ask us how: iamthetraveler@outlook.com'. The green screen with white lettering dissolved. The yellow, black, green continued to repeat.

"Mr. Truth, are you ok?" the voice of Deputy Skully asked.

"I need to use the restroom, and I'm hoping I can send an email. Is there anywhere I can do that?"

"I can accommodate both of those requests," she escorted him to the restroom.

"Thanks, don't know how bad it is sometimes until you're almost there."

"The terminal is not great, but you can send an email," Deputy Skully smiled amiably, indicating the terminal. "It's an old Mac from the school."

"Not great with these, which of the icons is for the internet?" He was lying, but a little human interaction was always a good thing.

"That one there. After that, everything is the same. If you just whistle, I will head back to lock you back in," she walked off.

After logging in, Clear entered his email account, not bothering to read the scads of unread emails. Instead, he went directly to compose new.

'To whom it may concern,

> When I left school, I considered going into the military, but I fell into what I had thought would be a lifelong career. As it turned out, after 18 years, I realized it wasn't. Having some notable successes as a private investigator, I believe I have skills that will be valuable on most teams. I'd like to hear more from you, if you need more information, please reach out. I've taken many personal missions after changing careers, which makes me realize I should have gone with my first path.

Clearance J. Truth
Private Detective'

Whistling, he got the deputy's attention after logging back out of the system. And for good measure, he deleted all history. He stood waiting for her to return him to his cell. After whistling three more times, he wondered if he was misremembering… *maybe I was supposed to head back to the cell myself.* After the fifth whistle, he just went to the cell and lay on the cot.

"Sorry," Deputy Skully said through the bars 10 minutes later. "My ex-husband called and told me he couldn't pay this month's child support or alimony… Oh, geez, look at me prattling on."

"You're fine, go on."

"Apparently, he's going to the Bahamas with his new lady," she chuffed a little.

"Tell him to take the kids if he's not paying the child support."

"That is a great idea," she walked off. "Thanks," trickled down the hall.

"You're welcome," Clear put his arms behind his head and dozed off again. Somewhere in his slumber, a high-pitched whistle pushed him deeper. To a small park north of Boston, Copp's Hill Terrace, he was setting up for a photoshoot with a college girl with hopes of becoming a model. He hated taking money to make amazing portfolios for diluted people, but he had bills to pay. After almost 20 years of doing this, his reputation for perfection at a fair price had him doing gigs like this weekly. "Miranda, we'll be starting this shoot on the granite steps across from the cemetery."

"Which outfit should I start in?" she held up the stack of dresses.

"I like the eggplant one, it will be accented well with the old stone. My truck is right there," he pointed to the teal bread truck. "You can change in there, lock the door so no one can mess with you. There's a vanity in there with three different light settings to make certain you get the lighting right. Set the switch to outside, afternoon. Put on enough makeup to look like you meant to do it, but not enough to look like you're going to the bar. Capiche?"

"I think so," she walked off, getting into the back of the truck.

Clear continued setting up the barricades, his permit gave him 20-minute intervals to stop foot traffic from walking through the area. Less than a minute later, a loud scream came from around the corner he had just set up the preliminary barrier. "Everything ok?" he ran toward the scream.

"No! Stop!" As he turned the corner, a man was mugging an older lady. It was her screams that Clear heard. The barricade he set up funneled the mugger right into him, sighting on the purse, Clear didn't see the knife that the mugger held. One man grabbed the purse, the other sliced the exposed left shoulder. "Leave it, it's fine," the old woman yelled.

"Here," Clear tossed her purse back to her and turned to give chase. "Stay in there," he yelled to Miranda as she opened the side door of his truck. The mugger continued his flight into the cemetery, grabbing a baby out of the arms of a young mother walking on the cobblestone path surrounding the landmark.

"Sarah! My baby!" she screamed.

"Stop chasing me, I swear to the heavens I'll skewer this thing on these finials," he held the baby up like he was about the smash it down on the fence spires.

"Nooo!" the mother's voice broke as she screamed.

"Set the kid down and you can go. Do something stupid and, well, stupid is as stupid does."

"Fuck you, pal," he dropped the baby, who flew around the cemetery like a popped balloon as Clear leaped over the fence. Landing feet from where the staircase turned back toward him, right where the evil bastard was running. Landing on the uneven surface, he fell left, cutting his shoulder on the odd decorative railing.

"Shit," he pulled his fully impaled arm off the metal post. The dead man was still under foot, literally, each of Clear's feet were on the shoulders of the man. The landing had forced the man backwards into a step, snapping his neck.

"You son of a bitch," the woman was screaming from above, her damnation to Clear continued. "You odious fiend, you killed my baby! I hope you rot in hell, you feckless ape," the screaming continued until the police showed up.

"We should probably get a wrap on that,"

Clear looked up into the face of a woman who appeared to be floating above him. "Clear, what are you doing here?"

"What?"

"How did you get here? I thought they took you to jail last night?" Evgeniya asked.

"Where am I?"

"On the deck outside Tux's rental property."

"How did I get here?" he asked stupidly.

"That is what she just asked you!" this time, Fainah spoke. "What happened to your shirt?"

"What?" he looked down to find the left sleeve of his polo shirt was cut off from his collar to under his armpit. In its place, he had a large bandage. "Fuck, I liked this shirt."

"Careful there," the two women said as he stood, swaying and showing he was still woozy.

"I'm fine, I'm fine. Did you find my bag?" Clear shook his head, trying to clear the cobwebs.

"We did, here you go," Evgeniya handed it to him.

"Thank you," he took it, but as he started to open it…

"Mr. Truth, I need you to come with me," a deep voice said, from right in front of him.

"Where did you come from?" Fainah spun, getting into an offensive position.

"None of that now," the man held up his hands in front of his chest.

"I just want to ask a question of Clearance." His smile looked like a foreign feature on his chiseled face.

"Go ahead and ask him," Evgeniya put herself in front of her boss.

"Evya, Fai, it's ok. I'm ok."

"Are you certain?" her Russian accent was strong as she doted on him.

"I am, thank you. If you could, see if Tux has a shirt he can give me," Clear patted them both on the back, and walked off with the stranger. "Sorry about that, they're kinda protective."

"Developing that much loyalty of anyone is impressive. I, by the way, am the Senior Helvetian, Commandant of the North American Honor Guard."

"Pleased to meet you."

"I think you're right, you do have some skills we could use. Before that, I need to know, do you still blame yourself for the death of that child?"

"I feel terrible that Sarah died. I gave that man a chance, I can see I didn't cause it, he slammed her head into the fence, not me," he never made eye contact, his eyes shot around, seeing it all again.

"The fact that you remember her name is not lost on me, but I'm glad you see that no matter what the mother said, you did nothing wrong. Choices that are made cannot be changed. The only choice to regret or blame yourself for is the one you failed to make."

Clear thought for a moment and then asked, "Sir, how did I get out of the cell?"

"I'll have to tell you that story another time,"

he started walking toward a helicopter floating in water off the shore. "The President has left the island; the transports will be running later today. The Secret Service are not looking for you, they may have heard that I pulled you into my personal team."

"Personal team, sir?"

"No sirs from here forward, you aren't military. Oh, and, Clear…"

"Yes, sir… um, yes?"

"Get some coconut oil for that arm of yours," he turned, pointing at the shoulder.

Chapter 22
Wait, You Want Me To Do What?

As each man entered the building, they signed in and turned over anything that could be used to record, photograph, or in any way document what they were going to see. Interestingly enough, none of them raised a concern about these actions. Each was given a seat assignment, some random, others established by one of the eight people standing center stage of the small Horseshoe Colosseum. Waiting patiently, they spoke to one another without the fear that their microphones were hot, as they controlled all aspects of this event. In front and above the shadow figures, the volunteers shuffled to their seats, which by their guesstimation, were more than three-quarters full. There were just over 10 minutes left until the doors would seal, and those left on the other side would double their regret at missing out on this golden opportunity to contribute to not only God and Country, but to the future of the free world.

The Senior Helvetian, Commandant of the North American Honor Guard, stood alone among the eight, staring off or perhaps watching for a certain section of the colosseum to fill in.

"The Senior Helvetian, each member of the teams we pre—" the only person on the main stage with facial hair, a regulation mustache, started to say.

"They're here?" uncrossing his arms, he panned the audience, looking for the remaining two members of the largest preassigned team, which happened to be the team he had personally selected.

"Yes, sir, they are," Mustache grinned and walked back to the group.

"Shall we boot up the scoreboards?" A tall man with sunken and unique facial features asked, while he calmly spun a silver ring with a square white stone around his index finger.

"I believe it is that time, yes," the Senior Helvetian replied.

"You's got it." Standing next to a raised table that looked ridiculously tiny beside the man with an enormous belly, who began pressing buttons, illuminating the two boards.

The audience quickly fell silent as each man looked up, beginning to read the posting, 'Welcome all, please take a moment to introduce yourself to the people in your immediate area. You will be spending a large amount of time with them. Not all groups are the same size, do not concern yourself with that.' Below these words, a timer, which had started at 10 minutes, counted down.

When the timer reached zero, the lights around the auditorium went out. Leaving the lights shining on the eight people, while their picture showed on the scoreboard being the only illumination in the large building. On the outside, an audible door closure and latch echoed in the building.

"Welcome, I am a Captain in the North American Honor guard, I shall be called Captain Cratchit," the tiny Asian woman looked like a child among the individuals in the center of the colosseum. "Before we begin and you understand clearly what the papers you signed upon entering today said, nothing that you will hear in this building may be discussed outside of we the North American Honor Guard," her arms took in the other seven figures next to her. "Or those in your personal groups," this time, she motioned to the people in the auditorium. "If you don't completely understand what that means, in its simplest terms..." she paused. "If you are on a date and you say that you joined a group with these crazy military types... Neither of you will wake up the next morning. We don't fuck about with warnings, this is the only one you will get. If you have a problem with that, leave now. The same rules apply as you've already walked in here. However, it will be easier to walk out now, the less you know, the less you will feel the need to discuss. Before we will say another word, I will give you one minute to stand, don't feel bad that you may have made a mistake, this will be your one chance to back out," she walked in a circle, the technique she had used to make people comfortable, getting them to start random chatting. As she had suspected, in this room, no one spoke. More importantly, no one got up and left. "Good," she returned to the line with the other seven.

"Greetings, I, as most of you know, am the Senior Helvetian," the imposing visage projected on the overhead. "In front of you, myself, along with these other seven people, make up what has been classified by the Unified Nations Accord as Byte. For those computer literate people in the audience, the meaning is clear, however, to make it understandable to the rest, a byte is made up of eight bits. That number never varies. everything has grown from those eight bits, from the very beginning of computers. That applies to the North American Honor Guard, which we are the first members," his body turned, his hands gestured, taking in the others. "You are the new members of the North American Honor Guard. Congratulations," he took several steps, separating himself from the others. "As the leader of Byte, I welcome you and hope you have what it takes to make it through whatever may come next. It is important to me that I thank you for coming forward in a time when the fate of the free world needed you to. It takes balls to raise your hand, throwing yourself into something not knowing what the challenge you'll be facing even is. This is going to be an extremely interesting day for all of us. Each and every person in this room has, whether you know it or not, been vetted by me. Additionally, other members of Byte interacted with you in one way or another as well. These bizarre interviews that got you here are nothing compared to what you will be going through in the days, weeks, months, and potentially years ahead of you. Leaving your sofa, lounge chair, or whatever place of relaxation you may have grown complacent in, was the first step," he returned, allowing the next of the figures to take their place.

Captain Cratchit advanced once more, "The North American Honor Guard was established by the leaders of the Unified Nations Accord via the Paramilitary Institution. The Senior Helvetian is the active member of PI from Byte," she indicated the leader. "The NAHG has representation of all 24 countries that make up North America. The stated goal of our organization is to change that number back to 23. Not every leader in the Paramilitary Institution supports the unification of the United States, these member leaders like the fact that Arch Master Base is a world power without a single nation holding its reigns," she stepped to the rear.

"Hello, I didn't get a chance to meet most of you's. But I'm very proud to stand in front of you's now. And beside you's later. My name is Captain Sebastianelli, but unlike these other leaders, I'd prefer you's call me Vito. Look, I'm not gonna stand before you's and lie, what you's signed up for here could get you's killed. If just not by the training you's are gonna go through, then by the elements in the world who don't like what the United States of America stood for, both foreign and those domestic, be they members of the UNAPI that Captain Cratchit mentioned, or other. And while it is our job to get you's ready to face whatever those who mean you's harm, I need you's to understand you's aren't military, we don't want you's to be military. That means you's are not to address us as sir or ma'am, you's are not to address us by our ranks. So, you's is probably asking yourselves, why are they giving their ranks? That is simple, we are military, we have a very clearly defined rank group system. You's don't and won't." Vito stepped behind Captain Cratchit.

"Those of you who met me, know me as Dutch, I am a Lieutenant in the North American Honor Guard. As the Senior Helvetian said, each of us have interacted directly or indirectly with each of you. In some cases, I, or one of my peers, may have killed people right in front of you. In other cases, we may have shot at you, I know I personally shot at a bunch of you. The bottom line, we needed to know who you were inside. This isn't ever going to be easy, this is never going to be fun. I honestly hope none of you thought it would be," he stepped to the rear.

The next of Byte stepped up, for several seconds, she said nothing, instead, looking around the room as if to make eye contact with each and every man in the auditorium. "Lieutenant Susan Branch, call me Suzi. Aside from outside elements, we needed to know that who you are on the inside wasn't going to get you killed as well. Each of you experienced a purging. That grand event was made possible by a device that I was part of inventing, it found one of your life's regrets. The purging made that moment in your life a passive distraction, not something that should bite you in the ass when you are faced with something that could trigger a memory. As the Senior Helvetian likes to say, you are coming to us with your past, our present, and the nation's future. We don't need you to be held back by your past. We need you to embrace this present, learn all you can from your brothers around you, so that we can form a new future for our fucked-up nation," the small woman stood, looking at the emotion she had stirred in the room, before stepping to the rear.

"Greetings," Mustache now stepped to the front of the eight. "My name is Sergeant Davis. As with Dutch, some of you may have seen me kill people, others may have seen me get killed by one of these assholes up here with me," this brought a dull laugh from parts of the audience. "I want you to know the duty that you are showing at this stage of your life is commendable. You should also understand, before you get to the interesting stuff, that you do have a few steps left," A man of few words, he walked to the rear.

"That is where we, the sergeants come in," a tall fat man took his turn stepping up. "We are the same bastards that your friends and family may have complained about, the ones that movies make look insane as they scream in the face of new recruits, spit flying everywhere and all of that was true when we were training military personnel. We had to break them, reform them, but not you, you, we need to form into a team differently. While I may personally love seeing a team built through mutual destruction if it doesn't. Military people of the world know other military people can sense something in them. That means if we forge you in the same furnace as our old recruits, it will show, whether you think it will or not."

"That was Sergeant Thumb, just call him Thumb. I am a sergeant as well, Sergeant Ernst. As I am the last one up here, I get to tell you that, after tonight, you have one month to get your shit in order, you'll be receiving an email with a location where you are to report to. Do not bring any personal items. We will supply you with everything you'll need. Expect that the clothes and anything you bring with you will be burned. That means if someone arrives in an expensive sports car or a custom truck, it will be a cube when they return from the first training. Remember, one month, look for the email, don't arrive with anything you want back. Dismissed."

Chapter 23
Overcoming the Need to be Invulnerable

The taxi arrived at the location given by the email, a small church, 'Truth Barn' in the foothills of the Smokey Mountains. "That'll be 115 SG," the driver said with a pleasant grin.

"Keep the change," Ananias tossed his wallet up to the driver, it had 1000 SG in it as he didn't know what a taxi ride would cost.

"Seriously? Thanks," he tried to hand the wallet back.

"Keep that too, I won't be needing it."

"Dude, did I just drive the richest man in North America to an obscure location to commit suicide?"

"Nothing like that, I'm meeting... well, nothing like that." He got out, closing the door. Watching the car drive away, he looked at his watch. "Fuck," the ridiculously expensive diving watch was such a part of him, he forgot to remove it. "Oh well. Hopefully, they'll donate it," there were no lights in the church, he looked at the printout again. Meet at the Peaceful Saw-Whet Chapel at 2p EST 14 Nov. The time was 1:45p, he arrived right on time. His father had always said to follow Coach Lombardi's rule of time management, if you aren't 15 minutes early, you're late. And after completely pissing people off, including one guy that sat next to him during the first meeting, he wasn't gonna be late this time. The door to the chapel was open, so he walked in and sat in one of the small pews.

"Ananias," a familiar voice said from somewhere at the front.

"Rolly?"

"Yes, sir. Step on up here, we have some last-minute items to go through before the next member of the team arrives," the young man stood from where he was concealed behind the pulpit.

"Of course, of course." Having only spoken with Rolly on the phone previously, Ananias was surprised to see how tall he was, "Cripe sake, son, you must be close to seven feet tall," he commented in spite of himself.

"Seven foot exactly. Made getting scholarships for playing basketball pretty easy, even though I sucked," he laughed. "I wrote up the terms for the new corporation, with the modifications we spoke about last week. I figured you'd want to look it over before you signed all that money over to the new team."

"Well, it's that, or donate it to charities that I know will just set up a trust to pay their own salaries," he took the docket and opened it, having worked with Rolly for several weeks couriering this docket back and forth, he knew most of it by heart. The sections he wanted redrafted were surrounding what would happen to his estate in the event of his death.

"Any concerns?"

"Not that stick out, geez, I miss the days of being able to scan through documents for last known changes on the computer," Ananias laughed. "I know we can't email this, but I do like that you are putting stickies to the marked-up page, and arrows to the changes. It helps, surely."

"Did you just call me Shirley?" the old joke still worked and they both laughed.

"Rolly, I really appreciate all you've done for this. You should take this," he handed the diver's watch over. "They're gonna make me throw it away, I forgot to take it off."

"I don't know if they actually will. It's probably just a test."

"Even better reason for you to take it, I hate failing tests," Ananias rubbed his wrists, an odd feeling not having his watch on.

"Well, thank you for this," he slid the watch over his wrist, it fit very well. "The remaining items we needed to address are the name of the corporation, and the air transportation purchases. For the name, the Senior Helvetian would like it to be named 50-Out."

"Seriously? What does that even mean?" the trillionaire cocked his head.

"I don't know for certain, to the best of my knowledge, your team are all above 50, and have decided to do a mic-drop... Out!"

"Oh, I actually quite like that," Ananias reached in his pocket, finding his favorite pen, he wrote in the blank line provided on the first page, '50-Out!' and then began initialing and signing each area it was required. "I think I've finished signing. You might as well keep this too."

Taking the pen, Rolly examined it, "Hold on, this looks expensive, is this an antique pen?"

"No... it's just a fountain pen, not very old at all," the older man smiled.

"Ok, good," Rolly slid the pen into his pocket.

"The plane I was looking at is a Spartan C27J, it's a good size for a tactical team, without being too large to be slow and awkward."

"That happens to be on the list that Byte gave me. Can you pilot one?"

"I can, recently had a chance to test-run one that is for sale."

"Please don't tell anyone else that, it may actually be an issue."

"I was told that looking but not buying was ok."

"Thank goodness. Ok, as we form the company, the purchase of the plane and whatever negotiated changes to it will go through the board of directors. Do you have a price?"

"100M SG,"

"Ah, umm... 100 million standard gold? Are you for real?"

"Rolly, that watch I just handed you is worth 500k SG and the pen was around 250k SG, I'm obviously not concerned about the cost of things."

"Wait, wait, wait... so you just nonchalantly handed me three-quarters of a million standard-gold?"

"Probably closer to an even million at auction," he bounced as his eyes jumped around, an odd thinking gesture. "Yeah, that's about right."

"Mr. Dare, I can't take…"

"The specifications that I requested on the plane…" Ananias ignored the young man who still held the items out to him. "Put those things away before we both get into trouble, think how stupid you'd feel watching them make the team throw all the forgotten items in the trash. Don't be foolish, young man."

Clearing his throat, he returned the items to their previous locations. "100M SG is a large purchase, I need to add a procurement level authorization to the document you just signed."

"No reason to get signatures again, you already have it. Section 2.3.17a states 'All capital purchases in excess of 200k SG or the combined three months' gross receipts, whichever is higher, shall require signatures of the BoD.' We have no receipts, therefore, all capital purchases in excess of 200k SG for company assets will require signatures of the BoD."

As Ananias spoke, Rolly found the section in the document. "That is impressive."

"Not at all, some areas in this type of document are very important to me," he handed the pen back to Rolly. "I'm not an expert in helicopters, but I can say this, if the chopper pilot on the team can fly a UH-1Y Venom, those have both attack and transport choppers with a good history."

"Isn't that the 'Huey'?"

"The UH-1N was the 'Huey'. The Venom was the upgraded cousin."

"The other purchase will need to be discussed

with Mason when he arrives. For now, tell me a bit about this watch,"

"It's a Rolex Sea Dweller Double Red, which is, of course, a nice watch, but what makes this one expensive is that it was owned by Jacques Verpeaux when he dove to 501 meters, sometime after that, he gave it to Jacques Cousteau, who dove with it for 10 years. I bought it from the great-granddaughter of Cousteau, her signature and a picture of her great-grandfather with the watch on gave the provenance the insurance company needed. But honestly, I never really cared about its value, if the insurance company did the research, authenticating it, I was cool with having a piece of history. Plus, it's a nice-looking watch," he smiled.

"Sir, I can just hold it so it doesn't—"

"Rolly, don't you think you deserve a Rolex?" Ananias gave him a disarming look, "I do," he winked.

"I, um," the young man was choked up, it was in no way the value of the piece that caused his reaction, this man had made him feel, well... important. Important in a way no one had ever made him feel before. "I do too, sir, and thank you," he looked down at the watch, blinking away a tear forming. The only issue was that a seven-foot man can't hide his face by looking down.

"What time do the others arrive?" the elder man walked away, pretending to look at the tiny church.

"All but Mason will be here tomorrow, he'll be here any min—" Rolly started, but the doors opened and in walked Mason, along with Blaire.

"Good morning, gentlemen. My name is Mason and this is Blaire, I apologize for not being formal, the email said no family names."

"Hello, I'm Ananias and this—"

"Oh my bubbling goofy fuck pirate, I didn't see you at the auditorium," Blaire cut him off.

"Never heard that string of expletives but, yes, you did see him. I pointed him out, this is the fuckwit who almost made me late."

"Sorry about that, I have a thing about signing my name without having a pre-read. I'm not the fastest reader, ya see," Ananias put his braid behind his ear.

"Mason, this 'fuckwit' as you called him, is Ananias Dare, the richest man in North America."

"I'd rather you stop using that name for me, nicknames tend to stick, and fuckwit doesn't feel like a good one."

"Yeah, ok, but are you really *The* Ananias Dare, actual descendant of Virginia Dare? I mean, I've seen pictures but you look much shorter... in the pictures, I mean," Mason finished the statement in a blur of words.

"Now you're being polite, I actually look tall in pictures," he smiled. "It's not because of posing, it's because my arms are so long, even next to someone taller, it gives an illusion that I must be stooping. Besides, I'm ok with being five-foot-seven, it isn't that short."

"My name is Rolly. We have some work to do, and I don't know if Blaire is approved to know the topics."

"The Senior Helvetian put us together a month ago," Mason nodded his head as he spoke.

"Let's take that as an approval," Ananias nodded his head along.

"K' fine. We need to purchase a helicopter," Rolly said.

"I already have one," Mason wrinkled his brow, confused.

"Not one to evac seven or eight people, you don't."

"Definitely not, I felt like we were cuddling the entire time we were flying," Blaire shuddered.

"You never once complained, I even told you that I wouldn't be insulted if you got into the back," the comment from Mason brought a laugh. "What kinda a chopper are you looking to purchase? Please don't say a Hughie."

"Nope, the updated cousin—a Venom," Ananias replied.

"If he can't fly a Hughie, I can't imagine a Venom would be any better," Rolly sat down on the steps to be more at eye level with the three other men.

"Oh, I can fly it, that's not the issue, I learned to fly in a Hughie. I would love to fly something with more balls."

"You're nuts, ok, he's nuts," Blaire looked from Mason to the other two. "That little chopper he had goes fast enough for any sane person, and if we're looking to go faster in one of those…"

"Relax, chief, my chopper goes 167mph, and a UH-1Y Venom goes around 190mph."

"Its size will make it feel slower," Ananias added.

"Unless you're up front cuddling with me," Mason gave a hoarse laugh.

"And then I'd be puking all over," Blaire shot back.

"As the others aren't arriving until tomorrow, and I know where a few air transports are for sale…"

"The papers need to be filed before we can purchase anything," Rolly said.

"Aww," the other three all moaned.

"You're like kids on Christmas. Fine, we can look. I'll call the law office, and we'll get the final details set for the financial transfers. We may be able to purchase something today."

"Yea!" they clapped together like teachers on a snow day.

"Did you arrive in your helicopter?" Rolly asked.

"As instructed in the email I got, yes. I was a bit worried because at the auditorium it sounded like anything we brought would be confiscated."

"Small difference, your helicopter will need to remain wherever we purchase the new one," Rolly commented absently.

"A trade-in?" Mason bristled. "This was my gramps' chopper, and one of the few things I have to remember him."

"No, no, nothing like that. None of us can fly," the younger man tried to placate the pissed-off member of the team.

"Look, here's the thing, if I just leave my shit everywhere, how will I ever get it home?"

"Jeremy," Blaire replied.

"What?" Mason spun on a dime.

"Remember when you picked me up, the man I gave the keys to my car to."

"Not so much, I remember you talking to someone after you scared the shit out of me."

"Yeah, him, that's Jeremy," Blaire nodded his head.

"Can he fly a helicopter?"

"Mason," Ananias' calm voice broke in. "I will make certain that your gramps' chopper is taken care of, nothing will happen to it, I give you my word."

"Like that difficult," Mason started out of the church. "Where are we headed?"

"Did he just play us?" Rolly asked.

"I believe that may have been the first of many to come," Ananias tossed a shoulder shrug and started walking. "Do you know where the Skyranch is?"

"Sure, maybe a 15-minute flight."

"Where is your chopper?" Rolly asked.

"Had to land a bit north of here, this barn truthfully had no room to land," Mason shot pretend pistols in the air to emphasize the joke.

"Does he do that often?" Ananias looked at Blaire.

"First time I've seen it, so I'd say no."

"Good," he kept walking, toward the location of the chopper. The track felt more like a washout from a rainstorm than a trail.

"That's your helicopter?" Rolly asked.

"Yeah, why?" Mason replied. Then, looking at the younger man, he said, "Oh fuck, this should be interesting. I don't know if this little girl was built for a seven-foot-tall person."

"Shotgun!" Ananias yelled running up to the helicopter.

"Not to be completely disrespectful to my elders, but... fuck you," Rolly shook his head, laughing.

"Oh, my virgin ears," the trillionaire swooned before hopping in the back.

"I think the trick will be for you to not get in until I'm absolutely ready to take off."

"But lean inside, if you accidentally stand up, you'll get cut in half at the belly button," Blaire winked as he walked to the other side.

A few minutes later, they were in the air, three of them an uncontainable rolling merriment. Rolly, on the other hand, looked much like someone preparing for a tornado, his head tucked between his knees and his hands behind his neck. Both hands giving a continuous single-finger solute. "If you bastards take a picture of this..."

"Don't worry, Rolly," the Senior Helvetian's voice came from the onboard broadcast system. "A picture wouldn't tell the entire story of this one. I have four 5G cameras videoing this."

"Fuck me," the young man sighed.

"Mason, take it to the southern tip of the peninsula. We have rented out the entire location. There will be four helicopters arriving. We will be purchasing one, after that, you'll fly to the Spartanburg Downtown Airport. I have four airplanes lined up there—"

"Sir," Ananias cut in.

"I have the unit you already looked at flying in as well."

"Perfect," he said, trying to hold in his childlike excitement.

"Oh, and, Mason, Jeremy will have a word with the curator at Skyranch, to get your chopper back to your personal hanger, where Olive O is."

"Thank you, sir."

"Of course. Tomorrow, we will be meeting the remaining group at Indian Creek Campground in Cherokee, NC. Be there no later than noon."

"Are we ok to bring the helicopter?" Mason asked.

"Good question, the folks at Big Cove Church have kindly obliged us in that. They did say there are a lot of overhead wires, but Pastor Brooks landed there safely a few years back."

"Why do I feel glad, I'm not going to be there," Rolly, for the first time since getting in the helicopter, laughed.

Chapter 24
And Then That Happened

Crash! The door flew open and three men rushed into the room. "You're late," the Senior Helvetian leaned against a podium. "This had better be good."

"Did you… see…" said Mason, who had been the first of the three into the campground's store. "Those wires?" his hands were on his knees, panting.

"I did. Tell us how the landing went," the tall man continued to lean on the podium. The room was small, but as the only stick building in this campground, it would serve its purpose.

"After two attempts, we decided that the rotors would need to be partially in the road," Blaire, panting just as hard as Mason, picked up the story. "So, Ananias and I lowered ourselves out of the chopper and we stopped the traffic on Big Cove Road."

"Which, believe it or not, was taxing as the cars were coming around blind corners, much too fast in my opinion," Ananias not quite as gassed as his counterparts, pushed his braid back.

"After we were under the wires, I hovered over until the rotors were out of the road," Mason finished.

"By the time we were done with that, we had a two-mile run to get here," Blaire added.

"Well, by the time we're done here," Captain Cratchit, who the three newcomers had not seen until then, did a pretty good impersonation of Blaire. "The group will determine what your punishment will be for your truancy," the small Asian woman took a drink of water, "Please take your seats," she pointed to the floor where four other men were sitting. From their positioning, they had been listening to those at the podium. "The only thing you missed was the declarations, which I'm assuming since you three arrived yesterday, should be nothing."

"Yes, ma'am," all three said.

"This will need to be said often, but it's important. Do not refer to any of Byte as sir or ma'am. We need you to not come off as military personnel," the Senior Helvetian stood from his position. "Now that each of you have declared the items you brought with you, I need you to hand your wallets to Captain Cratchit."

"Can I ask what may be a stupid question," Mason handed his wallet over. "If we're trying to not look like military men, how do we address Byte?"

"Let's get to that in a few minutes. Let me tell you how this all came to be and why I chose you seven for this specific team."

"This should be good," Captain Cratchit laughed.

"Enough, you," a faint smile touched his lips. "See, I didn't share with Byte what my reason for this group was. I'm getting ahead, let me start one step back, and then we'll progress into that. The discussions around a group of never associated individuals getting involved in helping the country move into the next century started three years ago. Its genesis came when the Paramilitary Institute, or PI, discovered that a sub-group from the leadership at Arch Master Base had gotten involved with the Congress of Governors to hold the Nuclear Missiles hostage. PI wrote the Unified Nations Accord in which Byte was formed. From there, we made up the founding members of the North American Honor Guard," he glanced at Cratchit.

"Seven of us were retired military, if you didn't guess, the Senior Helvetian is the only one still active. Just a side note, he is also the only member of Byte who will be imprisoned and most likely executed should this venture fail."

"Seriously?" a couple of the men on the floor asked.

"Yes, I will, without a doubt, be held up as a rogue and executed for treason or sedition. Don't worry yourselves about that. I have no intention of allowing us to fail. Captain, please continue."

"Of course. Over the course of the last few years, we have gone through several iterations of what we thought this company should be made up of. As we formed the common ideology early on, that being none in this group could have any military training."

"You've said that a few times. Why exactly is that so important?" Robert asked.

"If I could," the Senior Helvetian looked at the captain.

"Be my guest."

"Everyone, stand up, please. Ok, now take a few steps back... I know it's a small space, just make it work. Of this group, excluding us," he put his arm around the Captain's shoulders. "If any, who would you think could have some military background? Don't dismiss it and say none," this secondary comment made everyone look closer. "Ok, Blaire, any guesses?"

"Robert and Leif, maybe..." his voice trailed off.

"Mason?" he asked.

"I was thinking the same, Robert and Leif."

"Alright, Ananias?"

"I can see what they are seeing but I would actually say JaLen."

"Hmm, interesting. Why would you say that?" Cratchit asked.

"His physicality is immaculate, fingernails are not even dirty, though he obviously works with his hands."

"Ok, that's good," the Senior Helvetian replied. "None of you are actually what I would call military. Several of you are cut from the same cloth, and if we push you more, military people will see you as one of their ilk," he stepped back, letting the captain have the floor.

"It was decided, we would form a team of people that will be overlooked. Sorry, sit, sit," she patted the air. After the men had taken their spots on the floor, she continued, "Just as throughout the 80s and 90s the Russians had planted sleeper cells, in the 00s and 10s, the Chinese picked up the same practice. People that were just one of the boys, yet when called on, they brought about serious issues. We didn't want the teams embedded; we wanted the just overlooked. Take for an example, if Ananias there went to the Kremlin, they would be like yeah, so, he's been here 1000 times. The same goes for JaLen, if he showed up in England, they would wonder what building was slated to be imploded. There would be no concerns. Meanwhile, we could execute whatever we were planning right under their noses."

"The challenge that we will run up against is if you don't click together. I'm not picking on anyone here," the Senior Helvetian stepped up again. "But take, Clear, if you were working with Robert, together, you give the vibe of casing the world to either overthrow it or kill its ass. We need your keen insights to be a little less obvious."

"Is that what you guys do?" Mason asked, looking between the two men.

"Hold on, we're not there yet," the captain stopped either of the men from answering.

"Sorry," Mason sat back, looking up at the two leaders.

"No reason to be sorry. What we decided," she continued, "was to develop a team differently than military teams. We don't want to beat you into submission to learn the simple truth, if one fails, you all fail. We don't care if one or two of you fail to perform, as long as the team can adapt and move forward. We want the team to know what each cog in the wheel does, whereas in the military, you know what you do, the rest will do their part. You trust they will do their bit. Do you see the difference?"

"Sure, but in the private sector, most teams are formed to do their job. Driving this team differently, wouldn't that throw the whole thing into question?" Ananias asked.

"Ok, well, let's think that one through…" The Senior Helvetian once again took over the floor. "If you were taking a team to, say, Turkey to set up a new proxy server…"

"Mmm, my language," Blaire perked up.

"And you can only take seven people, of the team I would imagine you would have a translator, a couple of wiremen, a couple of hardware men, a trainer, and a foreman. Close enough for hand grenades. Anyway, if the translator got laryngitis, what would you do?"

"Hire a new one?" Leif asked.

"Fair enough, but what if it was a proprietary setup, that you couldn't do that?"

"I guess you would make certain one of the others could step up," Mason said.

"But if one of the wiremen step up, what happens to the work he was supposed to do?" the leader asked.

"Oh, I see where you're headed," Blaire nodded. "You need the translator to have the knowledge to take other roles if he can't perform, and so on."

"Exactly. And while the military may do redundancies on top of redundancies, the difference in our model is that the team directs itself to that conclusion, not us. We won't be there," Captain

Cratchit grinned.

"This is gonna take a long time. One Step, One Brick, One Rome. We will start with making you a business unit. Teams in business are successful when the unit hits its goals. To make this happen, we will start like teams in large corporations do, through team-building exercises. How many of you have been involved in something like that?" The Senior Helvetian asked. When only Ananias and JaLen raised their hands, he said, "Ok, let's start simpler then, how about the simplest form of team-building... How many have been in a three-legged race?" This time, they all raised their hands.

"There you go. I'd actually prefer it this way as, with this, we will have no distraction from preconceived notions of how this should go," Captain Cratchit clapped her hands. "Here's what your first assignment is, I want you to be able to tell me what each member of this team wanted to be when they grew up. Where they grew up. And what their mother and father's names as well as vocations were. Pretty simple, right?"

"Question?" Blaire asked.

"Go ahead."

"Do we need to be able to answer that for everyone, or can a specific person know the details of one other person?"

"Good question. Do you feel that a completely homogeneous team would have cells like that?" Before any of the men could answer, the front room of the campground's general store faded away.

"What the hell just happened?" JaLen opened his eyes, the sun was past high noon by a bit, but it wasn't starting to get dark yet. "How did I get outside?" This time, he stood up, finding that he was beside a large forest, sitting on the ledge of a mountain. "How the fuck did I get on a mountain?"

"This isn't really a mountain," Robert's voice spooked him, causing him to turn in place. "The best I can tell, we're in the foothills still."

"Um, dude," JaLen looked the other man up and down. "You're fucking naked."

"As are you, and them," he pointed at the other four men, still out cold. "What is your mother's name."

"What?" JaLen looked at himself, funny that the cool breeze hadn't made him realize the obvious earlier. "Seriously, what messed up shit is this?"

"Your tattoo turned out really good. I have a couple of blowouts on mine, but they're on old scars so I wouldn't blame the artist," Robert, still calm, continued to offer conversation points.

"Goddamn it, what do you know about how we got here?" JaLen stood to his full, imposing height, trying to control the uncontrollable situation. Realizing this, he laughed. "You woke up here too, eh?"

"I did, yes, about three feet from you," he smiled.

"Sorry, this is pretty weird, although I did wake up naked when I got this thing," he rubbed the eagle on his left shoulder.

"Tattooed naked? Well, then you should be old hat at this. After I got mine, I woke up in the basement I fell asleep in. But I think a full day had gone by, I was never even concerned enough to ask," Robert looked at the others as they started to wake.

"Who shat in my mouth when I fell asleep?" Clear asked, not even opening his eyes. "Probably the same asshole who took my clothes," he wiped his face and sat up.

"Took your what?" Mason opened his eyes. "How the hell did we get outside?"

"Clothing, took my clothing. Looks like they took yours too," Clear stood, turning around seeing Robert and JaLen a few feet away waving stupidly at him. "And took us to a cliff."

"This is stupid, just because we didn't know how a team-building exercise worked," Blaire added his voice to the confusion.

"Well, I will say this, I've never had the balls to have a team-building outing where the participants started naked. It's a good theme though, afraid and naked seems like it would work," Ananias laughed.

"Showing that you definitely have the balls to do it now though, eh," Mason laughed awkwardly.

"Any of us good with this outside stuff? Wait a second, where's Leif?" Clear asked.

"Down here!" a shout came from the cliff.

"Oh, shit!" the six men ran to the ledge.

"How did you get down there?" Blaire asked.

"I was looking for just the right place to scare the shit out of myself, and thought, hey, how about 15 feet down the sheer face of a cliff."

"Seems a bit extreme," Blaire shook his head.

"He's joking, they put him down there," Ananias laughed.

"Oh, that makes more sense," Blaire laughed. "I'm slow when I don't have my gummy bears,"

"How do we get him up?" JaLen peered over, seeing that Leif was on a small outcropping of stones that appeared to be the result of a collapse at some point in the past.

"Is up the right direction?" Clear asked.

"Do you need a gummy bear too? It's a hundred feet down," Leif asked.

"I climb, that's kinda my thing, and I don't see holds coming up, but it looks like he may be ok the other direction."

"Well, I don't climb, so get me up there! By the way, why are we naked?"

"Team-building," Ananias said as those at the ledge started looking for articles to help their stranded compatriot.

"To answer Clear's earlier question, I live on a mountain," Robert walked toward the trees.

"I live on a lake, doesn't actually mean I know how to swim," Mason said.

"I don't live in a house, I actually live on the mountain."

"Ok... ok, he's our outside guy, cool," Clear

said. "How do we make a rope?"

"There are red cedars in the Smokey's, their bark has a fantastic fiber that can be turned into a rope pretty easily. With that said, it isn't a five-minute activity. We need to get a camp set up, that will get us through the task."

"But, he's down there," Ananias commented.

"As in an airplane emergency, put the mask on yourself first. Yes? I promise, he'll be fine. Here's what we need to start. Everyone is going to look for a few things, some pieces of slate that may have broken from a larger stone, dead trees, seedling trees no bigger around than your wrist. We'll set up our camp just outside the tree line."

"If we work in teams, don't forget to get the answers to the questions," Ananias added, and then for good measure, he repeated them. "Where they grew up, what they wanted to be when they grew up. And lastly, their parents' names and vocation."

Robert walked over to the ledge, "Leif, how are you holding up?"

"I'm planning a lovely afternoon of personal contemplation."

"Lovely, eh."

"Most definitely," he added a posh spin on his reply. "Any plan to get me up there?"

"Initially, I was going to cut Ananias' braid off, but Rapunzel he ain't, that braid is barely a foot long. I'm going to apply some good old-fashioned techniques to get you out of there. But I wanted to discuss options with you."

"That's new, no one ever offers options, they just do what they think is right."

"This is a team-building endeavor, I figured you needed to be included," he gave a non-confident nod of the head. "Option one, we cut a small tree, or long branch and hold it down to you. And you do your best to hold on while we pull you up. However, your ledge doesn't actually extend out, it looks as if a part of the cliff broke away, leaving this concavity. The concern I see in that is if you slip and fall from the branch, you'll miss the ledge as you fall."

"I agree, the stick is a bad idea."

"I can make cordage, but this is a long process. You'll be here for a while."

"I think that is a great idea, what can I do to help?"

"I would say at least once an hour scream, 'did you guys forget about me?'"

"That feels right, I can do that,"

"Good, perfect. See you soon," Robert walked off into the woods searching for the right downed cedars. Returning 35 minutes later, joining with the team who had searched as the sun took its time going down. Finding a few outcroppings of slate, they used to successfully cut a few small trees, making six poles around five feet tall."

"Do these meet what we needed?" JaLen pointed to the pile of rocks and harvested poles.

"Absolutely," he tossed a few items he had returned with. "We need to make a fire pit, but first, I'll take this stone and this branch. Start by clearing an area down to the dirt in a ten-foot diameter. By clear, I mean no twigs, needles, or grass—just dirt. From there, we will need to have the fire pit itself, a three-foot diameter of stacked stones."

"That's fine and all, but fire, where do we get fire?" Blaire asked.

"I'll be using the inner bark from these saplings to make a small cordage. I'll use that to make a bow."

"He wasn't asking about hunting," Clear broke in.

"I know," Robert fought to keep his composure.

"Hey, did you forget about me!" Leif yelled.

"Not on your life, buddy!" Robert smiled inside. "Guys, I truly know what I'm doing. I'll show you as I go, but we have a teammate stranded."

"He's right, it's not like we know what to do," Ananias started scraping the slate, beginning the process of making a fire-safe zone. Though he didn't know it.

"I'll talk through the process of making the bow as you guys prep the fire pit," Robert sat on the ground, using the sharp piece of slate he pulled from the pile. "I'm cutting the full length of the sapling. The cut should go all the way through the bark and into the wood beneath," he sat quietly working for a bit. "Lot easier with a knife, but we're there. Now, I need to peel the outer bark from the inner. As these are living trees, it's a different process, but you'll understand," he peeled the entire bark off in a single piece. "Now that the bark is off, I'll use the slate to cut it into ribbons. God, I miss my knives," the task as before took a bit of time, but in the end, he had seven ribbons about a half-inch wide. "The goal for this is to keep it simple. We need to braid three of the ribbons together into cordage."

"When you braid them, they won't stay flat like a ribbon, is that ok?" Mason asked.

"Done some braiding, have you?" JaLen asked.

"My sister... yeah, what of it?" he got a bit put off.

"Nothing at all, have a feeling Robert is going to enlist your help."

"Fuckin' aye right I am. You head over here to help me, I'll braid these four and you braid those three into a five-foot-long cord."

"Can do," he dropped his slate, getting up from prepping the fire zone. Less than two minutes later, he was done.

"Knot the end. That is going to be our bowstring. But this is basically the same process as making the natural fiber rope to get Leif out," he said, pulling the items he gathered earlier from the pile. "First, we need fire, this naturally curved branch will be our bow. If you could, use a sharp piece of slate to cut notches in both ends."

"I got this," Mason took the branch, beginning to whittle.

"This dead birch bark will be our flashpoint, kindling. Anyone want to help by crumbling this up and make a nest of sorts?"

"I'm no bird, but sure," Blaire took the birch bark.

"The pieces I'll be working on will be the fireboard, a hand-block, and the drill. I have a bit of forming to do."

The six men worked in silence until, as if on cue, "Hey, did you forget about me?" Leif yelled, snapping the silence, and the team sat a bit straighter again.

"Fuck, we did! Thanks for the reminder," Robert replied and Leif guffawed, making the team laugh along. "We ready to make a fire?"

"Yeah," the team cheered.

"Let's build a bit of a teepee with the dried wood I set aside," he pointed to a pile of wood he had kept separate from the rest of the project. "Only bring about four of those pieces. Inside the stacked wood, put the rest of the birch bark I set there as well."

"Yes, sir," Ananias jogged over.

"Oh, I forgot one thing, you come up with any worms over there?"

"Sure, why, you hungry?" JaLen tossed over a night crawler.

"Perfect, if you found more, throw them over as well," he took the worm and mashed it into the hole he had made in the hand-hold. "He'll be the lubrication, so my hand isn't the side that catches fire."

"Gross," Blaire's chin disappeared into his

neck.

"Grow up," Robert harrumphed. "I like to make my friction fire a little different than some teaches, I don't isolate the coal the way most do with a leaf, I make a small nesting hole," he walked closer to the completed fire pit. "Let's dig a small hole, just big enough for that nest," he said, pointing at what Blaire was holding. "Place the nest in its hole, perfect." Setting all the premade components on the ground, "The drill wraps through the bow as such. Simple enough. The flattened end goes into the wormhole, while the whittled end goes on the fireboard. Lay the fireboard flat above the nest," Robert put his left foot onto it. "This stabilizes the base so it stays still. Put your finger on the string to keep it from getting loose and slowly work the bow back and forth." His actions displayed his words. "As you see, I'm leaned over so the pressure on the drill isn't all coming from my arm, which would be a nightmare. I don't remember if I said this, but on my fireboard, I attempted to, and was somewhat successful at cutting a notch leading to the hole the drill goes into. This allows the coals to fall into our nest." After some time, smoke began licking from the fireboard. When a few smoking coals fell into the nest, Robert stopped, moved the board aside, and blew a long slow breath into the nest. As the smoke got thicker and thicker, he reached down, grabbing the nest and continuing to blow long slow breaths. "This is where you earn your man-card." On the next breath, flames filled the nest, he calmly turned, and set it on the birch bark in the teepee.

"Fire from nature, very cool," Clear shook his head. "How do we use fire to get Leif up here?"

"Oh, I was just showing off. I have no plan."

"Piss off," Leif yelled from below. "He has a plan, he told it to me already."

"We figured," Ananias yelled back. "I'm guessing it has something to do with the sticks."

"Yup, once our fire gets big enough, we're gonna use it to harden and shape the saplings. And to save you guys from wondering, the stick will have a flat point. We will use that to remove the bark from felled cedar trees that have some natural retting started," he used the stick he had picked out earlier to prod the fire, making ready for more wood.

"Retting?" pretty much everyone asked.

"When a tree dies, moisture breaks down the proteins which hold the fibers together…"

"So, the tree is rotting. Why didn't you just say rotting?" Clear asked.

"Because it's different, and I have no problem letting you take over. I mean, fuck, everything I say you critique. I mean, I can critique with the best of them, I'm supposing when you were a baby off the clearance rack, you wanted to be Ram-Man from Masters of the —"

"Robert!" Mason cut him off, "Enough, don't be a fucking douche."

"I was just asking why he's gotta critique me 24-7, that's all."

"I have a feeling that is going to just be a thing. It doesn't feel malicious," Ananias attempted to placate the team.

"It isn't meant to be a critique, I really can't help it. I live by a series of rules, Truth's rules."

"Did he say Knuth's Tools? What the hell are Knuth's Tools? Can I have some? I collect tools," Leif yelled.

"No, Truth's rules," he yelled toward the ledge. "Example,

Truth's rule: If you don't ask clarification questions, you're not listening."

"Ahh," Robert said, "I get it, you're as fucking nuts as me. Cool," he proffered a hand, and the two men shook.

"Oh, Rammy, I love you!" Leif added background commentary. "I love you too, Man-at-Arms."

"Duce, you can't even see them!"

"Damn glad of that too, I don't want to see two beefy boys hugging!" that caused an uncontrolled outburst.

"Maybe we're ok with him staying over there," JaLen shrugged. "Fine, fine, fine, maybe not…"

"Retting and rotting are almost the same. People like me who live in nature see the difference. Some people see auras, it's like seeing a spark of life in a felled tree, an energy that lives there right up until it doesn't. That's where retting and rotting transpose," Robert said.

"I can see auras," Ananias and JaLen said at the same time.

"No comment!" Leif added his behind-the-curtain poke.

The team took the instruction, forming flat sharp ends on the saplings. On the other end, they created a rounded end. As they worked, they went through the questions, making certain Leif could hear the answers. By the time the sticks were formed, they found the sun attempting to set.

"I really don't wish to put this off because of light. I found three felled cedars not too far away, three of us can go get the bark, two of you, come with us, I saw a great deal of berry groves, you pick a peck, and one tends the fire. I'm not a teacher, I don't make assignments."

"I'll tend the fire," Leif yelled. "Fuck, that won't work at all. Never mind, I'm going to sit here and evaluate my life's choices."

"Sounds like a good plan," Mason replied.

"JaLen and I will help with the bark."

"I can pick a shit ton of berries, I used to go with my girlfriend to—" Blaire started.

"Mason, you ok with the fire?" Ananias walked across Blaire.

"Sure, I really don't want my junk anywhere near berry bushes," he smiled and sat down.

"Fuck," Blaire remembered all the tiny barbs.

"Bad choices were made," Ananias shook his head, following the group.

The five men headed off. "The berries are over there," Robert pointed, five minutes into the hike. "The older bushes are closer to the tree line."

"Cool, thanks," Blaire headed off.

Ananias held off, waiting to look for the safest entry point. "Blaire, hold up. If we go in over there," he pointed to the opposite side of the trees. "We may provide a higher level of due diligence to our more sensitive zones."

"Oh, yeah… small barbs."

The rest of the team continued off into the woods, each carrying two of the sticks they formed from the saplings they had cut down. "The felled cedars are right over here. I hate being slapdash, but we really don't have time to do this properly," Robert pulled his lips into a frown.

"What do you mean?" Clear asked.

"When I typically do things like this, I do everything I can to use everything that the good earth has to offer. Today, we'll need to only do what is required to get Leif up and off the ledge."

"That's reasonable, put it this way. As newbies, we would have lost a bunch anyway," JaLen added.

"True. Alright, there are two smaller trees right there. One for each of you," Robert pointed with the two sticks. "Watch me and then go do your best. The reason we're selecting these, they aren't rotting," the word had a little bite. "Never use the fat end of your stick under the bark, we formed this side for that," he ran his finger along the rounded blade they had made with the fire. "The concaved side of the point runs between the wood and the inner bark. Don't force it, the goal is to have as many pieces where the removed bark is the full height of the tree," he approached the log, inserting the stick under the bark. "You'll see the difference between retting and rotting as you do this, retting will have strands of fiber connecting the inner back to the tree still, rotting will just pull away," he pried up on the tool they had made. With his hand, he helped pry. After a few feet, he inserted the second stick, and in this fashion, he worked his way down the tree. "Like I said, we don't have enough time to really do it slow as it should be, especially around knots in the tree. For today, force around them. Go give it a try."

A couple of minutes later, "Ants. I fucking hate ants!" JaLen exclaimed as he pried the first part, and a nest of ants started running up his hand onto his arm.

"Most likely that one has entered the rotting phase, but we may get lucky. Like I said, but remember, try to get as close to the full length of the tree," Robert said as he continued to work at sectioning the bark off the log. 45 minutes later, all three men had pried the bark sections off the felled trees and started back to camp. Passing the berry patch, they saw both Ananias and Blaire still picking.

"You having that much luck?" Clear asked.

"No, actually, these bushes bite, you pick a berry and they bite your berries!" Ananias shot back.

"Fuck these bushes! I'm fine with going hungry!" Blaire added.

"Then, come on, keep what you have and let's head back. We can finish this and be back to the camp in a few hours," Robert replied.

"Sounds good to me," Ananias, turned and

started off to the area that had the least ball-cutters.

"What's the story with the stack of bark?" Blaire asked when the two parties joined up again.

"Let's get back to the camp, he'll explain the next steps to everyone. Did you really volunteer for berry picking having done it before?" JaLen asked.

"I told you, without my gummies, my concentration is pretty bad. I actually really enjoyed going to the berry patch, my brain went to a happy time," he smiled.

"That's understandable," Robert replied. A few minutes later, they saw the fire burning.

"Good job with the fire," Clear announced their return, making Mason drop the poker.

"Dude, you scared the shit out of me."

"Sorry. Not sorry," he laughed.

"Ass," he walked to them. "Need me to take anything?"

"Nah, we got it," JaLen led the way to the fire.

"What the heck? Looks like you brought back a tree," Mason laughed.

"Robert is just about to explain what we're doing," Blaire handed a bunch of his collected berries to Mason, and then headed over to the ledge. "Hey, Leif has fire."

"Yeah, Mason threw a burning bush at me."

"Bite me, Leif!"

"You want to try and catch some berries?" Blaire asked.

"Nope… bad idea, berries give me bird-like poop."

"Ok then…" he walked back just as Robert sat down for the lesson.

"Like the birch bark, the cedar has fibers, in this case, several layers of fibers," he pulled and a long ribbon pulled from the inside of the bark. "This is what we need to do. Pull as many long ribbon-like fibers from the pieces of bark we brought back. The longer, the better. If you can keep it to an inch wide, that would be perfect. If you can't start a ribbon, use a sharp piece of slate at the end to cut a couple of times, an inch apart."

"I get it, then we'll braid them like before," Mason said.

"Exactly. Now, tell me, Leif," he raised his voice. "What were your parents' names?"

"Selma and Edward."

"And they named you Sedulous?" JaLen asked.

"Apparently, it was a family name. Ok, next, JaLen what were your parents' names?" Around the horn, they asked and answered the questions, each man getting shit at some point or another.

"We have enough ropes, we'll need to tie them into a ladder, and then up comes Sedulous," Robert said.

"Fuckin' call me that again, and I'll toss you down here," he spat back.

"Touchy, touchy,"

"Not really, I'm just a dick when I'm hungry."

Tossing a rope over, "Tie that under your arms," Robert tossed their cordage ladder over next. "Four of us will hold the ladder, and two will guide you up."

"Alrighty. The rope is tied, let's go." Two minutes later, he was standing next to the others. "Let's start heading back." The team agreed and they started jogging.

"Guys, I have a stupid question," Mason said as they slowed to a fast walk a bit later. "Did you know any of the members of Byte before you found out about this?"

"I actually knew Ernst for six months, he kicked in my door the week he was elected sheriff of the town I lived in," Blaire replied.

"I've known Thumb for about the same period of time, he and I camped on the mountain," Robert said.

"Ever have a cop wake you up when you passed out in the gutter? That's how I met Vito, he was sent to arrest me and he found me passed out," Clear said.

"Arrest you for?" Ananias rolled his hand.

"Violating one of Truth's rules."

"Ok, why did you call the cops on yourself?" Blaire laughed.

"I think we need to buy a huge bag of gummies for such an emergency. I stuck my nose in where I wasn't paid to stick it. Punched a barbell boy in the xiphoid," he smiled. "After he woke me up, we got attacked by aliens."

"I kinda wanna hear that story. But I think I need some beer," Leif nodded. "Yup, at least six before you start."

"Ok, well, Dutch contracted me to steal a painting. And then I helped him cover up the murder of a realtor," Mason said.

"Eight beers for that one. Ananias, how about you?"

"I don't think so."

"Oh, someone doesn't want to play along." Robert poked.

"No, I mean, I don't think I knew any. Cratchit was my nurse in the hospital after I was found passed out somewhere, but I didn't meet her until after the stupid yellow, black, and green screens."

"Feels like half the story but... I'll let it go at that. Sgt. Davis tried to arrest me, but that was just the day before the Senior Helvetian reached out. I guess 'knew' isn't the right word."

"I almost knew Suzi. She picked me up in a bar," Jalen smiled.

"Naked mole rat fuck pig," Blaire blurted.

"I..." Clear opened his mouth to talk, closing it, he looked at Blaire. "How do you do that?"

"I don't know, my parents had a thing about expletives, I could use them only if it was in a creative way. I think it gave me Tourette's," the group laughed together, starting to jog again.

Chapter 25

Getting to Know All About You

The campfire was warm and the fish and rabbit that was already cooking on it smelled wonderful. "Congratulations on getting back to camp all in one piece. You did well and should be pleased. Go get some clothes on. Be back here in 10 minutes." After they all returned, "As you move forward, and get into situations, you'll need to know who knows what, in real-time," the Senior Helvetian walked amongst the group.

"What about the questions from the first assignment?" Clear asked.

"Do you's know the answers?" Captain Sebastianelli asked from the river's bank, one by one, they remembered they were to call him Vito.

"Yes," they all replied.

"Ther that's good enough for us," the big man walked to the group, his enormous belly leading the way. From the size of it, he may have eaten Captain Cratchit, as she was nowhere to be seen. Next to him, a huge dog barked and started running to the group.

"Constantine!" Leif dropped to a knee, holding his arms out. The giant dog ran him right over, lapping his face with big kisses.

"Catfish fuck gator bait," Blaire jumped back.

"You gotta teach us that odd language," Mason poked.

"Ok, ok, yes, yes, very exciting. Now,

everyone, take a seat," Vito patted the air, trying to get the group's attention. "That test showed you's that relying on an expert is important. It didn't take you's long to see that on the mountain. Personally, I thought the whole being naked thing was a bit over the top, but I was overruled. See, being naked made you's vulnerable on one front, so accepting help on another was easier. It's real psychological stuff. Or something," he said the last part under his breath.

"The second test will be a little less in your face as it were," the Senior Helvetian said deadpan. "You need to sit here and get to know each other."

"Not stupid shit like what position you's played in football," he crossed himself. "God rest the Gridiron."

"We want you to know who in your party may be able to pick a lock, disarm a bomb, hack into a government database, disseminate huge amounts of data, repair a dead car, throw a knife to kill someone, scale a large building…"

"Important shit that you's are gonna need to learn. The next team-building exercise, you's are gonna teach everyone a unique skill that you's have. First, you's need to get to know what that may be. We'll start with you's telling us what the skills you's want to glean from each other. But we," his hand went between him and the Senior Helvetian. "Get to determine how you's learn it. Next, you's need to know each other, I'll throw a picture with a problem to be solved on the projector. You's need to figure out who can solve the problem right then, and in that, you's get to know what we think you's should teach the rest of the team," Vito talked with his hands gesturing the key points.

"As I said a couple of days ago, One Step, One Brick, One Rome. We know this is going to be a long endeavor. That's ok, get to know your team. I'll even start the conversation, take Robert, you already learned he's a survivalist, what else do you think you can learn from him? With that, we'll leave you to it."

"The projector comes out tomorrow, if you's don't have answers, you's will run to the helicopter, sign the flip chart, each trip is a new flip of the papers, and then run back," Vito turned and walked off with the Senior Helvetian.

"Sir, you never finished the story of why you picked us," JaLen said to their backs.

"You's never told me that either," the big man turned, looking at his boss.

"That will need to keep for another day. Eat up, and get to learning about your team," he continued walking.

"This seems pretty straightforward," Ananias said. "Robert, what do you think you are good at, that we may need to know?"

"He named one, I can throw knives pretty well."

"To kill people?" Blaire raised his eyebrows, leaning back absently.

"Well, yeah, I've killed quite a few people."

"And you were never in the military?" JaLen cocked his head.

"Never was. Just seems over the course of my

life, I've been in situations where people needed to be saved. To save them, someone else had to die. My father was a Seal, he taught me a lot about, well, personal protection. As a kid, I competed in long-distance shooting. My dad was always my spotter, I learned how to be both the finger and the eyes from him. After he died, I went into bodyguard work, the people I worked with were almost always military, and they showed me more stuff. The day I found out about this," he flailed his hands absently. "Whatever this is. I had killed nine men who were plotting to kidnap a senator and her family."

"Get outta here!" Mason chimed in. "I heard about that from my neighbor. He's a senator too, and works with her. That was you?"

"It was," Robert nodded his head.

"But you seem so… well, normal," Blaire gave an uncomfortable chuff.

"Not really all that normal, but when you start running obstacle courses and shooting targets at four years old, this is what you get. Hell, at 17 years old, my dad got me my first truck, only, he had it sky lifted onto the top of a mountain. He handed me the keys and a GPS locator, and said if I wanted it, I had to find it and then figure out how to bring it home."

"That's fucking awesome," Leif's smile was ear to ear. "I thought my pop was tough when he gave me a broken car and said if you want a car, fix it."

"To be perfectly honest," Robert laughed, "I couldn't fix a car to save my life."

"Leif," Clear turned to face the skinny man.

"Aside from cars, are you what some may call mechanically gifted?"

"I think that sums me up. I like beer, broken shit, and big ugly dogs," he grabbed the jowls of his companion.

"Ok, a couple of stupid questions, what the fuck kinda dog is that? And is he gonna kill me in my sleep?" Mason asked.

"Constantine, high-five," Leif pointed at his teammate. The dog walked over and held his left paw straight up. Mason clapped the paw with his right hand. "Other one." Constantine switched paws, and Mason hit the raised paw using his right hand once again.

"Woof!"

"He's telling you that since he had to switch paws, so do you."

"You're joking," JaLen said.

"Not a bit... do it a couple of times, intermittently forget to change hands," Leif instructed Mason.

"Ok."

"Constantine, other paw."

The dog barked at Mason.

"What?"

"You didn't change hands yet," Blaire laughed hoarsely.

"Constantine, kiss," this time, he pointed at Blaire. Without any delay and his paw still in the air, he kissed the still laughing man.

"Gads, he got me in the mouth!" Everyone clapped.

"Too perfect," Mason hit the paw with his left hand. Instantly, the other paw shot up, and Mason clapped it with this right hand.

"Other one," Leif commanded. Switching paws, Mason clapped it with his right hand.

"Woof."

"That's insane," Mason laughed, clapping the hand with his left.

"Constantine's a good boy." Lief's balled fists rubbed on the beast's ears. "He's a Neapolitan Mastiff, weighs around 225 lbs."

"Why is he here?" Ananias asked.

"To be honest, I wouldn't be here if he wasn't. And I think the Senior Helvetian took a shine to him," he winked.

"So, Leif is a dog person who can fix anything. Robert is a survivalist who understands how to shoot a long way and kill shit," JaLen summarized. "I am a demolitions expert. I also help police around the world with bomb threats."

"Bomb threats?" Robert asked.

"If the local bomb squad has combed a building for bombs but were unsuccessful, they'll do a video-call with me through what they have. Sometimes, how to deactivate them once they do find them. But most calls start with how to reduce the impact or destruction if a bomb goes off."

"By just seeing a bomb?" Blaire asked.

"Pretty much, they send me pictures and videos. I give them advice on suppressing the explosion, then try to talk them through stopping it from exploding altogether. I can almost always coach them how to stop the detonation from getting to the explosives."

"You don't try to stop the detonator from going off?" Blaire again spoke up.

"Most of the time, no. Computers and electronics are Greek to me. Remember, the explosives don't blow up because a detonator tells it to."

"They don't?" all six were puzzled.

"No, the detonator tells the charger to fire. The charger tells the explosives to discharge. I see how the charger, like det-cord, attaches to the explosives. Separate those two items and the bomb doesn't go boom. The rest is Hollywood bullshit."

"That's interesting. I always wondered if I could make an unstoppable bomb," Blaire smiled.

"It can be done. Some bombs, once set, will explode no matter what, redundancies are a thing. Most bomb-makers don't work that hard."

"To recap, JaLen can make bombs, disable bombs, and engineer an implosion to maximize the bombs," Ananias said confidently.

"Who said anything about the last part?" Clear asked.

"He did, that's what demolitions experts do," he said, pointing at JaLen, then tucking the braid behind his ear. "And Captain Cratchit mentioned it yesterday."

"Oh, yeah, she did, didn't she..." Clear laughed.

"I was asking all that because I'm the gummy bear-eating computer nerd in the group I guess," Blaire said. "Circuits and collapsing redundancies are intriguing to me."

"So, then you make computers?" Mason asked. "Do you also know how to use them?"

"You know the answer to that already," Blaire's eyebrow rose.

"I'm helping the rest of the group. So, aside from being fluent in a completely bizarre cursing language, let's make it easy, what do you do to make money and live?" Mason prodded.

"Mainly, I do IT consulting, but that's just for benefits, for money, I make mining rigs to mine and trade Crypto."

"Wait, those are two completely different skill sets, aren't they?" Ananias asked.

"Yes. Which is why I said what I did," Mason smiled.

"I'm an electronics engineer, with a Ph.D. in computer science."

"Ah," Ananias pointed at Mason. "Now I see the earlier question. In your IT consulting, do you help with security?"

"I set it up for some, and break it down for others."

"That makes you a..." JaLen pointed an accusing finger at Blaire.

"Yeah, it does, I'm the hacker in the group I guess," Blaire chimed in.

"Hell yeah!" Leif whooped.

"Tell 'em your name," Mason prodded.

"The Teutonic Knight, at your service," he made a ceremonious bow, tipping an invisible hat and all. When he pretended to put the hat back on, Constantine stood, looking close, and gave a combination growl and chuff. "Dude, your dog just threatened my very existence."

"He really hates hats. Long story," Leif replied.

"Clear, what do you do?" Ananias asked.

"I'm a photographer turned private investigator. I think Nanny and I will be the group's surveillance trainers."

"Ok, I have a couple of stupid questions, Clear Truth Detective Agency in Boston?" Mason asked.

"Yeah, but kinda odd you'd know such a specific thing about me," Clear bowed up.

"I went to an invitational jam at your studio. You have an awesome traceur pitch, set up."

"Wait a minute, you're Mason Patrick? You're sick! Guys, I saw this dude training at an old farm, there was a silo…" he said, getting real excited. "You know how those concrete silos have bands around them to hold them together, the bands are usually about 36 to 42 inches apart. Anyway, this dude would stand on one at the top, and just let go. He'd drop down, letting three or four bands pass by before grabbing on again." When no one really understood, he explained, "He was 50 feet in the air, free fell 12 feet, and stopped his fall by shoving his hands between a half-inch round, metal band and the concrete of the silo. Whatever, they don't get it, you're sick," the most emotion Clear had showed since arriving.

"Thanks, but let's face it, I weigh about a buck 25, and I've watched you keep up with me and you're pushing what two bucks?"

"210 on a good day," he patted his tummy.

"Your hands must be able to tear phone books."

"Ok, ok, we get it we get it, there's a bromance kindling," JaLen cut in. "What was your second stupid question?"

"What? Oh, yeah. Who or what is Nanny?" Mason asked.

"She's my artificial partner at my agency."

Before he could continue, "You have an AI business partner?" Blaire's interests were raised.

"It's a long story. Yes, she is AI but not like that. Kind of like a virtual assistant for surveillance."

"We're all ears," Blaire waited.

"When I was a photographer, I decided it would be a novel idea to create collages of my patrons as they interacted with the real world. The cost of getting enough pictures of them to make a collage, especially ones that didn't know I was there, was ridiculously high, and I lost money on the first couple," he paused.

"Makes sense, cool concept though," JaLen commented.

"I reached out to a college in Massachusetts and found the right kid to help me, he needed summer work and had the right skill sets. We invented a new form of facial recognition. Basically, in a couple of days of running the program, we could gather 1000s of photos. It became too much real quick, he invented Nanny to help me. As an exchange for Nanny, he took the idea and started a new personal entertainment business, it's called 'Your Experiences' — "

"And how they affected others?" several of the team cut across him.

"You hired Josiah Yearly, Explorations of You, Josiah Yearly?" Ananias asked. "That 'Kid' is worth almost as much money as me. You say he came up with his E.o.Y. world-changing software from your idea... did you get anything for it? I mean, outside of Nanny?"

"One percent of the company. It goes into updating Nanny and other fun shit."

"So, you're well-off too?" Robert asked.

"I don't know about well-off, I didn't really need Truth's Detective Agency, it was more of a hobby."

"Back to Nanny," Blaire redirected the conversation. "How does she work?"

"I hate to tell everything about her, but even out here, she's with us."

"Get the fuck out!" Leif shook his head, "Let's see."

"Nanny, say hello through the phone JaLen has in the concealed carry pocket of his shirt."

"Hello, Clear," a British female voice came from the big man's armpit.

"That's impossible. My phone isn't only off, it's dead," JaLen reached inside his Hawaiian shirt, into a pocket sewn into his undershirt.

"Nothing is impossible," Blaire said. "It is scary but not impossible. Nanny, where are the nearest cameras to us?"

"She is 100% coded to me."

"Bummer," Ananias said. "Would be a good tool for the team."

"Still is. Nanny, where are the nearest cameras to us?" Clear asked.

"Inside the store, there are three. There are two at the Big Cove Church, one is always watching the helicopter," she said.

"I admit it, I'm a bit creeped out by that," Mason said. "I have a stupid question."

"He's got a goddamn lot of those it seems," Leif said to Constantine.

"How did you know he had a phone in that pocket?"

"It's one of my detecting things, I guess, he held his arm less free. Just caught my eye. Nanny confirmed it earlier. Before Mason asks, I have an ocular implant with a randomizing I/P address, whatever the fuck that means. Another of Josiah's inventions to help communicate with her."

"Now I'm creeped out too. What do you do for a living, Mason?" Robert changed the conversation.

"Hmm, Gramps would not be happy with me for this..." he started.

"He's a cat burglar," Clear replied.

"Wait. what?" both Ananias and JaLen almost fell from their seats.

"How did you know that?" It was Mason's turn to blow up.

"Private investigator, and I invited you to my Jam, duh."

"Ok, so we have a knife-throwing shooter, a surveillance, and an explosives expert, a hacker, and a cat burglar. This keeps getting better and better," Leif looked between each of his teammates before focusing on Mason, "I hope you can teach us some cool shit."

"Lock picking, safe cracking, or even how to defeat most surveillance. Sorry, Clear."

"Feels like a challenge," the bulky detective smiled and rubbed his hands together.

"Oh, yeah!" JaLen and Leif cheered.

"That leaves me, I guess," Ananias looked at them each in turn. "I imagine most of you know who I am and maybe even what I do. Truthfully, I don't know what I can train any of you on. I know he threw me a bone in his statement about disseminating huge amounts of data, and while I can do that, I don't know anyone who would want to learn, much less how it will be useful to this team."

"Based on our limited interactions," JaLen said, "you're kind of a, and don't take offense at this, a confidence man. You disarm people by giving them odd statements, which leads to hope or trust in you. You're a salesman, a leader of a group. You kinda ooze an inner 'fuck the world, and devil may care' attitude. I'd love to learn how to be like that."

"I just wanna know how the black streak in your hair stays so dark," Leif rubbed his hand across his own brown hair, mixed with grey. "I mean, shit, the rest of your hair is completely white, did it go right past grey?"

"It did, been this way since I was in my 30s, no dye either. Fine, I'll try to teach some techniques in gaining people's trust. I still think I'll be getting more out of your training than I'll be giving, but so be it."

"Um, forgive the — "

"Stupid question!" they all finished for Mason.

"Kinda saw that one coming. Did you forget that you're bankrolling this entire team?"

"What?" several inquired.

"Yeah, wait'll you see the plane he bought, the team name, and logo on the tail," Blaire said.

"Team name?" JaLen asked.

"50-Out," Robert said.

"How did you know?" Ananias asked.

"It was my call name, I left society after a moron let a kid I was protecting get killed. I had just turned 50, I did a mic-drop and checked out. 50-Out! The Senior Helvetian told me he was 'borrowing' it."

"Ok, that's kinda badass," Blaire smiled.

"If you say so. What's the logo?" Robert asked.

Instead of answering Ananias, Blaire and Mason pulled up their left sleeves, leaning into the fire as if it were planned, they all howled, "Seriously? How did you not guess that? We all have it on our left shoulder," Mason asked.

"Because that would paint us as vigilantes," JaLen said. "My assistant saw this," pointing at his arm. "She almost shit herself looking for cops to bust in."

"No, no, hold on... it doesn't show up unless he flips a switch. Come on, that's pretty cool, eh," Blaire said.

"Until then, it simply says 50-Out in a circle," Ananias explained.

"Gotta love it," the group said.

"Alright, how do we define who teaches what and when?" Leif asked.

"I know this, I want to learn lock picking first," JaLen interjected.

"Agreed," Ananias, Clear, and Blaire all said.

"I was worried I was the only one wanting to learn that," Robert smiled.

"Any other thoughts?" Ananias asked when no one disagreed. "Alright, Mason, since you're the first teacher, thoughts on a second topic?"

"I've shot a couple of times, but I'd like to learn more about pistols, and then maybe sniper wet-work."

This time, it was split, some wanted to learn about firearms, and some wanted to learn how to hotwire a car. Robert wanted to learn how to, "Blow shit up."

Chapter 26
Training a Trained Monkey

The morning came and the team had reached an agreement that the first three items they wanted to train each other in were ready to be presented. Vito walked up and petted Constantine, "Let me guess, you's want to learn how to train a dog as well as this. No? Mistake, this dog is awesome."

"Good morning, team," the Senior Helvetian arrived from the other direction.

"Good morning," they said, most of them did so with mouthfuls of food.

"Are you's ready to talk through you's first three?"

"We are," Ananias stepped up, as the group had decided he would speak for them.

"I guess I owe you 5 SG, they chose a leader," the big man shook his head.

"Yes, you do. Go ahead, Ananias."

"Lock picking. Hot wiring cars. Shooting handguns."

"All very good choices. All we had guessed and have the training plan all set up for," the men didn't look surprised. "As this is a team-building endeavor, and Robert has already taught you a bit, we'll start with him first, shooting handguns it is."

"I will be taking you's to the shooting range. By taking you's, I mean, I'll drive the UTV with the guns in it, and the boss sitting next to me, while you's all run. Be ready in 20 minutes. Oh, and these dishes don't wash themselves. Get a method of cleaning, the dishes and doing you's laundry too," he walked out. "Come on, big boy, let's go for a walk."

"Pardon me?" The Senior Helvetian raised an eyebrow.

"I was talkin' to the dog," Vito shook his head and walked out.

"I knew that," shaking his head, he caught up quickly.

"I can pull together a chart for the dishes and laundry," Ananias said after they left. "Any objections to having two men rotating teams? One clears the table and takes out the trash, the other washes dishes. Next time, on the rotation, they switch. Same with the laundry, one gathers the clothes, then does the washing and drying while the other does the folding and returning."

"You just came up with that?" Leif asked.

"Yes?" he looked put out. "Why?"

"I was trying to figure out how we were all gonna fit in there to wash our shit, and you devised a plan. I like it."

A short time later, they were running behind a covered UTV with a rear box full of flat green painted boxes. Pulling up to an area that looked like an odd baseball field, the backstop having been made out of sawn trees.

Robert stepped to the front of the group, "Rules one and two directly tie together. Always assume a gun is loaded and never put your finger on its trigger until you want the gun to go bang," he looked around the group. "Different people arrange those rules differently, but that's not important. For this training, I want you to assume a gun you are handling is loaded, as rule one. As some of you still don't understand, let me give you an example," he pulled his Bond Bullpup9 from inside his boot, ejecting the magazine before setting them both on the table, and walked back to the group. "Vito, is that gun clear and ready to be inspected?"

"I have no idea," he replied.

"Why? I ejected the bullets, didn't I? You see them on the table right next to it, don't you?" Robert followed up.

"I would not assume that."

"This is why he is being noncommittal," Robert walked up to the table and picked up the gun. Aiming downrange, he pulled the trigger, the gun went bang and he set it next to the magazine.

"How?" Blaire asked.

"For now, let's not worry about how. What is rule one?"

"Always assume a gun is loaded," they replied.

"Good. How do we clear a gun and make certain it's safe before doing anything with it? Some guns, it's easy because if their hammer isn't back, it won't shoot anyway. But that's still not good gun safety. If I want to show my gun to you, I open the cylinder," he pulled the gun from his hip holster, making certain to aim it downrange, he clicked the lock and pushed the cylinder out. "Other guns," he pushed the stem at the front of the cylinder to remove the bullets before setting it along with the bullets on the table. "Don't have a cylinder like the revolver, their bullets are in what, Mason?"

"The clip."

"Not unless you're shooting a gun like that," he pointed to the chassis-mounted 50 Caliber on the old jeep to the side of the range. "That gun has a string of bullets that 'clip' together," he said, pulling the gun from behind his back. "This gun has a magazine," he pushed a button, releasing it from the grip, holding it for the group to see. "Different guns have different calibers, as well as capacity, this is a .45 ACP, the magazine I have in it holds eight rounds," he flipped each bullet onto the table, counting as he did, "6, 7, 8," before setting the magazine beside the bullets. "Plus," he racked the slide back, ejecting and catching another bullet. "One in the chamber," he set the round down, and then racked the slide back a second time, locking it in place. "Which should answer the question of 'how', from earlier. Blaire, how did I shoot a gun without the magazine in place?"

"There was a bullet in the chamber."

"Correct. Onto rule two, do not put your finger on the trigger of a gun unless you want to make it go bang. There are no exceptions to that rule, these are not toys. These will discharge and kill people," he looked around the group. "Questions on rule two?"

"This is picky, but after I clean my guns, I always do a trigger test," Clear said, looking like he didn't really want to make the statement.

"I agree, and thank you for asking a clarifying question. However, for now, let's move onto rule three, which is to never point a gun at someone that you don't mean to shoot. That too is cut and dry, don't threaten a person with a gun. If you pull it out, shoot them," Robert waited, knowing everyone would look for support from Vito and the Senior Helvetian.

"Don't look at us," they quickly said when it happened.

"You obviously have questions."

"Yes," Mason looked nervous. "You're saying the only time someone sees you aiming a gun at them is the last thing they will see?"

"Pretty much. Because of our last rule. Rule four—never get cute, when you shoot someone, aim for what you can most easily hit. This area right here," he drew a circle with his hand taking in from shoulder to shoulder, down to his hip and over to his other hip, before closing the circle back to his shoulder where he had started. "This area is called center mass. A person can live if you shoot them there, but if you draw aim and shoot, that can't be your concern. Saving your life or the life of your teammate is your concern. Is that fair?"

"Fair," they replied.

"Question, what are you trying to do when you aim a gun at someone, Mason?"

"Save the life of yourself or a teammate."

"Excellent. For now, I'll be showing each of you how to hold a gun, and then we'll shoot enough to get comfortable with them. I'm not here to train you to be a quick draw or an expert level shooter that comes from putting in the time. Who has never shot a gun?" Robert asked.

"I haven't," Blaire raised his hand.

"Then you, my man, are first. What is rule one?"

"Always assume a gun is loaded."

"Very good, please step up. This," he held the pistol aiming downrange, "is an auto-reload, striker-fired weapon. Which means, every time you shoot it, this slider moves back and forth." He racked the slide a few times. "This loads the next bullet into the chamber, when there are no more, it locks back. Like so," he locked the slide back. "As you shoot the gun, remember, this slide is moving very fast, don't support it by the back. Is that clear?"

"It is,' Blaire replied.

"You load the weapon by putting the magazine in the bottom and racking the slide. If the slide is already back, releasing it will load it." He lifted the gun, pretending to put the magazine in place before releasing the slide. "Understand?" When Blaire nodded, Robert set the gun and the magazine on the table and stepped back. "You're up. Before you shoot, you need to know, the gun will recoil back, don't hold your arm straight, let it absorb the shock," he demonstrated with a finger gun. "Time for some hearing protection." He handed him a set of earmuffs from under the table. As Vito handed the same out to the others.

"Ok,' Blaire stepped up nervously, picking up the gun first, he racked the slide a few times. "Secured gun." Still holding the pistol in his right hand, and aiming it downrange, he lifted the magazine and looked at the bullets. "Why is there a red piece in the end of the bullet?"

"Next lesson," he smiled at the curiosity.

"Ok then," he put the magazine in place and racked the slide.

"Live weapon," Robert said. "Have at it."

"Ok then." Blaire aimed at a darker log in the backstop and fired. "Frat fuck beetle ass!" he set the gun down and stepped back.

"Live gun." Robert reached down and set the safety on. "Are you ok?"

"It felt like a hammer to my chest. Sorry, scared me a bit."

"In the moment feedback," Robert said. "Never set a live weapon down like that. Secure it with the safety at the very least. Understand?"

"No, what's a safety?"

"My bad," Robert laughed, and then explained the safety function. "Now, you need to shoot the rest of the magazine, reload and shoot the other. You know what to expect now."

"Yeah, yeah, I got it." He picked up the gun, took it off safety, and finished the lesson as instructed.

After Robert had gone through the entire line once, they were given a chance to pick out a gun of their own. He helped by letting them hold and fire the different styles. They each shot two magazines from their chosen weapons before the bell signaling the second training session was going to start.

"We will now be learning the art of hot wiring a car. For now, we'll take a look at this old jeep. We put a battery in her, but no one has had a key for her in… well, according to the owner of this campground, for generations."

"This is important, first, old cars like this Jeep don't have a steering wheel lock. As dumb as it sounds, hot wiring a car that has a steering wheel lock is useless. While I can show you how to get around that later, today, we're looking at a car where that doesn't matter," Leif walked over to the Jeep. "To start a car, you need a spark and gas. Before we get too stupid thinking this will start, let's look at gas."

"We did empty the gas fully and put in new," Vito said from the side of the Jeep.

"Perfect. Looks like they are setting me up for success. Still, let's continue what I was going to do. Do you all know what a carburetor is?" They all nodded. "Good, it's where fuel and air mix on their way down to the spark. The important part of all this is that you can flood an engine if you give too much gas, this means we don't want to just keep pushing fuel into the carb," he released the hood, opening it. "We do, however, want to see that fuel is going in. The throttle body is where you can see that," he noticed that there was no air filter housing over the carburetor. "If I work this," he pointed, "back and forth, it causes gas to be pushed in. I want each of you to look into the open carb," he put his finger in, moving the choke out of the way, not wanting to give too much information for the first lesson.

"What is that lever called?" Ananias asked.

"That's for the next lesson," he laughed inside. "Let's take this inside the car," they walked around the other side, "Take your turns looking under the steering wheel. You'll see several wires running up the steering column." They each did as instructed. "Questions?"

"Nope,"

"If you are starting a car and don't need to hide yourself, the easiest way is to use your knife and cut the red wire and the red/white cable. After you cut them, strip it back and twist them together. These are live wires and these old batteries can give you a poke. So, try not to let the wires touch metal," he pulled out a knife and performed the action, pulling the wires far out and let each of them get in and look. "Questions? And don't ask what the other wires are."

"Nope."

"Good, since we are in the middle of a field, we don't need to try and do the ignition start under here, but if you had to, the light blue wire is the next one to cut and tap on the other two like in the movies. For today, we'll use the starter solenoid. He got out of the car and walked back to the hood. Easy peezy, put a screwdriver or your knife if it has an insulated handle across these two poles," again, he pointed, this time to the unit on the fire wall with thick red wires hooked to it. "Everyone, raise your hands in the air," he touched his knife across the terminals and the Jeep turned over.

"I bet we can get that thing to run," Vito came walking up. "Just not today," he added as he saw Leif start leaning back into the hood.

"And as we don't have a pile of cars for you to practice on, we knew this would be a short lesson," the Senior Helvetian added.

"Let's head a little further down the river, I think you's are gonna like this next training," the big man rubbed his hands together. "If not, I think we'll like it." He drove the UTV down the river until they found a much wider and what looked to be a much deeper spot in the river. Hanging above the river was an odd bridge with what appeared to be five cages in the center. "As you recall, the name of the game here is lock picking. Let me point out to you's, the river here is 10 feet deep, and as you's can tell, from all the times you's has crossed it, it never gets really warm," he smiled.

"What this drill is set to do, is focus you with real outcomes, right from the start," the Senior Helvetian nodded his head. "Let's be honest, this one is all my design."

"And the next phase, well, that one's all me." It didn't seem humanly possible, but his grin rose above his eyes. "But you's gotta earn that privilege."

"For now," the leader shook his head. "Sorry, for now, we have five different style locks you need to open," he pointed. "You'll enter down here, travel into cage one, you'll have a time to pick that lock. Once you close the door, locking yourself into cage two, you'll again have a set time to either return to cage one, or progress to cage three. This process repeats until you're across the river."

"Sir, er... ah..." Mason stammered, trying not

to use the term sir. "Stupid question," he waited, knowing the jeers from the team were incoming, and God were they… "Yeah, yeah…" he placated the mob. "What happens if the time elapses?"

"That isn't a stupid question at all. You's see at the bottom of each cage, there's a trap door. If you's fail, you's will fall 20 feet into ice water. And then you's can curse the Senior Helvetian for thinking of this method of training you's," he belly-laughed, smacking his knees.

"I'm all for a challenge," Mason licked his lips. "Do I get to go first and then come back and show them how to defeat each one?"

"If you think I'm that big of a pushover, I've been too easy on you thus far," the Senior Helvetian grinned, pointing to a small bag at the entrance to the bridge.

Walking up, Mason opened the bag and grinned, "Alright, guys, let's start with some high-level lock picking and safe cracking," he held a see-through lock and a combination lock that had been cut from a safe. "The majority of this is touch. Let's start with this lock, it is a pin-style tumbler lock. Can you guess what it uses to keep just any key from turning it?"

"Pins," the group all said.

"Excellent, we're done here. Just kidding. The pins inside are of varying lengths, matched to the key to turn the plug. Inside the lock mechanism, there are technically two types of pins, drive and key, and they are held down by springs. These pins must reach the sheer point to separate and allow our plug to turn," he walked through the group, showing the see-through padlock, and how the pins lifted to just the right height when the key was inserted. "Any questions?"

"Nope."

"Excellent. In our training lock, you can see the key raises the pins to the sheer line, allowing the plug to turn. Lock picks, as you most likely know, are the tools of the trade, and take the place of the keys. Some are used to manipulate the pins, others to turn the plug. The tool to turn the plug is called a tension bar, or wrench. Remember, not all locks turn counter-clockwise. Before you attempt to pick a lock, start with setting the tension bar in the flat side of the slot, and turn it in both directions. I have personally never found a lock that doesn't have a small give in the direction it rotates. That is called manufacturing tolerances, they can't be perfect, so they allow error in the direction the key will be turned." Seeing a hand go up, he waited.

"I've picked a few locks, and I'm a bit confused," Clear said when Mason paused.

"By?"

"What is the purpose of the concern of the rotation, no, I mean, it's only gonna rotate one way and you'll see that pretty quick, right?"

"Ah, but the rotation and other tolerances build upon each other. Together, they are what make it possible for you to pick a lock. I told you about the first tolerance, the key rotation, the second, the pins are smaller than the pin chamber, understand?" When he nodded as if to say, sure whatever, he continued. "Ok, well, they are applying the pressure, and by using a single hook or even a paper clip, you can cause a pin to bind against the inside of its chamber. Never allow the pressure off the tension bar, keep working the pins, the process will work its way out as the tension moves from pin to pin until the plug turns."

"Oh, I get where you were going, sorry."

"No reason to be sorry. There are several types of picks—triple peak, city rake, all are used with different sized tension bars. And the tension pressure isn't a calibrated value. Next, the up position of a pin is not all the way up, remember what I said, you have drive and key pins, you want the drive pin up, and the key pins down on the other side of the plug sheer line. If you push the key pin all the way up, it is still stopping the plug from turning. The pin that matters is the upper pin, which doesn't touch the key. What is that called?"

"Drive pin?" Blaire replied.

"Is that a question?"

"No, it's my answer."

"Perfect. Let's go through each of you attempting to open a padlock. It looks like Vito has made certain there are seven sets of lock picks in here,"

"I did," he took the bag, walking through, handing the kits to the men. After 20 minutes, each of them, with Mason's help, had managed to pick the lock. After an hour, they were all understanding the process themselves.

"Very good. I say we move on to the combination locks. As I said, both styles use feel, however, these can also be sound. I sometimes use a stethoscope. That allows me to hear the tumbler gates fall into place under the fence. Let me show you the inner workings, and hopefully, that'll make the mumbo jumbo I just said make sense," he held up the cut-away safe lock. "This is your dial, it has the numbers," he walked through the line. "The dial is connected to the drive wheel or cam, I want you to notice the notch on that cam, I'll come back to that," he turned it around so the small black wheel was visible. "Now, on the rod that connects the dial and the wheel are three tumblers. Each of them has a groove or a cut-out in them called gates," Again, he walked through the line slowly showing the three tumblers and their gates. "This is very important, when I turn the dial, wheel three, the one nearest to the cam, spins first, after spinning the same direction one more rotation, tumbler two picks up, and another turn, tumbler one joins in. Picture the cam having a pin which protrudes into tumbler three. Tumbler three has a pin going into tumbler two, and it into tumbler one."

"Just saying… ZZZZ!" Leif's eyes closed and his head fell forward.

"I never said this shit was exciting, all y'all made the decision to learn this. I could turn you loose and let you see how cold the water is," Mason shrugged. "I mean, I know I can make it across," he emphasized the word I like a valley girl.

"Let me try and snazz it up a bit," JaLen said. "The cam is pinned to the third tumbler. Rotating three will spin two, the middle girl, who pivots to her man, tumbler one. A combination is set when you lock one in first and leave it be... uh... uh... middle two gets set by turning the boss cam two times, not once or thrice, just two... uh... uh... set two by stopping at her home... Boyeee... Then we bring it home with three... Boom! Open! Boom! Open!"

They all clapped. "Ok, fine, what he said. Let me tell you the rest and you can teach your fanboys," Mason laughed.

"No, that was my best attempt at waking up this crowd."

"Like JaLen said, when you have the right combination, this bar, which is called what, Robert?"

"The fence."

"Exactly, as the fence drops into the aligned gates, it takes this lever down, forcing this protrusion called the nose latch, into the notch I told you I'd come back to, called the contact area. Questions?"

"If I could sum up what I think I heard," Clear said. "In simplest terms, when the gates align, the fence falls in, taking with it the lever and the nose latch. When the nose fully engages with the contact area, this allows the safe to open."

"Pretty close, only the end is different, once the number is made, you change direction a fourth time, back to the contact area, and beyond to force the nose latch to retract the bolt. And wa-la you can open the safe." He showed the nose latch pulling the bolt back. "Any questions?"

"Is the boring shit gonna get exciting soon?" Leif asked.

"This concludes a very rushed entry to safes,"

he walked over to the bag with the props, starting to put the mock-up safe away.

"I don't think we learned how to crack a safe," Ananias said.

"Oh, I'm sorry, I thought I was just explaining the boring shit. Someone else is gonna take over now."

"I'd like to see some of the interesting stuff, and I'll shut the fuck up," Leif put a fake smile on. "Sorry, I need a beer."

"The beer is on the other side, along with Constantine," Vito said.

"I tried to tell you the only way to learn safe cracking is to start by crawling. As we're done crawling, let's get into the finer details that may not be obvious. When the three tumblers are stacked together, no matter how high-cost the safe is, they are not the same size. Once again, it's the manufacturing tolerances we will be taking advantage of," he smiled, walking back to the group, passing the safe around again. "Look closely, you may be able to see which wheel is larger. Questions?"

"Nope."

"Alright, those manufacturing tolerances can be manipulated by understanding where and how they can be monitored. That brings us to the contact points, those positions where the nose touches and the notch. It's finding these locations that makes safe cracking possible. You holdin' on there, Leif?"

"Yeah, this is good… I'm catching on."

"For us to find the contact points, we need to understand next how to find them." Walking to the group again, he showed the CCW rotation, "When we spin the dial, as such, we can find the right contact point. The nearest number being 3. Now we find the left, by spinning the dial CW until we feel the impact of the left side. Which looks like 97."

"Got it. When you go CCW, you can find the right contact point, and CW for the left one," Clear said.

"Correct. So, again, we play with the manufacturer's tolerances and find the largest tumbler's gate. We need to make certain all the tumblers or wheels are turning, so four rotations and stop on 0. Now you will fight through the right contact point as you continue past 3. Remember, touch, touch, touch, there is a very slight resistance change as you find the gate, and like the contact point on the cam, you attempt to find the edges of this as well. That's where the easy stuff stops because, although we found the number, we don't know which tumbler it belongs to.

To find which wheel it's on, we do some more trial and error. To start, we put the number we have on two tumblers and either add or subtract 20 from that number on the third tumbler. Rotating back and establishing the contact points again. If the fence is not in the gate, the numbers will remain where we first felt it, if the contact point changes, the fence has found a gate," Mason said.

"Ok, if our number is 38 and we put 38 on all the tumblers, the contact point's numbers will be different?" Leif asked.

"Yes, but it wouldn't tell us which the larger

tumbler is."

"Yeah, I got that, it was a question, different like what?"

"Oh, the gap between them will be smaller, 3 may now be 2.85, and 97 may be 97.25. Before we move on, I'm going to walk around and have a brief feelings exercise. While I do that, practice with your lock picks some more, this may take a while. Hey, I forgot to say, when you do the finer work, put your fingertips just on the lip of the dial, don't grab it."

"Me first!" Leif stepped up. Everyone walked away grabbing a practice pin lock. After an hour, "I got it." The bolt pulled back, allowing the safe to open. "That's a bitch, and tedious and boring but fucking cool."

"It is that!" Mason worked with each of them, showing how the second and third numbers could be found. In the end, only Clear was having an issue. "I must be a good teacher," Mason laughed.

"They all got it?" The Senior Helvetian asked.
"I was so close," Clear said confidently.

"In case anyone was wondering, he really wasn't. I'll need to work with him a bit, most likely, he has no feeling in his sausage-sized —"

"Hey, now…" Vito cut in.

"Fingers, I was gonna say fingers," the group spent a few moments with the entire juvenile humor thing.

"Alright, alright… I need a beer, let's do this," Leif interjected.

"I guess it's time to run the course," Vito said.

"I don't get it, are you saying we're gonna need

to do all that to open a lock up there?" JaLen asked.

"How do I know? They wouldn't let me up there. I think what I showed you will get you through gathering the first number, and most likely, the second. After that, it's a brute force method, if you have two, it isn't that hard to find the third that way."

"We have four hours left in the daylight. Let's see how you do," the Senior Helvetian walked to the water's edge.

"We secured lock picks at each gate, so when you fall, you won't lose yours," Vito guffawed.

"That's a really good idea," Robert replied.

After four weeks of training on the shooting range, heading to the dump to practice hot wiring, and falling from cages into a river, they had all passed the individual tests. The group scores on Vito's slideshow were equally as impressive. Not having been made to run more than once per round, in those cases, the slide had a random oddity that allowed Vito the pleasure of making them head to the helicopter. "Today, we're having our first team challenge," the Senior Helvetian greeted them at breakfast.

"This is how the day will play out. Everyone will have to start seven cars, and I mean actually start them. The final car will need to be driven to the firing range. At the firing range, you get to shoot seven different guns, the last being the gun you selected as your daily carry," Vito explained.

"The teams will work like this, Vito and I will be the captains. We pick names out of a hat for each event, the trainers do not participate. Therefore, we will each have three random members of 50-Out for each event," the guys complained about the trainers not being part of the scoring.

"Yeah, yeah, may I continue? I was just getting to the best part. The total scores for our teams will become a handicap for us on the final event," he motioned between himself and the boss. "These will establish the time delay for the team to enter the first cage."

"To make things interesting, Vito has suggested that we position ourselves in the cages up at the top. There will be three cages, each with seven locks. The order you enter the cage will correspond with the order your name is picked for the last event."

"Who holds the hats and determines the times for the events?" Ananias asked.

"That would be the trainers," Vito said. "The first timer starts when the door to the first car door is open, and it ends when your first gun is picked up at the range. Correspondingly starting timer two, which stops when you's have shot seven bullseyes, with seven guns."

"As Robert is the trainer at station two, he needs to go first on station one," the Senior Helvetian said.

"Are you's ready? We leave in 20 minutes."

After the first two events, the Senior Helvetian was given a 14-minute and 47-second head start due to a couple of lucky draws. With a huge smile, he drew his final team names and entered the cage, locking himself in.

Chapter 27
Relaxing with Firearms, Loaded Firearms

"Alright, you've been doing well with the slide show and, for the most part, the training," the Senior Helvetian looked over at Clear.

"What? I suck at cracking safes," the room laughed.

"Today," a 40-something woman walked into the room behind them. "Your team-building training will also test your communication skills. We're going to be doing a derivative of a classic training game called the block man challenge. The general way the game is played, one member of the team runs to the other side of the river, there, they will find a tent," she pointed to the small circus tent set up amongst the trees, roughly 100 feet from them. "Now, inside it they will find something. I'm not telling you what, this runner will have 20 seconds to look from the time they enter the tent. They will then run back across the river to help the team by saying what they saw. Only one runner can be off the porch at a time."

"Thank you, Suzi," the Senior Helvetian said. "Meanwhile, on this side of the river, there is one person who is blindfolded, that person will be the one reaching into the four boxes," he pointed to the boxes, which were all covered in black leather, each having a slit in the top. "The team will be given an option, either two pieces from the box they are awarded, or one piece from another. The team has the final say, the blindfolded person does get to provide input. Once drawn, the piece is placed on the inspection table, from there, the team decides where it goes. Today, I will be imposing one rule, Robert will be blindfolded for the entire challenge. Any questions?"

"Harsh," Robert laughed.

"Sir, you didn't tell them how they know which of the seven boxes they are awarded," Suzi added.

"Completely correct, this activity is time-based. When the runner leaves the porch on this side, they will hit the green button," he pointed to the box mounted on the railing. "When they return, they push the red one. Their time dictates the box that Robert gets to pick from. And I have a chart that tells me how the time equates to a certain box," he waved a piece of paper.

"And with that, we should be ready to do this," Suzi clapped her hands.

"This is gonna be easy compared to being on a mountain naked or trying to crack a safe to stop the Senior Helvetian from falling into the river," Mason laughed.

"Keep it up, pretty boy!" Clear shook his fist.

"It's ok, Clear, he's the one who failed at instructing his student," Suzi laughed. "I'll wave when I'm ready on the other side. Oh, and don't think I'm gonna be a pushover when it comes to the 20-second rule," she held up a cattle prod, laughing maniacally when she pushed the button and everyone could hear a hum. The laugh continued as she trekked across the creek.

"Could be worse, she could be your wife," Ananias cheerfully smacked the dumbstruck Mason on the back.

"Can you see anything?" The Senior Helvetian smiled as he finished tying the blindfold.

"No, I can't. Shit, I can barely breathe," Robert replied.

"Good."

"Whenever you're ready!" Suzi said over the radio.

"Whoever is going first, don't forget to press the buttons when you leave and return," the Senior Helvetian instructed.

"I'm first," Clear pushed the button and sprinted to the creek, carefully making his way across, he reached the other side. Realizing now, the tent was 20 feet higher than the river, he jogged up the steep embankment to the large tent. Stopping to catch his breath, he looked around the area, spying several targets in the trees that he hadn't noticed over the last few weeks. "No rush, the tent timer starts once you enter. The big timer started when you left," Suzi gave another laugh.

"You're a bit crazy, eh?" Clear asked, stepping into a very well-lit tent. Inside, he found seven display boards, on the top of each were disassembled handguns, below that, the pieces were reassembled in stages.

"17, 18, 19…" Suzi's voice was distracting but he made it out before 20.

"Shit!" he didn't properly take the large drop into account and he pretty much leaped to the creek bank. Reaching the other side, he hit the red button.

"This is important, be careful of the embankment, it's quite a rise, but it's a worse drop. There are seven boards with different guns, all in pieces. Also, there are several targets hanging in the trees," everyone waited.

"54 seconds, box four," the Senior Helvetian called out.

"Put your hand out straight," Mason instructed, holding the box out for Robert.

"Feels like the body of my Redhawk," he reached to the left, feeling the inspection table, he set it down before going for the second awarded piece. "Hammer assembly," he set the second piece next to the first.

"Small point of order. The runner needs to facilitate the discussion as to whether you take two pieces from the awarded box. In this case, it didn't really make a difference, but stay the course communication even in obvious decision points," the Senior Helvetian said.

"Got it," they all replied.

"I'm assuming the pieces should go on table four," Robert commented.

"Makes sense," Clear moved them and he took his place in the line.

"I'm gone," Blaire said before hitting the green button and heading off.

"And now you know why I made him wear that blindfold."

"Makes sense for certain," Clear, catching his

breath, wheezed.

"Sir," Robert's voice was pleading. "Please tell me this is just field-stripping and not full disassembly "

"Correct, though full disassembly will come later," the Senior Helvetian winked, forgetting Robert couldn't see.

"Your 20 seconds start once you enter the tent," this time, Suzi said as Blaire ran up the loose embankment to the tent. He didn't say a word as he ran right into the tent, straight up to the boards. Finding the boards that Clear had described, he found the one that had the barrel and trigger assembly Robert had pulled from the box, it said 'Ruger Redhawk' at the top. Along with the two pieces, he saw eight other items attached to the display board. "17, 18…" Suzi's counting drew his attention and he headed back, "Don't break your shit on the way down," she instructed. That in conjunction with Clear's warning, alerted him well enough that he slid down the decline to the creek.

After hitting the red button, "I don't have much to add, just get familiar with the boards."

"51 seconds. Box two."

"It's early, I advise we go for two pieces from box two, all agree?" Blaire asked.

After they all agreed, Ananias held the box up for Robert, "In front of you."

"Sorry," Robert, whose hands had been at his sides, touched the top of the box, then reached in. Pulling a stainless-steel frame body, this time, the grips were still attached. Robert ran his fingers around the grip and then to the trigger, which, on this unit, was also still attached. "It's another Ruger, this one is a 1911. Put it on table two." Reaching in again, grabbing a barrel, he removed and felt the bushing which was able to pivot on the barrel. "This is definitely a Ruger. Table two as well."

"You got it," Mason said, taking and examining the carved wooden grips and the barrel, then placed them on table two as instructed. He headed to the steps, wondering if it was worth just going to the other side, glancing at the boards and then returning. He stopped pushing the button, turning, he asked that question to his team. "Any value in just seeing how the time works, I was thinking just run in the tent, looking briefly and heading back. Thoughts?"

"I like it," Ananias replied. "Any objections?"

"Cool," he headed off when no one objected, pressing the green button. Trying to defy gravity, he sprinted up the steep side and into the tent. Seeing the stained wood grips on the second board, he turned and dashed out. Sliding down the incline, not even hearing Suzi's warning. Hitting the red button, "Time."

"42 seconds, box one," the Senior Helvetian nodded approvingly.

"I see no reason for us to not start the new box," Mason panted.

"Agreed," the team said. This time, JaLen lifted the box, touching it to Robert's outstretched hand.

"Difficult to tell," Robert held a black grip, rubbing his thumb on the texture. "This is a grip module, think it's a Sig, not going any further than that," they set it on the inspection table. Once again reaching in, he brought out another black piece. "And we have a slide assembly." Feeling it again, his thumb ran along both ends, and then the ejector slot. "I was right about it being a Sig, thinking a P365, but no bets just yet. Please put them both on table one."

"Yes, sir," Ananias took it, repeating the same feeling he had done, trying to understand what made him call it a Sig. Seeing the letters P365 on the slide, taking the grip module from the inspection table, he saw Sig Sauer in the grip texture. "I was going to repeat what Mason did. Just rushing across," Again, no disagreement, so he hit the button and took off. Sprinting into the tent, he found the word Sig, on board three. Turning, he ran out quickly, dropping to his butt to slide, he hit the bottom and shot into the creek, barely getting his foot under him. He hit the red button and waited.

"42 seconds, box one,"

"Good job, first repeat box," Leif reached for the box and then waited, glancing over his shoulder at Ananias.

"What? Oh, sorry, from what I saw on the board, there are only four pieces to the Sig P365. We should finish box one in my opinion."

"Here you go," Leif held the box out after they all agreed.

"Ananias is correct, two pieces left," he pulled out both the spring assembly and the barrel, setting them gently on the table.

"Good catch on listening to what Robert said," the Senior Helvetian gave a thumbs up. "But did you see enough on the board to put it together?"

"Maybe," he walked up to table one, placing the barrel into the slide assembly. Moving it in until it dropped into place. "The spring goes…" he held the 'oh' sound in goes while he snapped the piece into the half-moon cutout. "Here." Examining the grip module, he slid the pieces together, but they didn't quite work. "I guess not. Sorry, guys," he set the slide back down on the table.

"Actually," Robert, still blindfolded, smiled. "Is the takedown lever at six o'clock?"

"No, it's," Ananias looked at it, judging, "kinda at 4:30… maybe."

"It is not at six, it most likely reset. Move it to three o'clock, now, if you push up on the thumb lock, you can bring the take down lever back to six."

"That worked," he reintroduced the slide to the rails on the grip module, this time, it slid all the way back, Ananias set the thumb lock. A moment later, he released it, and it racked forward.

"Gun one complete," the Senior Helvetian announced and the team clapped. "You got lucky, not all guns have so little pieces. Although…"

"Is he giving hints or something? What is taking so long?" Suzi yelled over the radio.

"Leif, you better head out or she's gonna taze you for fun when you get there," JaLen chuckled.

"Great, of course it had to be my turn, she is a bit crazy," he mashed the button and jogged down to the river, seeing her standing at the top of the hill.

"Crazy am I?" she stood between him and the entrance, holding the cattle prod out.

"Fuck, yeah, you are," he went right up to her, stopped, and turned. "Problem is, I'm worse, let me have it," he wiggled his butt at her.

"Get in there or I will, you goofball," this time, her laugh was genuine. Looking at the boards perhaps closer than the others did, attempting to glean how the 1911 went together.

"17, 18, 19, 20, 21…" Suzi walked into the tent, finding it empty.

"Hehehe," Leif's laugh could be heard as a shadow passed the opening.

"Ass!" Finding the place he slid under the tent.

"Time," he pushed the button, arms crossed.

"72 seconds, did you stay in the tent past 20 seconds?" The Senior Helvetian asked.

"Just by a couple. Which box?"

Looking at the paper, "Box three."

"Guys, first crack at seeing inside the last box. I looked at the 1911 we have, there are eight pieces so we know we have six left. I didn't have a chance to study the Redhawk…"

"There are at least 10 pieces, depending on how they present it," Robert said.

"I agree," JaLen said. "Let's do box three."

"Group?" Leif asked.

"Three,"

"Here you go," JaLen took Robert's hand, leading it to the box.

"If you put my hand in your pants, we've got a problem."

"Well then, never mind, fuck!"

"We're back to an easy one," Robert pulled a grip module, feeling above the trigger. "Glock." Feeling further, "19. Great fucking gun," he reached to the left, setting the part on the inspection table. "And a spring assembly. Table three, girls."

"Yeah, he's all cocksure now," JaLen laughed, pressed green, and started up the embankment. Getting a poke from the waiting cattle prod in his right thigh. "Cain-Able fucking shit. Oh, God, Mason's language is catchy."

"Tell Leif that was for him," Suzi used the cattle prod as an extension of her arm, waving him into the tent.

"I thought it was because…" his words faded and he walked in the tent.

"For? What?"

"Did she find the note?" JaLen questioned caringly.

"Sorry?" Suzi followed him into the tent.

"Did your wife find th—" his words stalled. "I'm stupid, that was a test, you don't have a wife and you didn't leave her a note because she cheated on you."

"I have a wife, yes. But you're correct, the rest

was bunk, I have slept with a couple of men and hated it!" she put a weird flair on the words, "Mostly, it was a test to make certain who you were, and to see if you could get past the loss of your wife."

"Thanks for lying for me," he turned and faced her.

"I didn't, you completely failed the test. The man down there disagreed. If it were up to me, you wouldn't be anywhere near this camp. Take that for what it's worth," he started walking out, 'Buzz' she nailed him in the right ass cheek.

"Rat, God, ape, ass."

"23, 24..." she shooed him out, again, using the prod.

"Fine, fine, fine..." he ran out and down the hill. "Time."

"77 seconds... Do I need to do more conditioning with you gentlemen?" The Senior Helvetian asked.

"Nah, I thought that because she shocked me for Leif, I would have extra time. I was wrong."

"She got ya?" Leif almost pissed himself.

"Box?" Robert brought them back on task after letting Leif crack up for around 20 seconds.

"Three."

"I'm thinking we close out the Glock, I saw while I recovered from the first poke that the Glock only has four pieces as well. All agreed?" JaLen asked.

"Agreed,"

"Good, I need some heat on my ass, she

shocked the fuck outta me," he limped away as the team assembled the Glock 19 at Robert's instruction.

After 10 more trips up and down, they pulled the rest of the pieces for the Redhawk and the 1911. "Robert, you aren't allowed to help them," the Senior Helvetian said.

"Look I don't care how many times I run up there, I'm not seeing how this goes together," Blaire said after another two trips to see how the pieces went back together, he almost threw the 1911. "I see the slide stop is in place, but… fiddly drum stick frog dicks," he removed the slide cap, releasing the tension on the spring, allowing him to freely work with and latch the slide stop in place.

"Gun three completed," the Senior Helvetian announced.

"Hey, I forget to tell you," JaLen said. "I caught your bizarro cursing bug."

"Good, it gives righteous indignation to profanity," Blaire gave him the thumbs up.

"Sir, may I?" Robert implored.

"It's Mother, may I… and yes, you may," Suzi pulled the blindfold off Robert. "Have at it, I'm fixin' to prod the boss if you don't,"

"She really is crazy," Leif shook his head and watched Robert put the Redhawk together in a matter of seconds.

"Beers?" Suzi aimed the cattle prod at the Senior Helvetian, who nodded his head.

Chapter 28

Do You See What I Hear?

"Alright, today, we're flying to a new location. Get your rucks packed and meet at the storefront, 15 minutes," Sergeant Davis met them as they finished their breakfast. As everyone left, Leif started clearing the tables. "Recruit, I called for a 15-minute bugout."

"It's my turn to do the dishes."

"And?"

"I'm not leaving these kind people a mess."

"When your superior gives you an order…" Davis started.

"I typically ignore it. And unless you plan on doing these dishes, I'd stop holding me up," he scraped the remaining food from the plates into the trash. "Besides, we're not military, not supposed to act like military. So pt-t-t-t-t," he blew an extended raspberry at Mustache.

"Leif," the Senior Helvetian chimed in from behind Davis. "We got this, go get your stuff,"

"Can do," he finished scraping the remains from the plate he held before leaving it. As he left, he overheard, "Don't lose perspective, Sgt, we need independent thinkers, remember?"

In the end, Leif wasn't even the last one to get to the porch. "Where is Ananias?" Davis asked.

"Probably getting the sheets over to the laundry," JaLen replied. "It's his turn."

After an uncomprehensive series of grumbles,

Davis shook his head, "Ok, I have to ease up a bit," he looked at the Senior Helvetian, who winked. A few minutes later, Ananias joined them. "This time, I will give an order that needs to be followed, training is important, I don't want any cadence. But since there is an actual reason for cadence not just hear and repeat, the act of talking while running is better for your lung capacity. Since we are not doing that, I want you to sing your favorite song while you run to the helicopter. I want your rucksack in your hands and held over your head, we need to continue to work on your conditioning, military or not."

"Very true," the Senior Helvetian added.

"And since Leif and Ananias decided to be cute, Leif, you lead the team, everyone stays in line, Ananias, you bring up the rear. Stay in the center of the road, DO NOT move for cars. Let's getcha moving," he stepped aside, and Leif headed off with his rucksack over his head.

"I wasn't being cute," Ananias said as he passed the sergeant.

"Sure," Davis fell in, jogging behind the men.

"Come on, Leif, I can see why you're the never-ending pursuit. At this pace, you couldn't catch Covid-19," the Senior Helvetian turned, jogging backwards and starting to pull a gap. Leif ignored the ribbing, he had made several dozen trips up the road to the helicopter in the last three months. He knew full well, the speed he could maintain to get there, while singing. "What song are you singing? I can't hear you."

"Green Grass and High Tides, it's in a guitar

317

reframe."

"You cheeky bastard," the Senior Helvetian horse laughed.

"Hey, he said my favorite song, not my fault that song has 75% guitar duels. Oh, words... As kings and queens bow and play for you... OOOH, just for you!"

Behind Leif, JaLen was doing his rendition of a familiar song from the early 2000s. "Here's to us, here's to love for the times that we fucked up..."

"Hey, I loved that one," the Senior Helvetian slowed his pace and joined in, "Fill the glass because the last few days have kicked my ass!" The men high-fived.

"When I was, a young man..." Mason, whose voice was insanely good, sang. "My father took me into the city..."

"Holy mother pendulum shit!" Blaire gave another of his bizarre grouping of expletives. "You sound just like Gerard."

"He really does," the Senior Helvetian started running next to the cat burglar. "You, get back to your singing, oh, and, hey, sergeant I don't hear you either," he scolded Blaire and Sgt. Davis who was passing by on the opposite side.

"Sing, yeah, sing at the top of your voice! Love, without fear..." Sgt. Davis belted out a few lines as he crossed to the front of the column.

"When I was young, I was the nicest guy I knew..." Blaire started.

"Oh goodness gracious, is that why your girl

left you?" Clear patted Blaire on the shoulder.

"Yeah, yeah, I don't hear you giving voice to 'La Vendetta!', Mr. Critique."

"If I had a clue what that was, I'm sure I still wouldn't have a clue what it was," he laughed and began singing, as instructed with a glance from the Senior Helvetian. "If it ain't broke, you can bet I'm gonna break it." His relaxed speaking voice broke into a country twang, "If there's a wrong road."

"Love it! Love it! Love it! My pocket lighter sparked the fire," continuing to catch each song the team was singing. Reaching Robert, he had guessed one of two songs, and he had gotten it. A song by the first artist to be locked up for violating the speech ordinances at music venues after The Parting. Of course, Robert would be singing this song.

"...Wild like an untamed stallion. If you can't see my heart, you must be blind!" His face was front and center, the distance between Clear and him never wavered.

"More than that, his footfalls were exactly where the lead man's had lifted from." The Senior Helvetian noticed, and then questioned his decision momentarily on this one candidate. "Too close to military," he chastised, but then heard the trillionaire bringing up the end of the line, and he simply had to smile.

"The winter is forbidden until December and exits March the second on the dot," his voice distinctly impersonating Richard Burton. Paying no attention to a car honking its horn mere feet from his butt. "By order summer lingers..."

Deciding to take the pressure off his man, the Senior Helvetian fell in behind Ananias, as he did, the shimmying and skipping began along with a twirl here and there as he sang, "I thank God every day! I woke up feeling this way…" pretending to put on a burlesque show, the Senior Helvetian started pulling off imaginary gloves a finger at a time. "If I was you, I'd wanna be me too," Throwing the imaginary glove at the car, miraculously, his pace did not slow. After a verse or two, the driver started blasting the song he was singing over her stereo and even started dancing in the driver's seat.

Just before the song finished playing through for the third time, the line of joggers arrived at the helicopter. The driver waved and beeped as the car drove off.

The group ran up, touching the helicopter, and then turned to face their leader. By the time the Senior Helvetian reached the transport, eight sets of eyes were staring at him. Davis, his eyes blinking repeatedly, shook his head as if trying to clear cobwebs. "Nope, I can't unsee it. I'd pay to unsee it, but I don't think he even has enough money to make that happen," he pointed at Ananias.

"Turn the bass up," was his only reply.

After five minutes, the helicopter was prepped and Mason was told where they were headed. "We need to come in low, and when they reach out, only say, '50-Out'. Got it?" The Senior Helvetian spoke into the headset, having taken the co-pilot seat.

"Got it, sir. Question, if I may…"

"Of course. Is this a standard training place?"

"No, we are going to a sub-level of a private facility. We've put a lot of time and pretty much all the funds we had setting this up. Well, prior to getting our trillionaire infusion."

"I remember visiting this place when I was a kid, is it actually still open to the public?"

"Yes and no, social distancing pretty much killed them when it actually became a national law. However, with our money, the patriot who owns it keeps it open for special needs children. She flies families here from around the world."

"Does she know what you're doing, under her facility?"

"She asked if she could do what you gentlemen are going to be doing. My answer was a resounding no, I didn't want to be responsible for killing a national treasure."

"Why does that not leave me with a high level of comfort?"

"What, you don't think you can make it through training that I believe would kill a hundred-year-old singer? Moron," he perked up. "There it is," he pointed to what was obviously an amusement park taking up more than 150 acres.

"Are we in Pigeon Forge?" JaLen yelled up into the front of the helicopter.

"Yep!" The Senior Helvetian held his thumb up.

"Told you," he thumbed his nose at Leif, who

laughed.

"Why in the hell are we at an amusement park?" Blaire asked Davis.

"You'll find out," his grin was not exactly what could be misconstrued as comforting.

"Fuck," Blaire sat back.

"Aircraft," a southern bell transmitted over the headset. "Please divert from hovering over this air space. But ya'll can come on down and visit."

"50-Out," Mason replied.

"Aren't you the sweetest? On the Northside of the park, there's a teal-colored tin roof, can't miss it, long and thin-lookin'." The same air traffic controller instructed.

"Yes, ma'am, I see it." He responded.

"Land in the circular drive to the east. And remember to social distance, sweetie."

"I said, 50-Out only," the Senior Helvetian raised an eyebrow.

"You never lived in the south, did you? If I didn't give her a ma'am, she would'a shot us down with her SHIT-gun and then burned our remains for stinkin'," Mason shook his head as they approached the circular drive.

"You just make that up?" he asked after the chopper touched down.

"Nope. You ain't lived until to you've been reprimanded by a southern woman."

"Everyone. Single file, don't talk to anyone," Davis ordered.

"He ain't ever lived in the south either, eh?" Mason asked.

"Nope. Davis, take them in. We'll head in after the chopper is secured," the Senior Helvetian smiled at the pilot.

"Even after we get there, it'll be 10 minutes minimum, this many new men heading into a pack of southern hens, trouble," he laughed, but sure enough, the seven men were being schooled on etiquette by three southern marms.

"Pardon me, ma'am," Mason stepped up. "What a lovely shawl, could you direct me to the Emporium?"

"Thank you, young man," she tugged on the article around her neck. "Of course, we can help, if you promise to take these, 'uns, bless their bones, to the Dollar Tree and buy them some manners."

"Cross my heart."

"It's just that first building on your right, but there isn't a sale going on today."

"We have a private meeting, if you see any others looking for it, please let them know we arrived already."

"We'll keep an eye out for them, sugar bee," the three women stood up straighter as they headed off.

"You do know —" Davis started.

"Hush. He knows," the Senior Helvetian cut him off. They continued to walk right up and through the doors of the Emporium.

"Ok, I've been here at least 40 times, never been stopped and frisked like that," Mustache held his palms up "What gives?"

"When southern women see a group of men, they go into mothering mode."

"What? Why?" Blaire added his confusion to the question pool.

"Mainly because men are helpless creatures," Ananias replied.

"Exactly," Mason shook his head.

"At least they blessed our hearts," Leif added.

"Bones, she blessed your bones and she did that because all you're good for is fertilizing the cemetery," he replied.

"And she did it so kindly, it made me feel good inside." JaLen laughed.

"Now that I know how helpless AND worthless I am, let's head to the basement," Davis took them to the service elevator. "We'll all fit, get in," he pulled the manual doors open, and then closed them again.

"Next stop, Guinea Pig Central."

"You guys are testing my heart," Blaire exhaled.

"Don't worry, this will be the most insane training that Byte could come up with," Davis replied.

"Why shouldn't we be worried about that?" JaLen asked.

"We're not that smart," he replied, bringing laughter from himself and the Senior Helvetian which went unanswered by the seven.

"Kinda hating you guys now," Ananias shook his head.

The elevator stopped and Davis pulled the doors open, showing a small room with an exit that had a digital reader. "We had to add this to keep the matriarch of this place from coming down," the Senior Helvetian waved his empty hand in front of the unit, the door buzzed and he held open a door to a stairway, a blue hue illuminated the area. "The lights are UV purification lights, don't stare."

After 40 steps down, which everyone knew were 40 steps because Clear counted them off, they entered the operating center's brains, "Welcome to DollyBase."

"I can't believe you just said that," Davis shook his head at Clear. "Let's start here," the same blue lights showed a three-quarter view of a series of walls below them.

"Ooh, a labyrinth," Mason said.

"Actually, it's a maze," Ananias corrected. "More than one path into the center."

"Correct," the Senior Helvetian replied.

"Paintball? Are we gonna get to play paintball?" JaLen asked.

"Not really," Davis replied. "Everyone, take the seat with your name around the conference room table." Each of the chairs had an apparatus sitting on them and a wetsuit laying across them. "These units will be your cognition training uniforms. Inspect them, but do not place the helmets on just yet," he gave them a minute or so to look over the units.

"I think we're ready," the Senior Helvetian pressed a couple of keys on the keyboard built into the head of the table. A hologram of the helmets held in their hands popped into life, rotating above the table. "This helmet and suit will deprive you of 100% of your senses," the collective question rolled over the room. "Let's start with an example. Put your gloves on," he waited. "Everyone, place your hands out with your palms up and your fingers splayed. As such," he put both his hands out, chest level, then spread all his fingers wide.

"Robert, grab on to this," Davis handed the man an ice cube.

"What the fuck?" JaLen said. "I can feel it."

"Can you feel anything, Robert?" he asked.

"No, nothing at all."

"That was a small example. Pass the ice around to the others." Similar surprised expressions came from around the table. "When you put on and secure the helmet, just like the gloves, you will be given the sensory input of someone else. You will see what they are seeing. You will be able to talk, of course, but you won't actually hear your words. Additionally, the person who hears what you are saying will not be able to speak directly to you," Davis smiled at the group who looked both confused and intrigued. "I would like to point out, the suits will protect you from heat including fire and cold down to liquid oxygen. So, while you are wearing them, you will be safe, nothing you encounter her will damage your skin. It will get your attention though."

"Well it'll get someone's attention," the Senior Helvetian said stone faced. "Now that you have a very high-level understanding of what the suits do, the goal of this test will be to get seven people through the maze, pretty straightforward. Get dressed, but leave the helmets off until I tell you to put them on. I guess I should've disabled the feedback sequences for now," he punched a few buttons. "It shouldn't feel quite so odd. We're going to head downstairs and walk through the maze without the suits active." When the group reached the bottom of the stairs and approached the 12-foot-tall maze, each looked up at the bizarre structure.

"Sir, what is this material?" JaLen looked closely at the wall.

"That would be the same material that is in your suits, it's a combination of carbon fiber and different types of natural materials, we call it Dragonweave. It allows the walls to hold up to the same abuse that you can in your suits. As we enter, you'll notice different colors on the pathway, to our left, the orange indicates fire, and to the right, the blue designates water. As we're not suited up fully and we didn't put our locks in place, entering the orange area would be violating safety protocols, and I'm not about to do that... again," he grimaced. "To the right we go," they proceeded deeper into the maze, stopping, he indicated a recess in the floor. "If you allow your team to walk into these areas, several things could happen, all of them suck. Remember, the suits you have on are fire and frost-safe. The helmets have purification filters, so if you're in fire or frost, your lungs will not be damaged. Also, if you happen to find yourself submerged in water, you will have at least three minutes of oxygen. So, if you fall into multiple water hazards, you may be fucked," he led them back out of the maze.

"Ok, are we ready to start?" Davis asked. "Go ahead and put on your — "

"No, no, wait. Before we proceed, let me explain one more thing, I will be setting the difficulty level at 0 for our first go-through. To complete this training, the team'll need to pass level 11. And yes, that is my humor. 10 is as high as the actual difficulty goes, but at 11, the sensory sharing changes randomly every minute," he nodded to the sergeant.

"Put on those helmets and once we get upstairs, I will give you the thumbs up to enter," Davis and the Senior Helvetian left the area, heading to the control room. "Clear, you're in the front position, you are approved for entering the maze. I look forward to speaking with the team after."

"Listen to me, stop all movement, pass it forward," Ananias ordered, after they had all stopped, he said, "We need to work through this puzzle without killing ourselves. We know that Clear is in the front." Again, he stopped so that the message could be shared. "We need to know who is talking and who is hearing. I'm going to say my name. Whoever is hearing me, pass the message, X is hearing Ananias." A moment later, the statement, "JaLen is hearing Ananias," came back to him. "Perfect. JaLen, do the same thing I just did. Again, a moment later, he received and retransmitted, "Leif is hearing JaLen.

Jalen, please tell Leif to repeat the process." As they did, the communication chain proved out to be Ananias, JaLen, Leif, Robert, Mason, Blaire, and then Clear. "Let's do the same with visuals. Who sees Clear's display?"

"Robert sees Clear's display. I am waving my hands in front of my face, who sees Robert's display?" The comment went through the group.

"Blaire sees Robert's display. I am waving my hands, who sees Blaire's display?" And forward it went Clear, Robert, Blaire, Ananias, Mason, Leif, JaLen, and back to Clear.

"Perfect, that means, Robert, you need to communicate what you are seeing to guide Clear. Mason and Blaire will communicate that forward," Ananias waited. "Clear, when you get around 10 feet beyond the first concave section, stop, and, Robert, you start in," he paused again. "Everyone acknowledge with name and agree."

"Clear, agree," Came back. "As I am last in communication to Ananias, I am going."

"Clear is starting," Robert communicated forward, but Clear didn't bother when it got to him. "Clear is entering the Blue zone, take three steps and stop."

"Take three steps and stop," Mason repeated.

"Take three steps and stop," Blaire instructed Clear.

"Take three more and there will be an opening on your left hand, look around the corner and wait," Robert instructed.

"I am reaching the first opening on my left," Clear told Ananias, who communicated up the chain.

"If you go around the corner toward the left, the color is white, continuing straight, the color stays blue, and going right, the color turns orange," Robert instructed.

Clear did not move, instead, asking for clarification, "When you say if I go straight, does that mean, if I stay on the original blue pathway, or turn to the left and go straight?"

The question came to Robert, "Shit, sorry. I was assuming you were turning left. So, if you turn left and go straight, the color stays blue. If you turn left and then left again, the color turns white. If you turn left and then right, the color turns red." He waited, seeing Clear turn left, and then left again, he transmitted, "Clear has gone into the white zone."

"Jesus Christ, what did you walk into?" Mason asked.

After Blaire asked Clear, the question came around to Robert, "Clear, hug the right-hand side wall. There appears to be a divot that has filled in with snow."

"We forgot to do touch," Clear said. "Mason feels Clear, Mason, clap your hands," the team went through the same exercise determining the order of feel sensation, which went Clear, Mason, JaLen, Robert, Blaire, Leif, and then Ananias. "Can I move forward 10 feet, and let the next person go?"

"Robert, entering the maze, following Clear's path. Walking straight into the wall, turning right, following that until I feel an opening," he gave a bunch of information, knowing that most of the team didn't know what Clear had done. He also remembered that Blaire would be seeing his feed, but for direction to come to him, he would need to go almost all the way around the horn. He walked with his left hand on the wall. "I'm at the opening. I will walk diagonally to the wall on the right." As he started moving, Clear turned around so that he could actually see himself walking forward.

That approach got them slowly and steadily to the end of the maze, but as Clear stepped through the final opening, the floor let loose and he was under water. "I'm under water," Clear broadcast. As he did, Mason freaked out because the water was cold.

Robert also added his voice to the chain, "Calm down. Look around so I can see how to lead you out," Mason and Blaire conveyed the message, Clear turned his head back and forth. "Tell him to tread water in a circle," he did and a ladder revealed itself behind him. "Stop," the transmission obviously wasn't instantaneous. "I need you to rotate counterclockwise until about nine o'clock," he watched, and as the ladder got into his field of vision, he gave the order to stop again. "Perfect, swim forward, not all that far. Listen for it..." he let his words linger... "There," Clear reached out and grabbed the ladder.

"Gentlemen," the Senior Helvetian greeted them as they arrived at the control room table quite a few hours later. "I can honestly say, that was amazing. I never would have thought you would even complete the first go-through today. Much less the emergency action test. Fuck... damn, I'm geeked out!" he looked a bit like an old school pro-wrestler pumping himself up! "Today was a testimony of how leadership, teamwork, and communication all play a key role. Go get some rest, you earned it."

Chapter 29
Mission Day

"Wake up, this is no drill, kids," the room, moments earlier, had been filled with nothing less than the sound of silence (ok, not really... these asshats were snoring like mother fuckers after the non-stop pace they had been training in for six months, culminating in the constant mental drills of the sensory isolation chamber).

"What? Why?" Blaire said, trying to figure out if there was a fire in the tent.

"Wake up, he said we need to wake up," Robert gave a confident tone, inspiring them.

"Test day?" Mason looked like a pre-teen awakened by their grandfather to head out on a fishing excursion.

"No tests, we finally found where he is being held," the Senior Helvetian was almost on his toes in excitement. "If this team can get him out, we're ready to take this shit into the real world. You'll need to get to the 50-Out plane, Thumb will update you on the trip. Let's go, go, go," he pushed each man from his cot, directing him to take their pre-packed rucksacks. "Remember, talk to each other! Make certain each of you are in the right place at the right time," the leader punched his balled fists together as the team left. "This is good, this is right!" being the last thing that they heard as they left their sleeping area.

"0 Stellah 1, this is 50-Out," Ananias called out as soon as his ass was in the seat.

"All clear for taxi, upon your availability!" came the reply.

"All get in your seats, we're starting our taxi to the runway," he announced. "Hey, Clearance… We got you, bitch!" he laughed into the cabin speakers.

"Boom, Daddy!" came Clear's reply, in the six months they had been drilling and training, this group had gone from complete strangers to a team who would know which foot the other six would be standing on when the music stopped in a cake walk.

The plane began its taxi to take-off, Thumb jumped into the co-pilot seat. "Ananias, we're headed to the Pentagon. All flight plans have been filed."

"Why there?"

"A political prisoner who refused to leave Michigan was arrested, and that is where he is being held."

"Thumb, you know I was part of the brain-trust that ran the Pentagon after The Parting?" Ananias continued to look at his instruments as the plane continued its trek to the runway. "The odd thing, how could I have not known about prisoners in the building?"

"Did you know there is a bunker under the facility?" Thumb asked.

"50-Out, you are cleared for take-off," the tower communications officer said.

"0 Stellah 1, 10-4, wheels up in 45 seconds." Switching his cabin speakers on, "Attention in the cabin, this is your pilot, Ananias, the long-haired-hippy-historian speaking. We will be wheels up in 30 seconds. If you aren't buckled up by then, God help your eternal soul."

"You crack me up," Thumb laughed in the co-pilot seat.

"If we can't laugh, why bother? Here we go." The propellers started yelling and the plane took to the air. When the plane leveled off, "Thumb, where are we landing? You said the Pentagon, but there's not an airstrip there. My best guess would be Ronald Reagan but I've learned not to assume anything anymore."

"Yeah, that makes an ass out of Tom and Pete."

"What?" Ananias' headshot over to the huge man.

"Never mind, if you don't know the joke, you don't get to know the joke," he laughed to himself. "Yes, you are correct, we're landing at Ronald Reagan Washington National Airport. Interesting fact, the Pentagon was built on the location where the first Washington Airport was. Do you know what its name was?"

"Arlington's Hoover Field. What do I win?"

"The opportunity to put this baby on autopilot so we can go back and brief the team on what is happening," Thumb gave a small head nod and unbelted himself, leaving the cockpit.

"Ok then," Ananias checked all the dials, enabled the autopilot, and followed.

"Ok, gentlemen, listen up. We are landing in about 45 minutes, there will be a transport waiting on the tarmac. We will take that vehicle to a predetermined location, from there, we are on our own. Here is the mission, we are rescuing this man," a picture was projected onto the front of the cabin.

"Wait, he's really in jail?" JaLen asked. "I mean, I heard that rumor but…"

"He is and has been for 12 years," Robert answered.

"That is correct," Thumb jumped back into the conversation. "He's being held in the sub-levels of the Pentagon in cell 14-112."

"The Pentagon? How the fuck are we gonna…" Leif started.

"Stop, let's think this through," Blaire cut in. "They have the same security as other places. And not as good as others. Any system can be hacked."

"And any hardwired system can be defeated," Mason added.

"Clear, if I can hack into the system, can your Nanny keep track of the patrols?" Blaire asked.

"All I need to do is get into their video surveillance and let her loose," Clear replied.

"Ok, so getting in and knowing where people are, check. Thanks, Blaire," Ananias started. "Guys, I do have clearance to be in the Pentagon. I've been there a ton, but not in the sub-levels. Thumb, do we have any documentation to find the entrances? We need to determine if there are even access points from the main building or if they're all external and heavily guarded."

"Perfect questions. Here is a chart of the overview, the entrances, there is one in the main building, it was added after American Flight 77. But, no, it isn't connected to a main staircase, there is a ladder, believe it or not, through a hatch in the floor in the Engineering Review Complex."

"I know that complex. I can get us there when you get us in."

"You just said you had access," JaLen shot back.

"He can't use his access to get in, if he did, he'd leave a digital fingerprint," Blaire corrected.

"Oh, yeah, duh!" the big man smacked his own forehead.

"Here," Blaire took over the projector. "These are live feeds from the main level, and the outside."

"And he did that from his tablet and a satellite connection. Unbelievable," Ananias shook his head.

"You're connecting to our hub, can you text me the path to get Nanny to that?"

"Just did."

"Nanny, we need to start flagging all personnel movements, you have our transponder codes so that you can ignore us when we get there, yes?"

"Affirmative, Clear," the now-familiar British voice of Nanny replied over the cabin speakers. "I will begin my tracing now. I will fall offline for 10 out of every 42 seconds and then four out of the remaining 18 seconds of every minute. This pattern appears to be able to defeat their internal alarming," the video dropped from the screen.

Four seconds later, it came back, "While the video is offline, Nanny will forecast the movements of known entities and where they should progress to. Her estimates will improve with time," Clear explained.

"Blaire, do you have a plan for the heat registration when we cross the grounds?"

"Camera pattern recognition alarms are registered with the same PEDI – Eidetic registration platform. It monitors the actual alarms as well as the video image of the raw input feeds. That way, if the software is hacked, and alarm annunciation is defeated, the secondary feature of individual inputs changing will visually be triggered," he replied.

"Um, what does that actually mean?" Robert asked.

"I will overwrite the software, and Nanny will need to overwrite the security feeds."

"I can do that," she replied.

"What happens when she has to drop?" Leif asked.

"I'll need to establish dueling feeds with at least a .25 second overlap," Clear replied. "That way, one will block the other and we will never have a gap."

"How do we establish two separate satellite feeds?" JaLen asked.

"I'm using the satellite to hack the local phone company and using their internal landlines," Blaire replied.

"When we land, we'll have a good indication

of how the ground forces are moving. We'll have double redundancy on the alarm blocking. Mason, you ok with picking the door locks so that we don't need to get ourselves into those side programs and risk tripping some internal diagnostics or something?" Ananias asked.

"I got this," Mason just smiled.

"Alright, once we are inside, you know how to get us below. Do we have any feeds from down there?"

"Not yet," Blaire said, "I'm going through the Pentagon operator station. I've followed all the numbers that are programmed as internal."

"Wait, what?" Thumb asked.

"You know like dialing a four-digit number to call an office in your company," he replied.

"Ah, yeah, got it,"

"None of the internal numbers go down to the lower levels," Blaire continued tapping on his tablet. "Fuck."

"We ok?" Clear asked.

"Yeah, sorry," he said but stayed silent for a minute longer. "I ran across their creeper program, it's a good one too. I defeated it, so yeah, we're good. Alright, they set a secondary landline distribution via voice over internet protocol. I'm in it now, but this area has a much better fire wall."

"Interesting that they have more security in the lower section, are you certain that it is lower and not just the 'secure' lines to the generals?" Leif asked.

"Good question, I can't know until I break in fully, but I can say, the first lines were identifiable to every office and conference room on the main floor throughout the building. To me, it would be odd to have multiple lines in each of those offices but maybe as a phone center."

"Like internal communication, you mean? So you can message office to office?" Ananias asked.

"No, and yes. That could be VoIP, but this is different, this is a new dedicated web connection, trunk-line," he continued mumbling to himself as he worked on hacking into the secondary system.

As the team continued to focus on the planning, Ananias returned to the cockpit. After checking the instruments, he began the landing sequence. "All, we're starting our descent, you'll need to get in your seats and continue your conversation without me for now."

"You need me back up there?" Thumb yelled from his seat in the back.

"I'm ok," he broadcast. "Ronald Reagan tower, 50-Out nearing final approach."

"50-Cut, this is Ronald Reagan tower, you are clear to land on runway Oh 9r."

"Roger that, Ronald Reagan Tower, Oh 9r." He turned off the radio broadcast and let the team know they were in final approach.

Completing their taxiing near a small personnel transport, driven by Sgt. Ernst, "Welcome to Washington DC, previous home of the Nation's leadership, and current home of the New Roanoke capital, Croatoah."

"Thanks, Ernst, the team decided that they need to be dropped off at the parking area, between Boundary Channel Drive and 110," Thumb said as the team loaded up.

"Got it, across from the Marina. I know right where it is. Thumb, all the gear is packed under the seats," he jumped in and started the truck. "Slap the side when you're ready to go."

"Shall do," JaLen continued helping the team up to the bed of the vehicle. "All set." Being the last guy to get in, he slapped the side of the truck twice.

Away they went, "Radio check," Ernst provided.

"Check, check," Clear responded. A short drive and they pulled in and parked.

"Ok, I'll stay here. Give me a shout when you need the truck fired up."

"Clear and I are planning on staying here in the back," Blaire explained.

"I'm not allowed out of the truck either," Thumb added.

"Works for me, keeps me in the loop," Ernst shut off the truck and joined them in the back.

"Ananias, are you the radio lead?" Clear asked.

"I am. All communication to the group goes through me."

"Ok, right now, all guards are flagged and being followed."

"Copy that."

"When team lead gives the go, I will begin the alarm logging and PEDI registration mods," Blaire added.

"Team status," Ananias chimed in 10 minutes later. "We have followed the Boundary channel, currently beginning to follow the Connector south."

"Copy," Clear and Blaire replied back.

Ananias reported in two more times, and on his fourth check-in, said, "Team has past covered walk, along the southwest side. Current status of guards?"

"You are 500 yards from patrol. Will be arriving northeast of you in approximately 14 minutes," Nanny reported.

"Copy that. Blaire, time for you to shine."

"Check. Spoofing is currently active. You are good to go,"

"Copy, we are opening the door now. All clear to enter?" Ananias asked.

"No, not at all. Close the door. Repeat, close the—"

"Door is closed," Mason reported.

"What happened?" Ananias asked.

"There were nine more alarms than we presumed would become active when the door opened. We were covered and not detected. I will need more time to review where these other alarms came from."

"Current patrol status," Nanny's voice

reported, "147 yards."

"My recommendation is to leave the area," Clear added.

"Hoover Airfield," Ananias said.

"Repeat, recommendation to leave the area."

"Sorry, yes, we're leaving the area. I just realized there may be an access corridor through the old flight communication building for the Hoover Airfield. Which is why that building has a guarded entrance."

"Thumb, do you have any details on the building he's talking about?" Clear asked.

"The municipal building?"

"I believe so, yes, it looks like a municipal building anyway."

"Calling it up now, and I just forwarded you the information," Thumb replied.

"Best I can tell," Blaire started. "The trunkline to the Pentagon is connected to this building data hub as well."

"Let me know when we can open some eyes in there," Clear asked.

"Team status," Ananias reported, "Team, following Henry G. Shirley Highway, headed to the southern side of new target building."

"I have their surveillance cameras up," Blaire said.

"Current canine and guard patrol passing your trajectory now, do not progress toward the building," Clear ordered.

"Check, see them."

"I see no active infrared equipment, as soon as Nanny has control of the cameras, you're good to go," Blaire updated them.

"There are three sets of canine and guard patrols, Nanny has control of the cameras and is monitoring the three pairs, your team is good to go," Clear approved the entry and the five men raced to the fence.

"Team status," Ananias commented. "Dropped a red herring for the dogs. We made it to the first cooling tower."

"Red herring?" Thumb looked confused.

"Leif had several vials of Constantine's piss," Clear said.

"Brilliant," Sgt. Ernst laughed.

"Team lead, this system has the same PEDI eidetic system. I think you were correct, this is a branch of the Pentagon security. I have spoofing ready, let me know," Blaire waited.

"Team status, we are ready to pick the lock."

"Spoofing active, proceed with only the lock, do not access building."

"Next patrol 200 feet away," Nanny reported.

"Door open, status?" Ananias replied.

"Spoofing strong, enter and wait," Blaire held a fist up, shaking it.

"Team status," this time, he whispered. "Interior of treatment center. All quiet, do you have the location of possible access points?"

"There are seven doorways on the lower level, only two of them have security cameras watching them. Of those two, only one looks like you can enter from your side. It is 300 feet below you and due north," Nanny reported. "Additionally, there is a security access reader next to the door. I see no personnel in the area."

"I'll start working on the reader, let me know when you are ready." Again, they waited.

All went silent for 10 minutes, "Team status, ready to access tunnel."

"Team leader, there appear to be pressure pads inside the tunnel, as well as infrared, heat signature validation. Stay in a single file line, do not rush through the tunnel. One Step, One Brick…"

"One Rome. Check," Ananias replied. "Door open. Ok to enter?"

"Affirmative, follow each other's footsteps."

"Copy," 15 minutes later. "Team status, ready to leave tunnel. Do you have any update on what we may find?"

"There are no cameras on the other side of the tunnel."

"Nanny, you are breaking up real—" Ananias commented and then his transmission died.

"I don't know if you can hear me, I've got control of the alarms, proceed with caution," Blaire looked over at Clear. "And now we wait. I see the inputs coming in, they passed through the door, and now it's closed again. I overwrote the fire alarm that just came in, my best guess is they piggybacked the signals there. Otherwise, the leadership has incendiaries, and everyone is burning alive without help coming."

"Most doubtful, it's probably what we missed before, the fire systems are tied into their infrastructure. Pretty smart," Clear nodded.

"Another door opened. Here's something, in the code, I see 27 different references to block locks."

"Blocks? 27 of them?" Clear looked at the two sergeants. "Can there really be 27 levels of prisoners?"

"We have no idea," they both replied.

"Do you have a method of opening a specific cell?" Clear asked Blaire.

"Now that I see they have alarms hidden in the fire system we can, and have fanned them out as well," Blaire looked around seeing the expectant faces on the other three. "Sorry. When they open the final door, I will open cell 14-112, yes."

Chapter 30

Meanwhile, Inside the Underground Bunker

The momentum of the team continued forward, searching out their target. "Stop," Robert, who was point man, held his arms out. Turning, he put his hands akimbo, "I think we need to evaluate our performance thus far."

"What?"

"That's what they said good teams do, they evaluate during crisis…"

"Shut the fuck up," Leif laughed.

"But seriously," Robert grinned. "Do we know where we're going? We have all but lost our communication to the outside."

"Additionally, we know the path back will need to be different, the doors in the tunnel have no handles on this side," Mason added.

"Do you guys think we should double-back to re-establish communication?" JaLen asked.

"My vote is no, we know he's in room 14-112," Ananias commented.

"Cell," Robert corrected.

"Precisely a cell, yes, I stand corrected."

"In a cell, in America, for speaking about the love of country," Robert shook his head. "50-Out."

"Guys, if there are 112 cells full of people who did nothing wrong, are we actually going to leave the others?" Leif asked.

"I believe, if we fulfill this campaign, we'll

have a better chance to release the rest," Ananias hung his head, knowing that was the wrong answer for humanity, but the right answer for the team.

"I can see how you really feel," Mason touched Ananias on the shoulder. "We need to complete this, and only this... We all feel the way you just looked."

"Bigger problem," Ananias looked up. "I can almost guarantee that the 14 is a floor designation. So, it's most likely over 1500 people, not just 112."

"Fuck... I bet you're right. I hadn't thought about that," JaLen shook his head.

"I think I should go ahead and take the place of Nanny. Thoughts?" Mason offered.

"I believe you're the only one of us who could. I'm on board." Ananias replied. "Anyone disagree?"

"No, but, Mason, minimal radio communication. S'il vous plat," Robert added.

"Good plan," Mason silently jogged away.

"How the fuck does he do that silent running shit?" Leif watched, impressed.

"I could do it if I wanted to," JaLen nodded his head.

"Not even if that big butt was full of helium," Ananias said, straight-faced.

"See, I'm more impressed with that," JaLen chuffed. "How did he deliver that line without cracking up?"

"Would you morons shut up, I'm trying to be sneaky," Mason said over their headset.

"Sorry. Radio silence," Ananias replied.

"I've made it to the door, no cameras or guards spotted. Clear to head this way, guys, try to keep the chatter down."

"Go piss up a rope," Robert and Leif both replied.

"Stereo insults, impressive. Inside this door is a set of stairs," he reported when they arrived. "It's not locked," he pulled the door open.

They proceeded down, reading the plaques, getting more and more pissed. "This is the floor," JaLen commented. "14 cells 0001 through 0512. This is fucking bullshit."

"Before we walk in there, we need to remember that no matter what we see, we can't do anything about it today." Everyone looked surprised at Robert for the pragmatic statement. "The fact is, they emptied all the jails during the 2020 pandemic, just to fill them with people who disagreed with their opinions. The Parting stopped most of that from happening. This was their chance to make that right. Eh, Ananias?"

"Now's not the time for that," Leif interjected. "We have shit to do."

"No, let Mr. Tough guy have his say," Ananias stood and pulled his hair back. "You honestly believe I had any knowledge of this?" he smacked the plaque.

"You were the lead asshole in the Camelot think tank, everyone knows that group presented all the options for the Parting," Robert bowed up.

"Completely true, someone had to have ideas on how to stop the nation from falling into complete civil war. I stand by that, full of pride! If not for the ideas my team had, the simulations showed 10s of thousands dead every week for three years. That's between 1.5 and 3.2 million people dead, for those who can't count."

"Hey, hey, hey," JaLen took a crack at calming it down. "Enough."

"Fuck these retards, I'm heading in," Mason ignored the foolishness. Just before he touched the door.

"Are we prepared to kill innocent guards?" Leif asked.

"Seriously?" Ananias rounded on the much taller man. "These are NOT innocent men, they're oath breakers. They disregard all that is good every day they come to this place. Holding people in prison cells because they spoke out is their choice, and it's the wrong fucking choice! I'd kill every one of the employees of this place if given a chance." For the first time in six months, the passion that drove Ananias to join 50-Out showed in his eyes.

"There you go, Robert, clear enough for you?" Leif held his open palm toward the trillionaire.

"Yeah, I'm good. Let's do this," Robert turned, wiping his eye as he followed Mason into the dark corridor. After turning left twice, their path was blocked by another door, opening that presented a vast cavern. looking up and down showed only darkness.

"What the fuck?" a voice ahead of them in the darkness inquired. "Is someone there?" Four of 50-Out pulled their guns.

"No," Robert stepped in front. "Don't you recognize the voice? Blaire must have opened the cell for us," he walked forward. "Mr. Ritchie, we're here to get you out."

"You joking?" the stooped figure of a six-foot-tall, 80-year-old man asked.

"No, sir."

"What about the rest of these bastards?" his hands waved up and then down, taking in the floors above and below, his long stringy beard and his long thinning hair on his head were braided together to the front. The pulling and parting of the hair on his chin as his head followed the hands made him look like a crazy old prospector searching for a golden nugget.

"Sir," Ananias approached the older man. "Sir, we need your voice outside. Telling the world what is really going on."

"No one gave a fuck about me being here for years, why should I care now? Why should I give you my voice?"

"First, no one knew you were even alive, much less where you were," Robert said.

"Doesn't matter, I'm not leaving," he turned, walking back to the cell, his home for so long. "The war is over, evil won, just go home."

"No, sir, you're wrong," Mason stood straight, looking at the old man. "My Gramps used to say, evil has the ability to win battles, but never the war."

"But there have been so many battles," he turned, the tears running down his cheeks showed clearly in Mason's headlamp. "Good has gotten tired of fighting."

"Tired is no excuse, and I'm sorry, but you are coming with us," Robert stuck a syringe into the man's shoulder. "JaLen, you got him?"

"Of course, would've been nice if you gave me some kinda warning," he tossed the man onto his shoulder as if he were no more than a large bag of dog food.

"Team…" a speaker in the darkness crackled to life. "You have incoming. The path out is forward, you'll find another set of steps there," Clear's voice informed.

"I'll take the lead," Robert shrugged off his protective overcoat. "Drape this over him."

"I've got our six," Leif opened his coat as well.

"No time for heroics," Mason said as they started forward.

"Agree to disagree," Robert said as he unhooked the protective cover on his knives. His Redhawk already out and cocked. "Guess you'll get a chance to back up those words from earlier," he said to Ananias.

"Yes, I will," he pulled the hammers back on the two Kimber 1911s. "One Step."

"One Brick," JaLen added.

"One Rome," they all said and started to the exit.

The first shot sang out, Robert could only react, years of training cleared his mind. Self-preservation was cast aside knowing the higher ground the guards held was a superior position. Continuing to move forward, he launched knife after knife, the unsuspecting oath breakers fell one after another. "Stay close, don't hold the inner rail," he ordered.

"10 4," JaLen replied as shots from behind sang out.

"Leif?" Mason's concern showed in his voice. He turned, seeing the skinny man holstering his precious black Vaquero after fanning the hammer four times.

Slamming the door as he ran to join the others, "Blaire, if you hear me, lock the door to the stairs on level 14."

"Fuck it, lock the doors to the stairs on all levels and unbolt all the cells. Let the prisoners get some payback," Ananias shot the feet out of a guard who had leaped out of nowhere, landing a yard in front of Robert.

The klaxon alarm sounded and the cacophony of hundreds of voices yelling at once filled the stairway. "He must have heard you," Robert fired the last shot in his Redhawk, holstering it and, instantly, his Mossberg had left the sling on his back. The Shockwave fired twice, all went still. "Pick up the pace, we have the stairs to ourselves for now." Arriving at the top landing, he held a closed fist in the air and pointed to the lamp around his head before turning it off. Each man followed his lead. Their surroundings fell into darkness. "Reload."

"Listen," Mason said in the darkness. "The shadows know me, let me take the lead now."

"Won't help this time, they're right there," Robert pointed, lights and movement under the door jam.

"Let me do my thing," he looked up, seeing that while the stairs stopped on the landing, the infrastructure of them had not. He stepped onto the railing, launching himself into the open air where they had just come from.

"Wait," JaLen panted, still carrying their reason for having come here.

"Give him a chance," Leif said.

"I'm fine, relax," Mason's voice was above them. "Now we have the higher ground," he said in a whisper over the headsets.

"Be careful," Ananias whispered back.

"Radio check," Blaire's voice came through, still accented with static.

"Sit hard, Blaire," Mason gave their prearranged order for no more transmissions. Under the door, two flashbangs lit up the stairway briefly, followed by several gunshots.

When a third flashbang went off, Robert attempted to push open the door. "He only had two," the door, still locked, wouldn't open. "Blaire, open the door out of the stairway." A buzz let them know the request had been fulfilled. The door, however, was blocked with dead bodies.

"Mason?" Ananias whispered into the headset.

"Incoming below," Leif said, seeing bouncing flashlights on the stairs.

"Do you need me to help push the fucking door?" JaLen asked.

"That might help, yes," Robert stopped pushing as it was to no avail.

"Give him to me," Ananias said as JaLen passed.

"Ok," JaLen handed over the unconscious man and Ananias shouldered the burden.

"1, 2, 3," Robert counted and they pushed the door, which swung in effortlessly. The two men crashed in, landing next to Mason, who lay in a puddle of blood.

Leif rushed into the room. Closing the door, he leaned against it, "Blaire, lock the door we just came through," he demanded.

"Done," Blaire replied.

"How is he?" Ananias asked.

"Dumbass must've used the last of his energy to move the dead men," JaLen said, touching their downed friend's neck. "He's got a pulse. I'll see to him, you see about what we have ahead of us," his words were to Robert.

"Check," Robert drew his Shockwave again, stepping up to the door. "Clear, Blaire?"

"We're here," Came the reply.

"Can you see what we have inside the tunnel?"

"The tunnel is a choke point," Nanny's unemotional voice replied. "Several dozen men waiting on you to come through."

"How close are we to the access into the Engineering Review Room?" Ananias asked.

"Into the Pentagon?" Leif asked.

"Good thinking, they won't expect that," Robert said.

"He's right," Blaire's comment over the headset replied.

"JaLen, you and Ananias stay here."

"Robert, I know my way around that place. I need to go with you," the trillionaire handed Mr. Ritchie to JaLen.

"You three go, I'll stay with these two," JaLen laid the man next to Mason.

"Top off your guns, and balaclavas on," Robert ordered. A minute later, "Clear, get us to the access point."

"We have no eyes there, but knowing where you came from on the plans, you should continue straight past the door to the tunnel. After about 100 yards, there will be a retractable ladder."

"Got it."

"You sure, JaLen? I'm fine with staying here too," Leif commented.

"They aren't going to give up their position over there. Go on, they need you more than we do."

"Be safe," he headed off to catch the others.

"That's a dumb comment, what else would I do?" As the others left, he took the medkit from his rucksack, starting the process of field dressing his teammate.

Peering their heads through the access point into the floor of the conference room a few minutes later, they saw nothing. The small concussion from behind them gripped the team with concern as they slid stealthily through the hatch. "The door held, keep moving," JaLen eased their initial fears, but they knew their time was down to a precious few minutes.

"Location update," Ananias said, once again, taking the role of radio lead.

"We've established surveillance, no teams searching the Pentagon properly, there are several calls for additional assistance below. There are people in the cubes outside your location, advise no gunfire," Clear reported. "The people in the cubes have been given some type of order to hide under their desks."

"They're under an active shooter order." Continuing from the room, Ananias took the lead, trying to work through the fastest way out of this building to allow them to reverse back and reenter the municipal building. He took them into a small corridor with bathrooms, knowing there was an emergency exit less than 100 feet away. Leaving the isolation of the hallway, finding a desk with a secretary peering at them.

With the flick of his wrist, Robert unleashed a knife which killed the phone the secretary had lifted, presumably to call for help, while the other hand aimed his Redhawk at her. "We don't want to hurt you," Robert said in broken English that could have been a Russian. "Get up, you are with us now."

"I won't scream or anything just—" her next

words were stilled as Ananias punched her, and she toppled over in her chair. The two men looked at the trillionaire in horror.

"Ain't nobody got time for that! Keep moving. There's the exit," they entered another cube farm, staying low. "Disable the alarm on the door we're going through."

"Set off the one as far from us as possible," Leif added as they ran out into the night. "Which way to the building we were in?"

"I'm on it already," Ananias said, turning left and heading to the shadows along the building.

"Heat signatures?" Robert asked.

"I have your images, reading on the cameras on the other side, they are all mobilizing to chase the departing infiltrators. Good idea, Leif," Blaire said.

"The dogs have formed a wall," Clear said.

"Let Constantine loose as we approach. Let me know when you do," Leif said as they ran.

"Guys, Mason is waking," JaLen said. "As is Mr. Ritchie."

"Good, we'll need all of you in this fight," Robert said. "We're almost back to you," as he finished the statement, a dog leaped over the fence."

"Let him go now!" Leif yelled. Out of the darkness, the guard dog closed the gap. "Constantine, Einschlag!" the guard dog took the full impact of the mastiff, crumpling to the lawn. "Fass!" He pointed at the other two dogs as their handlers released them. The first shot rang out from the unconscious dog's handler, luckily, it missed Constantine. Leif's Vaquero barked six times before another shot could be fired, killing all three handlers. "Kriechen," he ordered his dog to lay on its belly, crawling forward, with one of the dogs still in his maw. The remaining dog, which had launched itself at the mastiff, landed, spinning instantly to reenter the fight. "Einschlag," the leaping dog had the misfortune of being rammed by the 225-lb. beast. None were dead, but the three guard dogs were dispatched.

"Fuck," Robert mumbled as they ran. "Don't forget to reload."

"Zielen auf, Constantine," Leif pointed back to the truck, and the dog ran off as the team continued forward. Placing his revolver in his shoulder holster and drawing two Glocks with extended magazines. "No time to load my baby, these will have to do."

The overriding concern that their teammates were going to be captured caused them to miss the fact that Clear had joined their sprint. Finally seeing him when they reached the door Mason had picked earlier. Stopping them from entering, "Nanny will see us approaching their team, when we have the best position, we'll get the thumbs up to attack," the team acknowledged the new plan. Creeping slowly, they arrived undetected.

"Now," Blaire's command sounded like an animal calling for a pack to attack a flock of innocent sheep. Within seconds, the two dozen men were all dead. The concussion that came from the distance pulled them from the carnage.

"JaLen, come to us!" Ananias ordered as they ran down the stairs to the tunnel.

"Already happening," Blaire said. "The three are running into the tunnel. Shadows approaching from behind them quickly."

"Can you lock the door on the other side?" Leif asked.

"No, it's held open by the rubble." He answered.

Clear launched himself off the deck, grabbing a sprinkler line. Dropping, he landed on the body of one of the dead men. Forcing his fall forward, everything happened at once, he splashed onto his stomach, pulling his shotgun from his back, aiming forward just as the door swung open. "Leap over me!" Clear yelled at the pivotal moment, his automatic 12-gauge acted like a blunderbuss, the glass pack he had loaded shot sharp glass particulate across the tunnel. All six shots having been fired, he rolled to the side, letting Robert push the door closed before helping him to push three dead bodies against it.

"They've retreated to regroup," Blaire replied.

"Move, move," Ananias put an arm around Mason, helping him up the stairs.

"Don't argue with us, go!" Robert ordered Mr. Ritchie, who complied and followed the injured Mason up and out of the building. Sgt. Ernst, who had pulled the truck onto the service drive, was waiting just on the other side of the fence.

"Come on, guys, run!" Thumb leaned out of the back of the transport, waving his hands. 30 seconds later, they drove off, each knowing that no camera, satellite, or drone had seen them, thanks to Blaire, Clear, and of course, Nanny. They arrived at the airport having run across no issues, and to that point, no radio commentary regarding issues at the Pentagon.

The 50-Out plane arrived at the hanger in Mexico. Mr. Ritchie, who had been given a sedative, was pushed on a gurney by JaLen, off the plane. Robert guided the wheelchair that Mason was sitting in. The team deplaned somber, knowing they had left so many back there. The Senior Helvetian met them with a smile. "I understand that you don't feel you can acknowledge this success, primarily due to the magnitude of prisoners you had to leave. I need you to understand this, the man you rescued will see that the world will know. Byte will see that he is safe while he does this. The important thing for you to know is that you performed as a team and you're learning curve continues to astound."

"You should be proud," the two captains walked up, putting to bed the concern that Vito had eaten Cratchit as she addressed them. "You're now a battle-tested team. You knew where each other were, and how you could rely on the others."

"But your training has only just begun," Dutch smiled, knowing that he had not yet gotten a chance to run this crew through his brand of training. "In the heat of Mexico, we'll continue to fold you into the most effective sword ever forged."

Ernst walked off the plane last, following Thumb. "We can worry about beating on them more tomorrow. Let's see to the wounded and get these men fed," the Senior Helvetian walked over and handed the gaunt man his ring, which he slid back on his finger, kissing the white stone.

"Gentlemen," Thumb got everyone's attention. "Tonight, we celebrate! Fuck your concerns for what you had to leave behind. It would've taken months of planning to coordinate getting all the prisoners out. You got this man out," he pointed to the gurney. "And you devised the plan to do that while in transport. I watched you bouncing ideas and rallying in a manner that a seasoned military force would envy. And since Mason won't be able to join us, I get his slice of pizza!" he added as the team started to smile.

"Not a chance, baby boy, I want an entire pizza to myself. And don't hold back on the anchovies," Mason said from the wheelchair.

"Somebody better have gotten beer? I think Leif needs a 12-pack," Blaire replied.

"Ananias here is buying," Robert patted him on the back.

"Seems fair," the trillionaire laughed.

"Senior Helvetian," Mason said from the wheelchair, "I have a stupid question."

"Of course, you do."

"Why us? You still haven't told us."

"We're still waiting on that too," Suzi crossed her arms. "I'd say now is as good a time as any. Or I could find that cattle prod…"

"Ok, you're right I owe you that. In this team, I see the individuals that made my homeland great, the progressives that had the strength to push for something new, the libertarians who had the consistency in their drive for freedom from government intervention, and the conservatives who unmistakably honored the people who formed the nation. This team embodies all of these groups, and being from the three new nations my homeland became, you see where your factions have lost their guiding principles. If the Parting showed us one thing, it's that everything can be replaced. Today, I say we started replacing the Parting with the Reformation. This is where I would normally salute, instead, in the history of the gridiron, I say all hands in," he held his right hand out. Mason stepped from the wheelchair, placing his hand on top, followed by the rest. "On three… 50-Out." He looked at Vito.

"1, 2, 3…" the big man started.

"50-Out!" they all shouted!

Not even close to the end…

Team-building for Non-Military Personnel

Keep Reading after this send-off, for a taste of misadventures to come.

This world has been quite enjoyable to build. Being a man who falls into the 50 and completely regretting not having served 'God and Country', it made sense to see how my friends and the Silver Lane Militia would handle being put into such an endeavor. Writing some of it required pulling some stories, experiences, and inspiration from people who did serve. I thank each of you, Joel, Rick, and Mark for both your service and your help in this project.

Needing to know what you think... Please leave a review. Without your feedback, no one else will stumble across this new version of team-building. If you liked it, don't be shy, tell the world... or the Senior Helvetian may pay you a visit.

The Audiobook is already underway, and we look forward to hearing our friend, John Pirhalla's interpretation of this introduction to 50-Out.

Lastly, if you enjoyed my writing, you may want to take a look at my other titles, 'Reaper's Revenge' and *'Birth of the Entities'*.

Love and Strength,

CV Reinhardt

Excerpt from "50-Out – Due Diligence"
Don't Call Me Puddin'

The night was full of sirens, explosions, and gunshots. The dog being led by the stocky man ignored it all, tonight, it had a mission. "Seriously, Constantine, I didn't bring a baggy," Clear looked around for cameras that would forward a ticket to him for not picking up canine excrement. "Jesus, I guess it wouldn't have mattered, I would've needed a shopping bag. Maybe we'll get lucky and they'll think it's a fire hydrant." After the dog stretched in a long downward dog pose, the beast started off again. "You know, I didn't know that was why they gave the name to that yoga pose.

"Any sign that he has a lead?" Blaire asked over the concealed earpiece.

"Only that he located the perfect spot to piss, and then take a monstrous dump," he continued to walk behind the dog as it surprisingly ignored the night sounds.

"Well, better he did it out there this time, I cleaned the plane for more than an hour and the smell is still here from last —" Ananias started.

"Oh shit, he's going," Clear interrupted.

"Again? Damn, what did he eat?" Robert laughed.

"No, he's got a scent. One of you tall fuckers should have taken him, I feel like a dwarf being pulled by a bear."

"You took him because you're the only one

strong enough to hold him back," Ananias replied.

"Besides, it's your Nanny who can't see anything in this area," Blaire added.

"You've got to be joking, she can't see where there are no cameras. Not her fault," Clear shot back.

"Whatever. Just show him whose boss," JaLen offered.

"Fine. Hold up there, Constantine," he pulled on the one-inch-thick leash.

"Grr, woof," the Neapolitan Mastiff turned, chuffed and continued at its break-neck speed. As he took a sharp left off the sidewalk, Clear lost his hold on the leash, which turned out to be pure luck because the dog jumped six feet off the ground and through a plate-glass window.

"What the fuck!" Clear exclaimed, weighing up his options, deciding that facing whoever was inside this building was far better than losing Leif's dog.

"Why did you stop outside the Pavilion Davioud?" Blaire asked, looking at the tracer on the headset.

"The damn dog jumped through the window," Clear leaped, his left foot finding purchase on a wrought iron railing around what looked like a small lower exit. Pushing off his right foot found the flower box outside the window Constantine had smashed through. Jumping again, he landed inside, finding the dog licking the face of its bound owner.

"Ok, ok, you dowsy dog, good job."

"Where's Mason?" Clear stooped and untied

his teammate's hands.

"They took him," Leif, having a free hand, pushed Constantine back. "You crazy mutt, I love you too."

"That's rather nice but I think relationships with co-workers—"

"Piss off!"

"Do you know what this is about and where they took him?" Clear finished untying his other hand. "You got your feet?"

"Yes, if you pull him back for a sec," Leif replied.

"Got him, ok, more info if you please."

"They took him because he stole some art from them. I had a hard time following but they took him to a place called—"

"The Louvre... Fuck! I need you to take your beast across the park. Ananias, JaLen, can you meet me at the Pyramide du Louvre?" Clear asked.

"Seriously? Why? I thought you found them?" Blaire asked.

"Not exactly. Mason was taken to the Louvre, and I don't fucking speak French. Leif is bringing his beast back to the truck."

"This is fucking stupid," Robert interjected.

"I agree, but sometimes we can't just walk in and kill everyone. Sometimes we need to see what higher lifeforms can offer," Ananias gave a big smile and stepped from the transport they were hiding in.

"Fuckin' ay, that just made me piss a little,"

JaLen said, jumping out to join the trillionaire. The two jogged up the Rue de Conde through several jigs and jags, eventually finding the Pont des Arts, which they crossed, seeing the Seine below. Once over the river, they had to bypass the Louvre properly, continuing to jog to the pyramid, finding Clear waiting.

The stout man greeted them with, "They have him down there somewhere."

"I've been there a lot. Let me lead, if asked, you two are my le Garde de Corps, bodyguards."

"Fine," they said and both followed.

.

.

.

.

.

Let's continue this adventure—you and I...